THE CURVE

A NOVEL

THE CURVE

A NOVEL

JEREMY BLACHMAN

CAMERON STRACHER

ANKERWYCKE

Cover and interior design by Elmarie Jara/ABA Publishing.

Printed in the United States of America.

20 19 18 17 16   5 4 3 2 1

Library of Congress Cataloging-in-Publication Data

Names: Blachman, Jeremy, author. | Stracher, Cameron, author.
Title: The curve : a novel / Jeremy Blachman ; Cameron Stracher.
Description: Chicago, Illinois : ABA Publishing, American Bar
    Association, [2016]
Identifiers: LCCN 2016000279| ISBN 9781634253260 (hardcover :
    acid-free paper) | ISBN 9781634253277 (ebook)
Subjects: LCSH: Law teachers—Fiction. | Law schools—Fiction. |
    GSAFD: Legal stories. | Satire.
Classification: LCC PS3602.L23 C87 2016 | DDC 813/.6—dc23 LC
    record available at http://lccn.loc.gov/2016000279

Discounts are available for books ordered in bulk. Special consideration is given to state bars, CLE programs, and other bar-related organizations. Inquire at Book Publishing, ABA Publishing, American Bar Association, 321 N. Clark Street, Chicago, Illinois 60654-7598.

www.ShopABA.org

JB: For Nina and Micah, hug-hug.
CS: For Adam and Erica, partners in crime.

Contents

In 500 words or less, or more, explain why you want to attend Manhattan Law School

[attach extra pages if you write real big]:

I want to go to Manhattan Law School because I've always wanted to be a lawyer, at least since I learned that firemen actually have to go into buildings that are on fire, and not just wear the hat and slide down poles. Besides, everyone has always told me I should become a lawyer, or at least my parents have, and even though they're both lawyers who don't know anything about me because they spent my entire childhood at the office, they've offered to pay, and that definitely sounds a lot better than getting a real job. Plus, it gives me three more years to hope they fulfill their big dream of dying at the office and I get all the money they've spent their lives hoarding as a substitute for love.

I also want to go to Manhattan Law School so I can do things you can only do at law school, like tell your friends you're a law student so they stop thinking you aren't doing anything useful with your life. I don't know when everyone got so concerned with having a career, but it is pretty lame. Call me a socialist, but I believe our taxes should support us.

Truthfully, I want to go to Manhattan Law School because I want to meet the girl in your brochure, on page 7, with the Mardi Gras beads. Is she really a student? I tried to reverse image search, but I could not find anything. See, that's the kind of lawyer I know I can be: someone who can do a little research on the Internet before I bother asking a stupid question. My parents always complain about associates who waste their "precious time" with nonsense. At least on the Internet, no one knows your parents are douchebags.

Finally, I want to go to Manhattan Law School because, from what I'm reading about the school, it looks like you will accept me. And that's important, because without a student ID, my parents will stop sending me money.

1

The Clock Strikes One

A<small>S THE CROW FLIES, IT'S</small> less than three miles from Wall Street to the banks of the Gowanus Canal in Brooklyn. The last crow who tried it, however, got sucked into the jet engine of a 727 landing at LaGuardia Airport, and then spat in pieces into the murky depths of the water. Ever since, the crows have steered clear of Gowanus. Navigating flight paths is difficult enough; it's the indignity of being discarded into a Superfund site that really gets them.

But not everyone is as smart as a crow.

The gray brick building that teetered at the Eastern edge of the canal, near Twelfth Street, was filled with human beings who should have known better, but didn't. Its entrance marred by pigeon droppings, the building had been designed by an architectural student with one eye and no ruler. None of the walls met at right angles, and the ceilings drooped in the middle like pancakes weighed down with syrup. If the students who sat in those crooked rooms were more alert, they might have noticed the metaphor.

Instead, they were playing solitaire.

Not just solitaire. Minesweeper. Hearts. Online poker. Checking their fantasy baseball teams, watching movie trailers, browsing through profiles on OKCupid, Tinder, Hinge. One guy in the corner, sweatshirt, baggy jeans, downloading a pornographic movie so raunchy it was illegal in eight states. Not that he knew (or cared) about the statutory violation—even though that was the law he was supposed to be studying.

A girl in the back row was buying and selling stocks in real time, her screen filled with market tickers. A middle-aged man, a stripe of pale skin still visible where his wedding ring used to be, was on a Skype call, watching his daughter crawl for the first time, in a house he was still paying for, three time zones away— evidence of a former life, a dead end he thought law school would give him the tools to escape from. But all it was doing was adding $50,000 a year to his debt load. His baby girl knew just about as much law as he did—and, sadly, was a heck of a lot more employable.

None of this was a mystery to their professor, Adam Wright. He had been in their seats not much more than a decade earlier—albeit nicer seats, in a newer building, at a school with an endowment, and with a rational reason to believe his law degree wouldn't be worthless. The Internet connection was a little slower back then, the earphones a little more conspicuous, but he knew all his students' tricks. He could tell by the books on their desks whose pages never turned, the smiles that didn't fit the words he was saying, the way their eyes darted back and forth, back and forth. He did not have their attention. He merely had their attendance, hyperlinked from the absent recesses of their brains.

He sighed, and shifted his focus to the seating chart he had made the students fill out on the first day, in the hope that the threat of being called on would force them to do the reading and pay the slightest bit of attention. He thought it had worked—until he read some of the names on the chart. He was pretty sure the joker selling drugs via Craigslist in the third row wasn't going to answer to Donald Duck. And if the woman in the fourth row on the aisle, buying the drugs, was actually Lady Gaga, she'd clearly borrowed this morning's outfit from a boring, impoverished friend.

And then the sound of a cell phone, as if the entire second row playing first-person shooting games on their laptops wasn't insulting enough. Adam made a point to remind everyone to turn off their phones at the start of each class—but there had yet to be a class where he got through fifty minutes uninterrupted. He recognized the ring tone. What was that song? It reminded him of a younger, hipper period in his own life. But then he heard the lyrics and cringed: "Fuck tha police!" This was what a law student had chosen for a ring tone?

Adam watched as a young woman in the second row—olive skin, gleaming black hair—fumbled for her phone . . . and answered the call.

"Yo 'sup," she whispered. "Torts."

At least they respected him enough to whisper, he thought.

"Yeah, it's a total joke."

He tried to focus on the lecture notes in front of him.

"You know, the new guy with the Labradoodle hair."

He could stand it no longer. He searched his seating chart, praying she had written down a real name. "Ms . . . ah . . . Ms. Fortunato," he said.

"Fuck," she said, as all eyes turned to her. "Gotta go. Sext me later." She swiveled her phone back into its case, bejeweled with cubic zirconium. It fake-sparkled like the smile she gave him.

"Hey, Prof," she said.

"Could you please tell us the facts of *Palsgraf v. Long Island Railroad?*"

There was a slight gasp among the students, which may have been related to the question but, more likely, meant there was a blip in the Wi-Fi. But Adam pretended the gasp was for him, and that the students were actually, suddenly, afraid.

Although the practice of calling upon students was still fairly common in law schools, Adam hadn't set out to be one of those old-fashioned, rigid interrogators. He started out as part of a kinder, gentler breed of faculty, eschewing the Socratic method for something resembling a real, authentic dialogue about the law. He believed students learned very little from having their arguments shot down and being made to feel foolish. Instead he believed in coaxing the answers from them, and making them feel like partners in the search for fundamental principles like Duty, Care, and Causation.

But he was coming to realize no one ever did the reading. Leaving him no choice but to bully them all into submission.

"Uh, what page is that on?" Ms. Fortunato asked. "The red book, right?"

Staci Fortunato, said the seating chart. A marketing major at Syracuse. Adam imagined she'd skated by on her looks and charm. Probably never met an assignment she couldn't seduce a teacher to let her avoid. Unfair assumption, but Adam was suddenly cranky.

"Page one-thirteen," Adam said. "And, yes, the red book. The one with 'Torts' on the cover. Because this is Torts. Or at least it's supposed to be." Adam was surprised Staci had even acknowledged his question. Most students, if called on, would simply ignore their names. Yes, the professors had the chart in front of them—but would they really challenge a student who pretended not to be there? In fact, if "being" meant "present," they might not have even been pretending.

"I think I skipped that case. Maybe I have the wrong casebook? Mine's blue, and I don't see anything about a railroad."

Adam stared at her with what he hoped was a menacing look. "I'm sure it's there. Can you skim the case quickly now?"

"Like, here?" she said.

"Yes."

"It may take me a few minutes. I'm a slow reader."

A slow reader? Then don't waste our time. Call your mother and ask her to pick you up. Tell her you'll be living at home while you look for a different career. This is what Adam's own Torts professor might have said to him when he was a 1L at Harvard. But, of course, Adam didn't say it. Although he wanted to be one of those professors who struck fear in their students, who made them feel that if they didn't do the reading, they might as well not show up at all—the time and place had changed. When Adam was in school, professors still gave C's. Now, a C was the new F, and an A– the new B. At Manhattan Law School—which wasn't in Manhattan at all, but on the banks of the Gowanus Canal in Brooklyn—even the curve was curved. If a student got a C, it meant either he didn't show up for the final exam, or he'd been caught in a compromising position with the professor's golden retriever.

Adam looked at Staci, her wandering eyes and her lost soul. Her petite frame squeezed into a low-cut blouse, her hair and makeup perfect. Why was she here? What cultural forces had driven her to waste hundreds of thousands of dollars of her parents' money and sit in class as if she were waiting for a manicure at her favorite salon? Did she realize she wasn't a kid anymore, and was staring down the barrel of the rest of her life?

The truth was he felt bad for her. It wasn't her fault her parents had expectations. And it wasn't her fault the system let her slide for all these years. She tried her best on the LSAT, but the logic games were a mystery. Why would the girl in the puzzle have to sit next to Jacob, but avoid Kevin, Linus, and Mark? Why couldn't she just invite them all to the table for bottle service?

Adam held her gaze, and Staci's eyes flickered, then turned away. In that brief instant, however, Adam saw something: call it shame. It was just a spark, but he saw it before it was gone and it gave him hope. After all, wasn't that why he left his big corporate law firm and took a teaching job at this third-tier school? The glimmer of intellectual engagement; the possibility of making a difference in a student's life; the challenge of educating a new generation to succeed in a complex world. He didn't become a professor to use his pulpit to embarrass the weak and ill-informed. Instead, God help him, he had hoped to inspire and provoke them.

He looked up at the class and asked for a volunteer.

Daniel Hamburger's hand shot up in the front row. It had become a familiar, and rare, hand. He rattled off the facts and twisted procedural history of *Palsgraf* with confidence, speaking in complete paragraphs and even concluding with a critique of the majority holding. "Query," he said, "whether proximate cause is so attenuated as to preclude recovery for a set of events—although implausible—not impossible to foresee."

It was a command performance, earning Hamburger the envious stares of several classmates, and the rolled eyes of the rest of the class who, although relieved Adam wouldn't have to call on anyone else, wouldn't hesitate to push Daniel into the Gowanus Canal should the opportunity arise.

"Excellent answer," Adam said, as Hamburger beamed, the grin on his face just as bright as the guy in the back who was checking his fantasy baseball scores. Adam couldn't help but feel a tiny drop of pride in Hamburger's performance—a student who cared enough to do the reading, even if he was the kind of guy Adam had hated at Harvard. At least Daniel Hamburger gave Adam the feeling that all was not lost. Coupled with his sympathy for Staci, he thought that maybe—just maybe—he could turn around these students' academic futures.

Just then, the woman next to Hamburger leaned too far backwards and her chair slipped out from beneath her. Her arms windmilled, and she went down, taking her coffee, laptop, and a stack of papers with her. It was as if a small brown shrapnel bomb exploded as students on both sides jumped out of the way. In the commotion, a soft-covered book tumbled from Hamburger's desk to the floor, landing not far from Adam's feet.

It was a teacher's guide. The same one Adam used to prepare for class. The one he'd use to write the exam questions. The one that the casebook publisher assured him was never made available to students. Hamburger saw him looking and shrugged. The shrug seemed to say at least I tried.

Adam felt sick. This was not what he expected when he gave up the town cars, Manhattan co-op, and Hamptons share for the idealized life of an academic. But no one warned him teaching at a place like Manhattan Law School would be like this—disappointment, frustration, and a feeling of pointlessness nearly equal to his work at the law firm. In fact, when he was hired, no one had said anything about the teaching at all. Instead, the faculty committee asked about his scholarly intentions, reviewed his meager writings, and called a couple of the partners who'd supervised his work. No one bothered to see what he would be like standing in front of a classroom or told him what to expect. It turned out he was a prop. A babysitter. A dartboard on which the students flung their disdain.

But he wasn't prepared to fold. Not after only three weeks. Not yet. "Let's review the case as a class," he said, when the student picked herself up from the floor and the laughter died down. Adam grabbed a piece of chalk and turned to the old-fashioned blackboard. He rarely used the board—his penmanship showed it—but things couldn't possibly get any worse. He scribbled as quickly as he could, the chalk making a reassuring clacking sound and kicking up puffs of dust as the words took form. Even as the bell rang he powered on. "I'm going to ask you to stay in your seats for another minute or two," he said to the board. "I want to get the facts up here and give you a few questions to think about for when we pick it up tomorrow."

He raced to get it all written down, a concise diagram reducing the case to its simplest parts—the train in the station, the passenger rushing to catch it, the dropped package of fireworks, an explosion, pandemonium, and poor Mrs. Palsgraf struck by the falling clock. He looked at his creation for a moment, pleased that he could turn a disaster into a true teaching opportunity. He turned around, ready to call on anyone who could read. No advance preparation necessary.

But the room was completely empty.

Manhattan Law School Tenure Evaluation—
Form Revised 12/83
Tenure Evaluation Form–CONFIDENTIAL

Faculty Name: Laura Stapleton
Height/Weight: Approx. 5'7", 130 lbs.

Evaluator: Jasper Jeffries

Section 1–Background and CV. Laura's credentials (BA, JD, Yale) were excellent prior to arriving at MLS. She has done nothing but distinguish herself while on the faculty here. Laura adds racial and ethnic diversity that allow the school to meet its quotas, and her youth and attractiveness help us better appeal to men and lesbians.

Section 2–Teaching. Laura's students consistently give her excellent evaluations. Of the two students who completed her teacher evaluation over the past four years, both have given her high marks even while scribbling vulgarities about the administration on the rest of the page.

Section 3–Scholarship. Laura is very attractive. And her book was nominated for a lot of awards. I hear it is good.

Section 4–Miscellaneous. Laura has yet to fully embrace the "administrative responsibilities" we like to see in our full-time faculty, but we expect with some additional incentives she will step up and take a leadership role on our grading committee. In the meantime, we continue to monitor her email.

Tenure: __X__ Yes ____No

2

Love Me Tenure

THE METAL VAT IN THE faculty dining room steamed with "Golden Delicious Chicken," or so claimed the placard on the rickety folding table. In truth, its color was closer to lead than gold. As for its taste, no chickens had been injured in its preparation. But at least it was pasteurized. The faculty insisted on this after an outbreak of giardiasis traced back to the "homemade" muffins served in the student cafeteria. Now, although the food was mostly tasteless, it wouldn't kill them. Not today, anyway.

Laura Stapleton lifted the serving spoon and stifled a grimace. She had seen legal briefs that were more appetizing. If she had a choice, she wouldn't be eating here. Not that there were a lot of other options in the wasteland that bordered the land of waste on which the campus sat. But anything would have been better than the tasteless food and colorless company. Face time, however, was everything—especially when most faculty rarely showed their faces outside of scheduled classes, hiding from students in their locked offices or home in their apartments. If Laura wanted to advance up the academic ladder—better committee appointments, fewer teaching responsibilities, more money for research assistants—she would have to eat and greet in the dining room.

As the only woman of color on the faculty, Laura was both constantly celebrated and consistently underestimated. She was trotted out for every candidate interview, accreditation meeting, and panel discussion involving anything linked to anyone of ethnicity. At alumni events she was positioned front and center. Her picture was photoshopped into most of the brochures released by the marketing department, and placed on virtually every page of the law school's website. On the other hand, her scholarship was viewed with suspicion and, occasionally, disdain. Her subject matter—civil procedure—was mainstream, doctrinal, and, to the disappointment of many on the faculty, entirely unrelated to her race. She had yet to propose a class on Racism and the Law, the Civil Rights movement, or the Voting Rights Act, and had not written anything titled, "The Founding Fathers of Bigotry: A Race-Based Interpretation of *Marbury v. Madison*." This was a huge frustration to the Promotions and Tenure Committee, who would have loved a good reason to reject her appointment when she came up for a vote. Instead, she wrote articles on perfectly normal topics, cited by an appropriate number of journals and judges, and her book on the ascendancy of the federal judiciary was published by Yale University Press and nominated for a National Book Award. So the Old Guard had no choice but to grant her tenure.

Laura took her tray and looked for a safe place to eat. Old Man Porter sat at his usual table in the corner, gumming his mashed potatoes, having lost his teeth somewhere between his home in Queens and the International Tax elective where he taught three students about new regulations in East Germany, Czechoslovakia, and the Ottoman Empire. Rochelle Tucker sat over by the window, reapplying her lipstick and adjusting her brassiere. She was gunning for tenure any way she could, and she didn't care who knew it. Rumor was she had even paid Old Man Porter a call—during visiting hours, of course—but no one wanted to think too hard about that image, let alone investigate the truth. At the large table in the middle of the room—the only one with a floral centerpiece—sat the school's Associate Dean and two of his faculty henchmen, along with the Chief Marketing Officer, who had managed to lose the rights to the law school's domain name to a porn site. Now the new website sat, uninvitingly, at *seemanhattan lawschool.com*. (It had been effectively parodied in the student newspaper as "Semen Hat and Law School." Sadly, this was now how most students and faculty remembered the address.)

Steering wide of the Dean, Laura sat at the table near the (broken) fire exit with some of the other junior faculty—second-class citizens in the professorial pecking order. They, at least, were tenured, or tenure-track. The non-tenure track faculty—contract employees and adjuncts—didn't even get a table, or chairs; they took their lunch to go in recycled Chinese food containers that still bore a faint trace of moo goo gai pan, and ate in the stairwells. As the conversation swirled around her, Laura poked at the shreds of chicken on her plate. After a couple of bites, however, she discreetly spat the unchewable parts into a napkin and gave up. She sipped instead from her bottle of Perrier, which, untouched by the food service subcontractors, at least had some effervescence.

"Mind if I join you?" a voice asked.

She looked up to see one of the new faculty hires hovering with a plate stacked high with the crusty ends of the chicken. He was tall and lanky, with floppy brown hair that he really should have had cut. Laura cleared her purse from the seat to her left.

"All yours," she said, and resumed fake chewing.

"Adam Wright," he said, extending a hand.

"I know who you are."

"You're Laura Stapleton."

"I know that, too."

If Wright was offended, he didn't show it. He smiled and sat beside her, then asked her to pass the hot sauce.

"Just finished teaching?" she asked, softening her tone. She regretted being sharp with him. He seemed harmless and inoffensive. One of a steady stream of young faculty who would last a few years, then be passed over for tenure. Barely anyone made it, and the number had only dwindled in recent years. The tenure system protected the perks and privileges of an entrenched oligarchy, and kept a younger generation from challenging the status quo. Laura was an exception to a jealously guarded rule.

"I guess you could call it teaching," said Wright. "Pleading is more like it." He picked up the bottle of hot sauce, noticed the expiration date, and put it back on the table. "Thanks for letting me join you."

Laura nodded. "Why not? We're on the same team."

Before Wright could respond, they were distracted by a shout coming from the center table. "I'm telling you," Prof. David Wheeler had said, loud enough for the whole room to hear, "it is not even a debate. The *Emancipation Proclamation* was a complete bust." Laura felt Wright looking at her, while a silence fell over the room. It was, Laura knew, exactly the reaction Wheeler hoped to provoke.

Wheeler taught Constitutional Law and had been named one of *New York* magazine's 100 Most Influential Lawyers in 1983, an honor he still had taped to his office door. He also ran the school's mostly ignored program in "distance learning," Web-enabled course offerings that recycled videotaped lectures for the Internet, packaging them with the promise of an "online J.D.," an unaccredited degree that was worthless yet cost $1,500 per credit hour. He was a big man whose hair grew entirely on the lower half of his head. Now, he called over to Laura. "What do you think, Professor Stapleton? Did the slaves get a bum deal?"

Laura refused to take the bait. Like all bullies, Wheeler was best ignored. He took a perverse glee in tormenting her to compensate for his extremely small manhood—not that Laura had personal knowledge, but she knew the type.

"Emancipation is overrated, don't you agree?" Wheeler's voice could crush glass.

"Laura, come join us," said Associate Dean Jasper Jeffries. Although Erwin Clopp was officially the law school's dean, Jeffries was the true power behind the throne. He was everything Clopp wasn't, physically, mentally, and otherwise. Muscular, bald, and clean-shaven, Jeffries could pass for a mascot on a bottle of cleaning fluid. Clopp, on the other hand, with his white hair, white beard, and mellifluous voice, looked and sounded like Burl Ives in *Rudolph the Red-Nosed Reindeer*. Jeffries made all the decisions while Clopp was rolled out for faculty and board meetings.

Laura glanced at Wright. She didn't want to be rude, but she couldn't ignore a direct invitation from Jeffries. The other junior faculty members at the table had resumed their conversation, studiously ignoring Laura and Jeffries for fear of being singled out.

Jeffries saved her from the Hobson's choice by adding, "Bring the doofus."

"I think he means you," said Laura.

"Charming," said Wright.

"It's a term of endearment," Laura assured him. "You should hear some of his insults."

She stood and waited for Wright, then took her tray and moved to the table in the middle of the room. Wright followed, squeezing into a chair between her and Rick Rodriguez, faculty advisor to the *Law Review*. A former Supreme Court clerk, Rodriguez was a rabid Republican and staunch immigration foe—and extremely, almost preposterously, gay. He was trailed constantly by a coterie of young, handsome students he was advising, although there was talk that some of these young men weren't even enrolled at the school. But no one bothered to check. As long as they didn't cost the school any money, no one cared who Rodriguez kept in his closet, or what they did there.

Laura pretended to listen to Wheeler pontificate. She snapped to attention, however, when Jeffries laid a thick finger on her forearm. She turned just in time to see the woman from marketing—who may have had a name, but Laura couldn't recall it—glaring at her. Was she jealous? Impossible. And yet that would explain a lot of things, like why Laura's name was misspelled in the alumni magazine and why her photo on the website was a hideous shot taken without her knowledge when she was sick with the flu.

"Laura, my dear," said Jeffries. "How is the book coming?"

Laura was working on a follow-up to her book on the federal judiciary. Although it earned her the enmity of her colleagues, her first book made her the most-recognized scholar at the law school.

It helped that publication coincided with a bruising Supreme Court nomination battle, which made Laura a minor celebrity on NPR. It also gave her a certain amount of clout, which she was loath to exercise, but quietly wielded during the tenure process when Jeffries questioned her "administrative responsibilities."

"Truthfully, I've barely started."

"That's a shame," said Jeffries, as he fingered her arm. "A brilliant and beautiful mind like yours should be focusing on her scholarship."

"It's been so busy with the new semester."

He lowered his voice. "You would have plenty of time for your writing if you had accepted our proposal."

"I know," said Laura, being careful with her words. "Unfortunately, my answer is the same."

"I thought recent events might have changed your feelings."

"What events?"

"Your living situation."

"Excuse me?"

"That lovely building you live in. It's going co-op. I assumed you'd heard. It would be a shame if you couldn't afford to buy your apartment. All that time and effort you've put into fixing it up."

For the last ten years, Laura had rented a beautiful apartment in Park Slope that she could afford because the landlord loved her and was too lazy to raise the rent. But if it were true that it was on the market, even at an insider price it would be beyond her means. She hoped Jeffries was wrong, although she suspected he probably wasn't.

"Then I better start saving my nickels."

"You'll need more than nickels."

"I appreciate the concern, Jasper, really. But I think I'll manage."

"It's your decision. Although I must say I remain mystified."

"It's not that mysterious. I'm just old-fashioned that way."

"I've always admired that about you." Jeffries's finger inched along her arm like an oily caterpillar. "But remember, we're in this together. Sink or swim. One big happy family."

The three men were not her family, Laura thought, and she would be damned to sink with them. But she didn't respond. She caught Adam observing her, his brown eyes like question marks, dark and uncertain. A spasm of guilt racked her insides— or maybe it was the food. She clenched her jaw until the feeling passed, but it left her hollow and shaken, and the taste in her mouth was like something had gone there to die.

From: Staci Fortunato <staci.fortunato@seemanhattanlawschool.com>
Subject: Next Week's Assignment
Date: September 5, 11:20:06 PM EST
To: Adam Wright <adam.wright@seemanhattanlawschool.com>

Hi Prof. I didn't buy the casebook for the course because it was really expensive. I know you said it was important to do the reading before class. Could you email me the pages we're supposed to read? PDF is fine. Thanks.

From: Staci Fortunato <staci.fortunato@seemanhattanlawschool.com>
Subject: Last Week's Assignment
Date: September 8, 12:14:29 PM EST
To: Adam Wright <adam.wright@seemanhattanlawschool.com>

Not sure if you check your email regularly, but I never heard back when I asked you for the book pages. That's why I could not do the reading. If you get this message, could you email me the pages—last week's and this week's? And I guess next week's too. Thanks.

From: Staci Fortunato <staci.fortunato@seemanhattanlawschool.com>
Subject: DO YOU CHECK EMAIL?????
Date: September 11, 2:13:55 AM EST
To: Adam Wright <adam.wright@seemanhattanlawschool.com>

Okay, I guess you're not checking email. Do you have a Snapchat? I was going to get the reading from the library, but the librarian said I could not just take the books home for the rest of the semester. Whatever. I cannot believe we're having class on September 11 anyway. I thought we were off, so I scheduled a massage. But I'll do you a favor, prof—if I show up, I'll wear my twin towers bra. Peace.

3

The Priapic professor

A WEEK HAD PASSED SINCE ADAM sat next to Laura in the faculty dining room. A week during which Adam spent his time plotting, scheming, and hoping to accidentally run into her again, without success. With their offices on separate floors, it was a challenge to engineer a random encounter, and apparently one meal per week was the limit of Laura's appetite for culinary danger. No matter how long he lingered at the lunch table he didn't see her. He was supposed to be working on an article that would keep him employed, but instead he spent his time trying to map out her most likely route to class. He even ventured into the faculty reading room where he found Old Man Porter asleep in a puddle of drool. But no Laura.

At most schools, he could have merely waited in the lobby for her to pass. Indeed, during the cash-flush 1990s, Manhattan Law School had spent $7 million constructing a magnificent main entrance atrium—cathedral ceilings, imported wood, great legal quotations from history etched into the walls (some without errors)—but the ventilation ducts had been accidentally reversed and blew exhaust from the street into the atrium. As a result, even though it was the only entrance to the school, it was impossible to wait there for more than a few minutes without being overcome by carbon monoxide fumes and the ever-present stink from the canal. The security guards wore masks and worked in short shifts, while everyone else held his nose and walked through briskly.

Adam tried to sit in the atrium each morning and casually read the newspaper at one of the old Apple IIe computer terminals. But his vision blurred before the modem finished dialing up the server, and he found himself taking regular walks around the building, where the particulate concentration was not as severe. On his fifth day of circling, when he had almost given up on seeing her again, he nearly ran into Laura as she raced around the corner, a cup of coffee in her hand. Adam's hands were stuffed in his jacket pockets, and his head was down as he gulped fresh air like a drowning victim.

"Adam?" she asked, as he narrowly missed colliding with her. "Are you okay? You seem like you're . . . lost."

"Oh, no, I just come out here for the fresh air sometimes," he replied, flustered. "My office gets a little claustrophobic."

"I can imagine," Laura said. "I was in a closet my first two years. People kept coming in looking for paper clips."

Adam laughed. "Last week the janitor asked me for cleaning supplies."

"Well, don't stay outside too long. You might come back to find him sleeping in your chair."

"I was just heading in. You?"

"Teaching at ten-thirty."

"We should grab lunch sometime," Adam blurted before he lost his nerve. "We never finished our conversation."

"That's true, we didn't," said Laura. "Give my assistant a call and we can set something up."

And that was how he and Laura ended up in a Carroll Gardens coffee shop, the kind of place with exposed brick, bearded hipsters, and overpriced milky beverages. Laura looked radiant as always, in a yellow blouse and black trousers that cinched high at the waist, while he felt slovenly and underdressed. It was warm outside, and his pants itched uncomfortably. He scratched at his legs, then rubbed one foot against his other ankle like a praying mantis. His hair felt suddenly too big for his head, and his skin felt sticky and loose.

Laura didn't seem to notice his awkwardness. She stirred three spoons of sugar into her coffee and shrugged when she saw him watching. "I have a sweet tooth," she explained.

"I'm not judging."

"No, it's a serious character flaw. Goes right to my hips."

"You can't possibly tell."

"Oh, I can tell."

"Well, we all need a good character flaw. It's like a well-placed mole. Accentuates the positive."

"I have others."

"Moles?"

"Character flaws."

"Let me guess," said Adam. "You hate children."

"I love children! As long as they're not mine."

"Dogs, then."

"I love dogs. I've got a retriever mutt."

"You put empty ice cream cartons back into the freezer."

"I hate people who do that."

"I'm stumped, then. What else could be wrong with you?"

Laura's eyes flicked toward the fire exit. She took a healthy sip of her coffee. Then she asked, "Do you like it here?"

"In this café?" Adam replied, a little thrown.

"No, I mean at MLS. It's not exactly Harvard."

When Adam first announced his career change, friends told him how much they envied him. After all, everyone in the rough-and-tumble corporate world was stretched too thin and too far, overworked, underpaid, unappreciated, and generally miserable. The work, at best, was amoral; at its worst, it was positively corrupting. The academic life seemed like the idyllic antidote, despite the pay cut. Only his brother, Sam, understood the complicated motives and emotions, how the choices their father made years ago cast a shadow over nearly every aspect of Adam's life.

"The students are a mixed bunch," Adam said carefully.

"What was your first clue?" Laura cocked an eyebrow, a neat party trick.

He allowed himself a smile. "I had a student take a phone call in Torts the other day. Then she emailed me to ask if I could send her the reading. I couldn't even come up with a response that wouldn't get me fired."

"That's nothing. Two students were suspended last year for having sex in class."

"Sex?"

"S-E-X."

"Like actual intercourse?"

"Well, no, I don't think so. We didn't get into the details. There was digital manipulation, shall we say. And they had to replace the chair."

"Wow. At least back in the day we snuck behind the library stacks to make out."

"Professor! I'm shocked."

"Same old, I suppose. Every generation complains about the next. Soon I'll be saying, 'That's not music; it's noise.'"

"I already do."

They shared a chuckle, then Adam said, "But students really are different today."

"They wear less, for one thing."

"True. And all their devices—you can't get their attention. And if you do, there's this sense of entitlement, like what have you done for me lately?"

"It's the customer service version of higher education."

"The consumer is always right."

"Exactly."

"For two hundred thousand dollars in debt, they want something for their money. Even if it makes us feel like short-order cooks."

"I suppose I don't blame them, but someone should teach them not to email their professors and ask for the reading material. What will they do when they have jobs?"

"They don't get jobs."

"Is it really that bad?"

Laura nodded. "It's bad. No one wants to tell our students the truth."

"Well, it's not as if their eyes aren't open."

"True, but we still don't level with them."

Adam had seen the glossy brochure and marketing video produced for the school at great expense by some NoHo PR firm. Reviewing the materials, you would think Manhattan Law School students had perfect hair, skin, and teeth, and liked nothing better than to read *The Federalist Papers* while paddle-boarding in the Central Park reservoir. Adam knew the reservoir was really a sound stage in Queens, and the "students" were unemployed actors, but he wondered if the real students—or, more importantly, their parents—did.

"You think it's different at other schools?"

"I don't know," said Laura. "I'll report back to you soon. I've been talking to the Dean at Berkeley."

"UC Berkeley—in San Francisco?"

"There's another Berkeley?"

"No, I mean—that's a serious school. Top ten. Congratulations." Adam tried to keep a straight face, but he felt like he had been sucker punched. They just met, and now she was leaving? Whoa, slow down, he told himself. No one is going anywhere today. Drink your coffee. Breathe. Stalking a woman he barely knew was surely not the best way to date her.

"The thing is, I'm not sure I want to move."

"Why would you stay if you could teach at Berkeley?"

"I'm a New Yorker. Born and raised here, and lived here all my life. Besides, I'm comfortable at MLS. Sure, there are problems, but at least I know where the bodies are buried."

"There are bodies?"

"You know what I mean. No institution is perfect. In the end, you live with the imperfections you can handle."

Adam understood, better than anyone, a life with imperfections—banging on the windows to get inside. But sometimes you couldn't keep them out; sometimes, they crawled up underneath and then it was them, or you.

Laura glanced at her watch, which Adam took as a bad sign. "Are we late?" he asked.

"I'm sorry," she said. "Directed Legal Studies. I should probably be on time, even though my students aren't."

"How'd you end up teaching that class anyway?"

"It's a long story. The short answer is I didn't get to choose. Call it a form of penance."

"Did they lighten your teaching load?"

"Are you kidding? I don't even get paid for it."

The school's administration was notoriously cheap, which Adam knew from his negotiations over salary with Dean Clopp, who offered him a new lamp and a box of staples instead of the additional $5,000 he requested. Yet law school was also a big business, a money-making machine that produced steady returns. At sixty grand a pop, and 400 students per class, MLS took in $72 million in annual tuition revenue alone. Even with the drumbeat of bad news about jobs and the legal profession generally, applications still exceeded available places by a margin of three to one. Given its low-budget location and lack of amenities, the school was like a corporate raider's plum waiting to be picked.

Laura cleared their cups and the empty packets of sugar. "Should we walk back to school together?" she asked.

"If you think you can be seen with me," said Adam.

"I'll take the chance."

It was unusually warm for the end of September. Laura carried her jacket over her shoulder and Adam was in his shirt sleeves. The streets of Carroll Gardens were tree-lined and flowered, and bustled with delis, markets, restaurants, and bars. Adam felt a sense of peace, a serenity that comes in the presence of a kindred spirit. Maybe he was seeing the world through Laura-colored lenses, but it had been a long time since he met anyone who stirred his soul, and even longer since his last real relationship. Jane Van Dyke had been his law school girlfriend, and they continued to date for a time after graduation. But it was the same old story:

she lived uptown; he lived downtown; and then she cheated on him with her boss. After that, he hunkered down and focused his excess testosterone on the law.

Was it too much to hope that Laura shared his feelings? He was relatively attractive, clean, and had all his teeth. Why could it not work out between them? He knew he was getting ahead of himself, but he couldn't help it. He felt like a schoolboy with a crush on the prettiest girl in town. Here she was walking next to him, lithe and loose-limbed, while the breeze rippled the leaves on a sun-dappled afternoon and blew his cares into the far reaches of Queens.

Laura grabbed his elbow as they stepped around a particularly treacherous pothole and held it one second longer than absolutely necessary. Her touch rippled down his arm into the tips of his fingers. He stole a quick glance and saw her smile, a flash of white between red lips, and that was enough to give him hope.

They turned the corner, talking about nothing consequential, and ran into a student Laura knew. He was thin and furtive, and wore a wool cap, although it was sixty-five degrees. Laura introduced him, but Adam didn't catch his name. The boy looked anxious and preoccupied, and Laura soon released him.

"He's going to be late for my tutorial," she said.

"Where's he going?"

"I don't know—to get a coffee?"

"Doesn't look like he needs any."

She shook her head. "Some of these kids are lost souls. I don't know what they're doing in law school in the first place."

"Where else would they go?"

"Prison?"

Adam looked back after the boy, but he was gone.

A knot of students smoking cigarettes lingered outside the school's entrance. Adam envied their careless indifference to health and breath. It was illegal to smoke near a school, but the students puffed away, defiant and proud. Once there were protests against apartheid; now there was smoking.

Adam and Laura made their way through the smokers and entered the atrium. It was foul-smelling and hot, but Laura did not seem anxious to leave. Students streamed past, backpacks like heavy weaponry. A herd of young men in baseball caps were shouting about last night's football game. A group of young women with belly rings and tattoos laughed uproariously at something one of them said. Everyone was texting, talking, walking, posting, snapping, chatting. A stranger couldn't have guessed this was an academic institution, where the next generation of lawmakers and judges were being trained.

"I'd like to ask you a favor," said Laura.

Adam stopped, then started. "Okay," he said.

Laura looked away. A small bird had flown into the atrium and was fluttering around in confusion. It banged against a window as if it expected it to open, then flew back up to a ledge where it rested before making another attempt.

"Don't say anything about Berkeley," said Laura.

"Of course not!"

"And if you know anyone there, they don't need to know what goes on here, either."

"What goes on here?" Adam asked, confused. He scrutinized her face for a clue, but her brown eyes reflected no light, just the flatness of someone who doesn't want to be asked more questions.

"Exactly." She pursed her lips and nodded, then held out her hand to shake goodbye. It felt awkward to shake hands as if they were strangers or business acquaintances, but the hand was waiting there and Adam took it. Laura shook briskly, her palm warm but not inviting. Her smile polite but demure. Then she turned, disappeared into a throng of students, and was gone. Adam slowly made his way in the opposite direction, betwixt, befuddled, and not a little bit priapic.

Search

Gary Deranger
@derangeredspecies
Student of the law, student of the world, GLD + AMK 4ever
Brooklyn, NY · garyderanger.tumblr.com

9,001
TWEETS

300
FOLLOWING

300
FOLLOWERS

  Follow

Tweets

Gary Deranger @derangeredspecies
Jury decisions have to be unanimous? WTF???

Gary Deranger @derangeredspecies
Whenever I try 2 b early to class, I pass a pigeon on the street who just needs some TLC and then I rip his wings off and try to bite him. And then I'm late. #kidding

Gary Deranger @derangeredspecies
Your love's got me lookin' so crazy right now. Crazy right now. Crazy right now. Who wants a cheesesteak?

Gary Deranger @derangeredspecies
"Even if you don't miss the transfer deadline by three weeks, you're still never going to leave this place" (what the brochure should say)

Gary Deranger @derangeredspecies
I think Civil Procedure was invented by the devil. Also, my Civil Procedure professor is the devil.

Gary Deranger @derangeredspecies
A Doritos Locos Taco, filled with El Pollo Loco chicken, served in a mental hospital, would cause a break in the space-time continuum.

Gary Deranger @derangeredspecies
If you're served with a restraining order is that a good excuse to treat yourself to Pinkberry?

Gary Deranger @derangeredspecies
AM your old phone number was so easy to remember, pls change it back

4

Lost in Translation

GARY DERANGER DID NOT SET out to be a stalker.
In the beginning, he was simply looking for signs of regret. A frown, a faraway glance, a quivering lip. If he'd learned one thing in law school—and he hadn't learned much more—it was that intent was everything. There was no crime without a guilty mind. But when her ISP started spitting back his emails, and she blocked him on Twitter and Gchat, unfriended him on Facebook, and changed her cell phone number, he really had no other choice. She had broken up with him in April, right before exams, claiming she needed to concentrate on studying for finals. Then she disappeared from all the places he used to find her: the student lounge, the Starbucks they frequented, the women's bathroom next to the shuttered library. He spent the rest of the spring and summer in a mounting frenzy of longing, searching for her like a hypercaffeinated paparazzo (Starbucks made him buy something if he was going to sit in there all day). He camped out in front of her building until some local hoodlums tried to set him on fire. Then he spent thirty-two hours straight at LaGuardia Airport when he heard a rumor she was flying home to visit her parents. His repeated encounters

with the Port Authority police landed him on the "No Fly" list, even though he hadn't flown since his first panic attack eight years ago. The Administrative Law judge who heard his appeal told him he had crossed the line, and warned him to leave Ann Marie alone.

By the time school began again in the fall, she had dropped the classes they had in common and seemed to know exactly where he'd be waiting in the halls. On the rare occasion he was able to get close, her friends intervened with a well-timed shove or a shot of pepper spray. She traveled in a pack like the Queen of England or a major party presidential candidate. There was always a giant lug beside her—a thick-skulled future prosecutor—willing to take a bullet. Gary's only option had been to follow her to class and peer through the shatterproof windows while she unpacked her books and laptop and took her seat in the front of the room. He was always an outsider, looking in.

On this day, as the students streamed into the classroom, jostling him as he stood by the door, he watched her chatting with the girl on her left, a brunette in a bustier, the kind of girl who might normally catch his attention if she had not been sitting next to Ann Marie. As it was, he could no longer even remember the names of most of his classmates. They morphed into a giant faceless blur, indistinguishable in their tank tops and cargo pants, tattoos and hair gel, bleached teeth, and depilated follicles.

That Gary was still in school was something of a small miracle. He had passed his second semester classes by the skin of his teeth, with two C's, one C–, and a D. As a result, he was forcibly enrolled in the law school's remedial program, something euphemistically called "Directed Legal Studies," or "DLS," but more commonly known as "Law School for Dummies" or "LSD." This required him to attend special workshops focused on test-taking and essay writing, and a course devoted entirely to basic English grammar. The school's ostensible purpose was to help him raise his grades, but really it was to keep him paying tuition. Every student lost was a $60,000 check down the drain.

Not only did the DLS program keep them in, but the school structured it so that a DLS student couldn't fulfill all of his requirements in just three years. Sure, Gary could quit. But quitting meant his already-spent tuition would have gone to waste, something he vaguely remembered was called "sunk cost." Even more important, quitting meant losing Ann Marie forever. And this, more than anything, was the reason he continued to read and outline for his classes—barely enough to follow his professors' lectures, but sufficient, he hoped, to stay in DLS.

If Ann Marie saw him peering through the window, she didn't acknowledge it. Not that it was easy to see through the glass, caked with years of law student spittle. The girl in the bustier continued to talk to Ann Marie as she pulled her books out of her bag. The class had filled, and nearly half the seats were occupied. Students had their computers open in front of them, already Tindering for potential dates or browsing the day's deals on Scoutmob. Two students were furiously finishing a game of Words With Friends. Gary stood on his tiptoes, mentally willing Ann Marie to look his way, until he felt a meaty hand on his shoulder, uncomfortably heavy, flesh swollen and loose, attached to a large, ursine creature.

"Are you in this class?" Professor Wheeler asked, his breath like a dead squirrel.

"No, I . . . uh . . . I," said Gary.

"And the reason you are blocking the egress is . . . ?"

"Uh, no reason."

"Then please find no reason somewhere else." Wheeler stepped past him with a sneer, leaving Gary wobbling in the door frame. The class stared out at him, and for one instant he caught Ann Marie's eyes before they dropped to her keyboard.

But that was enough. She had seen him! Never mind that he had been humiliated; it was worth the price of embarrassment for just one look directly into those velvet blue eyes, so dark they could be black. Gary remembered how they used to stare up at him as they made love, slowly closing as Ann Marie's excitement mounted, then fluttering awake in surprise.

Wheeler had already begun his lecture. A student in the front row squirmed nervously as Wheeler peppered him with questions about the day's case, a monster Con Law decision that had radically changed the world just before the casebook was written in 1942. Even through the clouded glass, Gary could see the sickly expression on the poor student's face and the beads of sweat that stood out on his forehead. Constitutional Law was a required course for second year students, even though it was the least likely subject any of them would encounter in their careers (those who were lucky enough to have careers). It was like teaching plumbers about the molecular structure of H_2O. Interesting work if you could get it, but worthless when there was a leak.

Gary considered waiting for the class to end in the hope of catching Ann Marie again. But he was already late for his tutorial, and had been warned that two absences would mean an additional "administrative fee" in order to continue participating. He was in enough debt that it would take three hundred fifty-four years of minimum payments to pay it off. He took one last lingering squint through the glass, then turned and headed for the elevator. The police tape across the doors reminded him that they were out of service. Panicked, he raced the other way to the stairs. If he wanted to be on time, he would have to sprint.

Although the law school spanned ten floors in one large building, the elevators were temperamental, prone to mechanical failure, and, prior to the tape, had caused no less than a dozen students to miss final exams, class-dropping deadlines, or days of sleep. Last week a librarian had been trapped for eight hours until school security noticed the alarm had been pulled and quickly finished lunch in order to go and rescue her. They found her chewing pages from Powell's treatise on Property, half-crazed from glue and the Rule Against Perpetuities. Now everyone except the fully tenured took the stairs. (Their elevator, the school's lone functioning one, was no luxury ride either, not since a queen hornet flew in and built her nest there.) So the stairwells were overwhelmingly crowded with students, staff, and the members of the faculty unfortunate enough to lack both job security and health insurance, all trudging up and down, most too out of shape to be in a stairwell in the first place, moving slowly, panting, resting, taking a break for a snack.

Gary followed a young woman with a tattoo of a fox (or possibly a squirrel) just below her waistline. As he leaned in to examine it closely, he nearly tripped on the feet of a man he assumed was one of the school's "nontraditional" students: old people who had lost their jobs and believed that saddling themselves with additional debt would save them. Gary yelped, frightening the tattooed woman, who escaped quickly into the herd.

"Sorry," said the man.

"Fuck!" said Gary.

"Excuse me?" The man seemed offended, as if it were Gary who had tripped him, and not the other way around. But now that Gary's eyes refocused, he realized he had seen the man before—it was the new Torts guy, Professor Wright, who had been outside walking with Professor Stapleton.

"Tourette's," Gary explained, faking a spasm and a series of eye tics. Then, spotting a pair of fire doors above them, he quickly pushed past Professor Wright, hoping he wouldn't be followed. When he got out in the hallway, he ducked into a bathroom stall where he waited a good ten minutes before safely (and uneventfully) resuming his trudge upstairs.

Professor Stapleton's office was on the eighth floor, near the faculty dining room. The hallway smelled of sauerkraut, rotten eggs, mold, and wet dog. It was a faculty smell, familiar to Gary from too many closed door meetings with associate deans after his first semester when the law school started talking to him about the Directed Legal Studies program, issuing him a glossy brochure he could show his parents in case they wondered where his tuition money was going and why it seemed like he would never actually earn his degree. Prof. Stapleton's tutorial met in a small conference room two doors down from her office. When Gary arrived, the other four students in the tutorial were already there. They avoided looking at him, as men condemned to death often avoid looking at their fellow inmates in the hope of eluding their fate.

"Welcome, Mr. Deranger," said Professor Stapleton. "Glad you could join us."

"Sorry I'm late," said Gary. "I, uh, I was talking to Professor Wheeler, and then Professor Wright."

Professor Stapleton regarded him quizzically, but if she thought Gary was lying she didn't call him on it.

The class was conducted in workshop format. The students wrote short assignments each week, and then, led by Professor Stapleton, reviewed each other's work. Gary imagined the class might have been helpful if he could actually concentrate. He liked Professor Stapleton. Besides dressing better than most professors—always wearing both a top and a bottom—she seemed genuinely interested in helping him. Too bad Gary spent most of the tutorial scribbling pictures of Ann Marie in the margins of the other students' papers.

It was not as if he hadn't had other girlfriends. And it was not as if Ann Marie was the first woman to have broken his heart. She wasn't even the first to call the cops—that honor went to his high school prom date, who flagged down a policeman when Gary refused to stop dancing. On top of her car. While she was driving. On the highway. But Ann Marie had been his anchor during a difficult first year, when his self-esteem and confidence were attacked by professors bent on making him feel stupid and impotent. Each day they chipped away at his façade, and each day his ego cracked a little more. His hold on reality, never strong to begin with, began to fracture. His very self began to split. He went from being shaky but secured to unmoored and dangerously unbalanced.

Now he forced himself to focus on the faces of the students talking. He saw lips moving, eyes raised. There were three other men and one young woman, the woman vaguely attractive in a Staten Island kind of way: wavy black hair, olive skin, plump arms exposed in a halter top. The words she was speaking sounded to Gary like "blurbedy, blurbedy, blook." He nodded and smiled encouragingly, then scribbled some more pictures of Ann Marie.

The class might have lasted an hour, or maybe it was only twenty minutes. Gary knew in theory it occupied a seventy-five minute block on his schedule, but time was just another subjective measurement like space or sanity. It seemed like mere seconds before Professor Stapleton was giving them their assignments for the following week, although Gary saw his notebook was thick with scribblings and blunt pen marks like fence posts.

As the students were packing their belongings, Professor Stapleton asked Gary to stay. He felt his neck burn while his classmates picked up their books and rushed off to their next courses. He knew the news wouldn't be good, and they did, too.

When the room emptied, Professor Stapleton sat in the chair opposite him, so close he could see a chip in her white incisor and smell her lilac-scented shampoo.

"I'm worried about you, Gary," she began.

"Me?" Gary asked.

"Your writing assignments are marginal, at best. You barely even completed last week's drafting exercise. And I know those aren't notes you're scribbling on your classmates' papers."

Gary flushed again, then looked down at his fingernails. Boy, were they dirty. When was the last time he had washed his hands? When was the last time he showered? He was suddenly conscious of a bitter smell rising up from his armpits, and was embarrassed to think Professor Stapleton probably smelled it, too. He squeezed his arms close to his body in the hope of trapping the odor before it escaped, or at least muting it enough so it could merge with the cafeteria odors.

"Is something going on?"

"Going on?" Gary repeated.

"Something at home? I mean, with your friends, or a girl-friend, or something?"

Gary looked up at Professor Stapleton. She was old—at least thirty—but except for some crow's feet around her eyes, her skin was smooth and unlined. In seventeen years of schooling, Gary never had an African American professor before, and he found his thinking muddled by his parents' prejudices. Although they were semi-educated people, his father believed the Nation of Islam blew up the World Trade Center, while his mother insisted it was the Jews.

Now, as Professor Stapleton waited for an answer, Gary wondered what his father would think if he ever dated a black woman, and then his mind wandered to what it would be like to date Professor Stapleton, or any professor. To someone who hadn't been touched by another soul in months, even Professor Wheeler's firm grip earlier had been strangely appealing.

"Everything's fine," he said. "How's everything with you?"

"Me?" Professor Stapleton arched an eyebrow.

"With teaching and everything." Gary shrugged. "I mean being the only black professor?"

Professor Stapleton raised the other eyebrow, and for a moment Gary wondered whether he had gone too far. Then she said, "I appreciate your concern, Gary. But we're not here to talk about my problems. We're here to talk about yours."

"Well," Gary took a breath, and something slipped inside of him. "I have been a little distracted. My girlfriend and I broke up."

Professor Stapleton nodded. Gary continued. "But everything's fine now. We're friends and all. It's just hard sometimes."

"Have you talked to anybody about it?"

"Talked? Like to a therapist?"

"Or to the school counselor? He's in his office most days until noon."

"No. I've just talked to my friends." In fact, Professor Stapleton was the first person to whom he had admitted that Ann Marie and he had broken up. Although he suspected his parents sensed something was amiss, every time they asked about Ann Marie he invented some story about a party they had been to or a cute south Brooklyn restaurant they discovered—authentic Vietnamese food served by gun-toting three-year-olds, for instance. It played into everything his parents imagined Brooklyn life was like. As for friends, he had none.

"If you ever need someone else to talk to," said Professor Stapleton, "I'm always here."

For a minute, Gary felt like crying. He wanted to lay his head on Professor Stapleton's lap and let himself go. He was so tired. At night his sleep was punctuated by staccato dreams that left him disoriented and exhausted. During the day he was assaulted in class by a teaching style that resembled machine gun fire. But he still had enough of a grasp on reality to know that a student should not lay his head on the lap of a professor, not if he wanted to remain in school and out of a mental institution. His instinct for self-preservation won out against his fundamental craziness, and he bit his lip to stop from crying.

"I appreciate that," said Gary. He stood to leave.

"Gary?" She stopped him.

"Yes?"

"Your work. It has got to get better."

"I know."

Professor Stapleton held his eyes, and he grew mesmerized by their complicated shades of brown speckled with green. If he squinted, they appeared to be slowly rotating like a kaleidoscope. The feeling was not unlike the first time he had smoked marijuana in college: everything spinning and slightly beyond his reach. Back then, he had laughed with his roommates at how easily a beer bottle evaded their hands, how difficult it was to navigate the doorway. Now he grasped the side of his chair to steady himself.

"Then buckle down, do the reading, and put some effort into your writing—at least use spell-check. Otherwise, Gary, you're wasting both of our time."

Gary nodded and stood still, until he realized Professor Stapleton was holding open the door and it was time to leave. Then his feet carried him out of the office and down the hallway where the smell of wet dog wrapped him in a shroud. Most days, Gary felt like a wet dog himself. And looked like one, too.

Office of Career Services   Manhattan Law School

Summer Job Opportunities

** Do you want to work in the canal this summer?
New York City's Department of Environmental Protec-
tion needs law students to rescue fish, unclog pipes,
and do light legal research to help defend the city
against toxic torts. Free summer swim permit.

** Top Law Firm seeks summer associates. Immediate
client access, plenty of office supplies, air-condi-
tioned. Must have own vehicle. Contact Charles Top
for more information.

** Looking for law students with strong academic
records, drug- and disease-free, to spend the summer
as an egg donor and surrogate. Good performance may
lead to nine-month contract.

** M&A? How about M&M? Dylan's Candy Store is opening
a new Brooklyn location and needs cashiers, assistant
managers, and people to dress as Skittles. Two faculty recommendations required, as well as coursework
in Food & Drug Law.

** Be a teaching assistant! Your law school education
prequalifies you to assistant teach at Gowanus Private Day, a nursery school on a barge in the middle
of the canal where the kids play with garbage from 9
AM until noon. Apply at our website, bargeintoschool.
wordpress.com.

** The federal government needs lawyers to staff its
new "Don't Go To Law School" educational initiative.
Sharing your experiences can help prevent future
young people from making the same mistake you did.

** Am Law 100 firm seeks assistant summer associates to help our actual summer associates with their
clerical tasks. Work beneath some of the city's top
future lawyers and beside some very excellent secretaries. Pay is minimal, but with our firm's name
on your resume, maybe someone else will give you an
interview.

** Law Firm & Hospice seeks summer associates to help
with legal work and provide comfort care to the ter-
minally ill. Must be able to read quickly.

5

Where Jobs Go to Die

THE STUDENT CAFÉ WAS NO more than a dirty corner on the law school's second floor, with a coffee urn and some week-old pastries wrapped in plastic. "Made in Brooklyn," claimed the lettering on the wrapping, which gave everyone the warm fuzzies—and later, the cold sweats. The half dozen tables overflowed with case books and study guides, and students crowded around them like bums at a trash fire.

Adam sat at one of the tables with four of his five "mentees," first-years in his Torts class, whom he was supposed to advise, guide, and steer clear of the pastries. His fifth mentee was just now making her way past a giant mimeograph machine the school finally retired in 2003, stopping every few feet to say hello to a classmate, plant a kiss on a cheek, and receive a high five or a pat on the ass. Her dark hair fell perfectly to the top of her shoulders, and her teeth shone like a predator's. Staci Fortunato was every boy's dream: lush, dark, and dangerous. She lured men in, then bit off their heads.

When Adam arranged this meeting, he had emailed all the students. Only Staci replied. Considering their first encounter in class, Staci was surprisingly cheerful and friendly, as if she'd been his star pupil rather than a first-class slacker. Of course, most of her communications were entirely inappropriate, but at least she responded. The other four students he had to track down by calling their emergency contact numbers, one of which turned out to be the cell phone for the student's drug dealer.

Now that student, greasy-haired with muttonchops, waved to Staci, who slalomed toward their table. Adam sat up straight, and kept his hands clear of the filthy surface.

"'Sup, Prof?" Staci asked as Muttonchops lifted his size-14 feet off the seat of the chair he had been saving for her.

"Hello," said Adam, not exactly sure how he should respond, and trying to maintain his dignity amid the squalor. "I guess that's all of us. I'm sorry we had to meet here. I didn't realize it was so . . . limited. Next time we can go out for something to eat."

"I have a friend whose advisor took them for sushi," said Muttonchops, whose name, Adam recalled, was Gregg.

"We could do that," said Adam.

"I don't like sushi," said Gregg.

"No biggie," said Staci. "Most people don't even meet their faculty mentors."

"I heard there are some professors who don't even come to school," added Samantha, an unnaturally tanned brunette who sat on the aisle in Torts, and seemed to make far too many bathroom trips for a seventy-five-minute class.

The other two students at the table were also in Adam's class, although one of them—Peter—had yet to attend, and the other—Derwin—appeared not to know it. During class he sat in the second row flipping through his Contracts case book as if he might find his Torts cases there. Right now he appeared to be asleep.

Technically, Adam was supposed to guide these students, answering questions they might have about law and law school, and otherwise making them feel as if the administration cared about the education they received. In reality, he had not been given any instruction on how to accomplish these things, and no money to facilitate them. He tried to strike the right balance between friendliness and formality; hence, the student café. But he realized he had made a mistake the moment he saw a squirrel scurry out of the top of the coffee urn from which he had just filled his cup.

"So tell me a little bit about yourselves—something I wouldn't know from Facebook." This was a question Laura had suggested. An icebreaker that would get them talking. Instead, it spawned complete silence.

"Anything," Adam added helpfully.

"I'm bi," said Samantha.

"Everyone knows that, Sam," said Staci.

Samantha shrugged. "He said anything."

"He meant anything that nobody knows."

"Then why didn't he say that?"

"I used to be a gangsta," said Gregg.

"A gangsta from Scarsdale," said Staci.

Gregg looked deflated. "I've been to Compton."

"In a tour bus."

"Facebook is lame anyway," said Samantha.

Adam tried a different tack.

"How about questions you haven't been able to ask your other professors? Maybe questions about grades? Or study groups? When I was in law school everyone said to join one, but I didn't think it was very helpful."

"How do we get a job?" asked Peter, pulling out a notebook and pen.

"Good question. Cutting right to the chase."

"My Dad says that," said Samantha.

Adam wasn't quite old enough to be Samantha's father—although he realized, biologically speaking, it wouldn't be an impossibility. Maybe that's what the students needed: a hip professor who spoke their own language and knew which social media sites were still cool. But even if Adam knew the difference between a tweet and a tag, which he didn't, that wasn't him. Instead, he decided the best tack was honesty, integrity, and a good dose of realism.

"It's a difficult market right now," said Adam. "You're competing against a lot of students from some very good schools."

"Your old firm is hiring," said Staci. She waved a flyer she had picked up from the career counseling office, also known as The House Where Jobs Go To Die. "How can we get an offer there?"

Adam was impressed that Staci had bothered to read his faculty bio on the law school's website—and that she managed to find it. But she had no chance of getting hired, especially as a first-year. "You should probably think about an internship or volunteering at a nonprofit this summer," he told her.

"What firm are we even talking about?" asked Gregg.

"Cranberry, Boggs & Pickel. The one that did the big oil spill litigation. Remember, it turned all those seagulls that yucky brown color? In Louisiana?"

"I thought that was Katrina."

"There was a hurricane, too. The firm proved the seagulls were brown to begin with, and got the case dismissed."

"Those firms pay like a hundred seventy-five grand," said Peter.

"Yeah, but you've got to defend cigarette companies and Nazi war criminals," said Samantha.

"You don't have to defend cigarette companies," said Staci.

In fact, as Adam recalled, the firm's litigators had a lucrative practice defending some of the leading tobacco companies. But he didn't mention that.

"If they pay so much, why are they interviewing here?" Gregg had been in law school for less than two months, yet the pecking order of law firm recruiting was painfully obvious to everyone. The top firms treated Manhattan Law School like a leper colony, avoiding its grounds and shunning its inmates.

"Because you worked there, right?" Staci asked Adam.

Adam explained that one of the firm's top partners, Howell Goldreckt, was an MLS alum. He threw his weight around—literally—to hire at least one summer associate from the school. It wasn't a pretty sight, but it was effective.

"You have to be on *Law Review* to get an interview," said Peter. "With straight A's."

"Not everyone on *Law Review* has straight A's," said Staci. "I know a guy, he told me he had a B– average first year. He got on through the writing competition."

"Everyone except Associate Editors get on through the writing competition."

"I know, but he had B's and C's and he still got on."

Adam had not been on *Law Review* at Harvard, but he was familiar with the grueling competition. Over a three-day weekend, students had to weed through several thousand pages of source material and edit a one hundred page article. Many of the successful candidates stayed awake for seventy-two hours straight. It was rumored that President Obama himself went to the emergency room with heart palpitations and a ruptured bladder after he turned in his packet.

"*Law Review* is a great credential," said Adam. "But there are other places to work besides a big firm."

"Like where?" asked Peter.

"Professor Copeland is hiring this summer."

"Yeah, a nanny," said Staci.

"Isn't she too old to have a nanny?" asked Samantha.

"Not her, Sam," said Staci. "Are you brain damaged?"

"Sorry we can't all be Rambda Lambda Ding Dong."

"Rho Lambda."

"Isn't that for lesbians?" asked Gregg.

"No, jerkoff. It's a leadership organization. You have to be elected."

"I don't know. Sounds hot." Gregg leered at her.

"Ignore them," she said to Adam. "Would you write me a letter of recommendation?"

"For the nanny job?"

"For the law firm."

Staci gave him her sweetest, most seductive smile. Truthfully, it was difficult to resist. But Adam did because, for one thing, it was a violation of school policy to accept sexual favors from anyone except third-year students. In any event, whatever pull he had with Howell Goldreckt wouldn't work for a first-year who didn't do the reading—despite her good looks. Goldreckt might be a letch, but he was also a savant, and he expected his associates to keep up.

"Like I said, you should focus your attention on other possibilities this year," said Adam. "Getting good grades should be a priority. The jobs will follow."

"Next year, then?"

"Sure. We'll see."

"Thanks, Prof!" Staci gave him another enticing smile, and Adam felt himself blush. By the time he regained his composure, the conversation had morphed into a debate over the best places to work in the summer (Nantucket was a top choice, followed by Jackson Hole, and then Taos), and from there into a discussion about whether global warming would make it harder to get a good summer share in the Hamptons. On the one hand, Gregg argued, rising sea levels would create lots of new beaches. On the other hand, said Samantha, hotter temperatures would make more people want to take vacations. Peter suggested they get Al Gore to speak on the topic at the law school. The students then asked Adam if he knew Al Gore. Adam said he didn't, but commended the students on their ambition.

This started another round of conversation about whether it was better to marry someone who was rich or someone who was famous. At some point in the conversation, Derwin woke up. He blinked and looked around like a hermit crab coming out of its shell.

"Yo, dog, what up?" asked Gregg.

"Huh?" said Derwin.

This provoked a round of laughter at Derwin's expense, and even Adam couldn't help smiling despite his best efforts to keep a straight face. It was comforting, he knew, to find someone more guileless than oneself. In the cutthroat world in which these students fought for jobs, a classmate like Derwin was a blessing. He lowered the curve and improved the odds for the rest of them. For a moment the students basked in the communal glow, warmed by their gratitude for the dimwitted and daft.

But they didn't read the fine print. None of them did. As the students gathered their books, and Adam exhorted them to stay on top of their classwork, only Derwin lingered behind. English was not his best language—though it was his only one—and many printed words were beyond his grasp. Even before his collision with the UPS truck, he had never been the sharpest tack in the box. Once, he lost his way in his own apartment and ended up living in a closet until his roommates found him rambling about liberating General Tso's chicken. Another time he mistook a flower pot for a hat and knocked himself unconscious. Yet in a pinch he could read, and even write, although not at the same time.

He scanned the flyer Staci left behind. The law firm was seeking summer associates—that much was true. Top dollars paid for summers spent dining in midtown, frequenting Broadway shows and Yankee Stadium, yachting up the Hudson. But there, at the bottom of the page, was the contact information for a different career counseling center, one located on the other side of the river, at another law school in a faraway borough. In her enthusiasm, Staci had picked up the wrong flyer, delivered by a postal clerk who didn't know the difference between Gowanus and Greenwich Village.

Derwin made a move to tell her, but then stopped, distracted, lost in space. By the time he regained his bearings he had already forgotten, and Staci was a faint blur in the distance, a smudge of red and black. Whatever it was, it wasn't important. He shrugged on his backpack and put his best foot forward. Then he followed with his other one, too.

The Manhattan Law School Law Review is published four times a year in print only by the students at Manhattan Law School. Annual subscription rate is $525, cash or money order only, hand-delivered to the offices of the Law Review, 1 Gowanus Canal Breezeway, Gowanus, NY. Not responsible for delays in publication due to fire, acts of God, nuclear war, toxic events, or complete breakdown of civilized society.

6

House of cards

THE *LAW REVIEW* DIDN'T HAVE a proper office. It had, instead, a mildewed windowless room in the sub-basement, between the boiler and the overflow cafeteria storage facility, filled with boxes of potatoes and freeze-dried meat that had been around since the Eisenhower administration. The room was previously used for mothballed equipment by the Director of Maintenance. He died while snorting bleach in an incident buried by the school and never reported to the police. As lawyers, they knew better than to involve the justice system. To punish the maintenance department for causing trouble, however, the room was converted into an office to house the law school's student elite.

Asher Herman was the *Law Review*'s Editor in Chief. He was not the smartest student on *Law Review*, although he was the most enthusiastic. On the short side, with unruly brown hair and perpetually wet lips, his one outstanding feature was a prominent nose that kept watch over the rest of his face like a hawk. Now he and his nose sat with his fellow editors in a corner of the room they had converted into an editorial suite by erecting partial walls constructed from old exam answers. There was the Managing Editor in Chief, the Articles Editor in Chief, the

Editor in Chief of Notes & Comments and the Editor in Chief of Comments & Notes, as well as the Online Editor in Chief, the three Supervising Editors in Chief, and the two Editors in Chief at Large. In the outer room, about twenty Associate Editors in Chief were hard at work at the copy/scan machines, shouting to be heard over the noise from all the whirring, clicking, jamming, and cursing.

"Vermouth! We need more vermouth," said Charlie Spires, the Managing Editor in Chief. He fancied himself a future Hollywood mogul and never lost an opportunity to sound like one.

"Duly noted," said John Tarantula, Supervising Editor in Chief #1, whose job consisted of ordering liquor for Charlie, drinking liquor with Charlie, and maintaining restroom supplies.

"The condom dispenser in the women's bathroom is jammed," said Binky Paratha, the Editor in Chief in charge of the publication's nonexistent website.

"I'll email the Dean," said John.

"And the overhead lights don't work."

"That's because they're video cameras."

"Isn't that illegal?" Binky had worked on Capitol Hill prior to law school and she vaguely recalled a scandal involving a Congressman, a bathroom stall, and a videotape.

"Not in a federal prison."

"But this is a law school."

"Yeah, and I'm Santa Claus."

"Not funny, John. If someone's taping me trying to buy condoms, we have a serious problem."

"No one's taping you, Binky," said Asher.

"Yeah, and you shouldn't be using those condoms anyway," said John. "I thought you had a latex allergy."

"That was a yeast infection."

"You win. I move to buy a box of condoms for the women's bathroom."

"Seconded," said Charlie.

"Any objections?" asked Asher. "Seeing none, the motion is approved."

With the important agenda items out of the way, Asher turned to the unpleasant task of publishing legal scholarship. "What's up next in the pipeline?"

"Federalism," said Willow Summer, the Articles Editor in Chief, who was anything but willowy.

Nods all around the table. Federalism was a solid topic. It had constitutional notes with a bouquet of states' rights and a whiff of musty British history. Not everyone was sure what it meant, but it sounded smart, and that was all that mattered. None of the editors had done very well in their classes, at least not by traditional measures, but they enjoyed the patina of their faux meritocracy.

Willow distributed a stack of printed articles from the pile in front of her. Asher took a quick look at their first pages. They certainly seemed impressive. Each page crammed with footnotes, headings and subheadings galore, lots of Roman numerals and Latin words, a complete lack of anything resembling spoken English. They were exactly the sort of gaseous claptrap that bestowed accolades and tenure on their authors.

"Looks perfect," said Asher. "You'll assign the Assistant EICs?" The question was directed at Supervising Editor in Chief #2, a young woman named Raya Kurdle who chewed on her nails, although she had no nails left to chew.

"Is this volume three?" asked Raya.

"Four," Asher reminded her. "Three is the Symposium on Pets' Rights."

"I thought that was two."

"No. Two is Queer Theory and the Law."

"Got it." Raya made a note in a marbled black book she used to schedule important quarterly events, like her next meal.

"And make sure they use the good scanners. Last time everything came out blurry."

"Good scanners. Check."

Asher squinted at the agenda, but he couldn't read the print because the page was soggy with Red Bull and doughnut crumbs. "Is there any new business?"

"Jobs," said Charlie.

"What about them?" asked Asher.

"When are we going to get them?" Charlie had received straight C's in his first year, but now that he was on *Law Review* he expected better. "I mean, what the fuck are we paying for?"

"Dean Jeffries says they can only give us the grades," said Asher. "It's up to us to get the jobs."

"How can we get the jobs if all they give us are grades?" complained Charlie. "Can't they call some firms? For all the money we pay, you'd think they could punch a few numbers."

"I heard Naomi is working for Trapp & Dore," said John Tarantula. Naomi Stein was an Associate Editor in Chief who was also President of the Jewish Jurists Society.

"Yech," said Willow. "You couldn't pay me to work for that firm."

"No one is," said John.

Willow glared at him, but stayed silent. The two had a history, dating back to first year when John drunk-dialed her and professed his undying lust, only to realize he had the wrong number. Since then, they pretended the call had never occurred, and circled each other warily like welterweights.

"We are the best and brightest," said Charlie. "If we can't get jobs, what hope is there for everyone else?"

"Very little," said John.

"Fuck that," said Charlie. "If the school wants my money, they better get me a job."

"You had a job," Asher reminded him. Charlie's father owned a waste management service in New Jersey and pulled more than a few strings to get his son hired last summer. "No one forced you to throw up in the back of that partner's car."

"It wasn't my fault," said Charlie. "The guy was a terrible driver."

"The car was parked."

Charlie shrugged and winked at Raya. He loved playing the drunk Casanova. In truth, he was just a drunk.

Raya smiled back. Charlie wasn't attractive, but there was something appealing about his oversized belly and large bank account. Raya felt most secure beneath a man who outweighed her by at least one hundred pounds and could write a check that didn't bounce like a Super Ball.

"Maybe we should set up a committee," she said.

"Good idea," said Asher. "Raya, Binky, Charlie, and John. You'll be responsible for keeping track of the hiring situation. If things don't improve, we'll create a PowerPoint for Dean Jeffries."

"That'll show him," said John.

Asher ignored John's sarcasm. He already had a headache from the stress of running this meeting, and severe gas pains from all the Red Bull he had been drinking. He wanted a job as badly as his classmates, but believed his law review credential would eventually get him hired somewhere. That's what the deans had promised him, and why he joined law review in the first place. Yet so far only four law review members had received permanent job offers, and three of them were lowly Associate Editors (no Chiefs among them), selected for law review based entirely on their grades. It had begun to make him wonder whether law review—and law school, in general—was one giant scam.

The irony was not lost on him.

He rationalized his cheating by telling himself that students at other schools had their own unfair advantages. No one in this world ever got ahead without the help of someone else. Whether it was a well-placed uncle, a college roommate, or simply a good word between the sheets, an unfair advantage was the American way. The cards were marked at birth and dealt to the highest bidder.

"Is there any other new business?" Asher asked. He peered at the agenda, and then back up at John, but both were inscrutable and needed a good cleansing. "Seeing none, the meeting is adjourned."

The editors pushed back their chairs and made their way out of the suite. Willow snuck another doughnut when she thought no one was watching, while Charlie looked at his watch and declared it was never too early to start drinking. Raya said she would join him, but Asher begged off. What he needed was a couple of aspirin and a gallon of water. He knew if he went out with Charlie things would end badly, as they often did. He couldn't afford another night in front of a toilet or in a police precinct.

At that moment the door opened, and a tall blonde woman entered. A current of nervousness rippled through the editors, and there was an imperceptible quickening of movements. The Associate EICs finished up their jobs at the copy/scan machines and tucked their papers safely into folders. Willow flipped the articles she was carrying so that only their blank white faces showed. Even Charlie covered his mouth when he burped.

Everyone in the room knew Ann Marie Kowalski. She was one of those pesky Associate Editors with grades too high to be ignored. Exempted from the write-on competition and the special orientation for write-on editors, the five Associate Editors were given the most demanding tasks that required travel to the far reaches of the Bronx and Staten Island. Last week one of them was sent to the special Polish War Veterans museum in Pittsburgh, and he had yet to return.

Asher smiled at Ann Marie in a way he hoped was welcoming but felt stiff and fake. He didn't enjoy keeping the Associate Editors in the dark about the inner workings of the *Law Review*, yet he accepted it as one of the hazards of the job. The risks were obvious, and both Dean Jeffries and Professor Rodriguez, the *Law Review*'s faculty advisor, drummed it into him on the day they approved him as Editor in Chief. Since then he felt like Lot's wife every time he was around Ann Marie: paralyzed by fright yet unable to look away.

"Sorry," she said, when she saw him staring at her. "I just had to get my new assignment."

"No!" said Asher, with too much vigor. "I mean, no worries. *Mi casa es su casa.*" He gestured around the room, feeling thirty pairs of eyes surreptitiously observing him.

"Thanks." She brushed a wayward strand of hair from her lips. "It's a lot to get used to so early in the semester. But I'm really enjoying the work."

"It's very rewarding."

"Yes . . . well. Guess I should get to it. Nice talking with you."

He watched as she made her way to a computer terminal, admiring the curve of her hips and the outline of her butt in her jeans. Lost in a reverie, he almost allowed her to sit down right in front of a screen on which another editor had uploaded a scan of a recent article published in the *NYU Law Review*.

"Asher!" shouted John from across the room.

Asher snapped awake and bolted toward her. "Ann Marie!"

Startled, she turned around. "What? Did I do something wrong?"

"It's nothing," said Asher. He was panting like a puppy. "It's just we have a different assignment for you, that's all." Asher's mind raced through possible tasks he could give Ann Marie that would get her out of the room and away from the monitor.

"What kind of assignment?" Ann Marie asked warily.

"An important one," said Asher. "You're not allergic to latex, are you?"

CRANBERRY, BOGGS & PICKEL LLP

DEUTSCH :: ENGLISH :: ESPAÑOL :: FRANÇAIS
PORTUGUÊS :: РУССКИЙ :: 中文

FIRM | Active Cases
LAWYERS | Delinquent Clients
AREAS OF PRACTICE | Fugitive Alumni
LOCATIONS
TOILING HERE
NEWS, EVENTS AND DENIALS
CONTACTS
HOME

Home :: Firm

About Us

Tools 🖨 ✉

"Cranberry, Boggs & Pickel has a broad and deep understanding of how the legal system works. Their lawyers use every possible tool to help us capitalize on the deficiencies of others. We view our relationship with CB & P as a true partnership, until we choose to go in a different direction."
—FORTUNE 500 CEO

WHO WE ARE

Cranberry, Boggs & Pickel LLP was founded in 1931 by lawyers with the goal of proving to their former law firms that they had been unjustly terminated. Now led by world-class legal minds Stephen Spivey, Michael Weirhammer, and Cepeda Wilkins, and female lawyer Ursula Font, along with the experienced and physically sturdy Howell Goldreckt, the firm is in top position to supply clients with the legal services they come to us to find out they need. Our Corporate Department works in the areas of mergers and acquisitions, capital markets, leveraged restructuring, business financialness, project estate, asset telestructurement, intellectful representating, and complex transactions of all types, with multinational corporations and individuals throughout the world. We also provide free snacks in our offices.

7

Point. Game. Match.

O UT!"
    "Out?"
    "Out!"

Adam knew his shot was a good six inches inside the line, inside the squash court, inside an exercise club so exclusive he wasn't even allowed to know its name, despite having been invited to play there once a month by Howell Goldreckt, the attorney who had made possible his escape into academia. If Adam cared at all about squash, he would have argued the call, but instead he cared about getting off the court alive, with no damage to his reproductive organs or his relationship with a man who could, with one phone call, make Adam's job go away. And so he gave up the point and the game went on, fourteen points for Adam and three points for Goldreckt. After all, cheating can only get a man so far when he weighs nearly three hundred pounds and it takes a full four minutes to find the ball when it's sitting right at his feet, because he can't see his feet, and the ball is practically invisible to him because it isn't food.

Two points later Adam finally put away the winning shot, which glanced off Goldreckt's fleshy face and caused the law firm partner to let go of his racket and fall to the ground. Supine, he looked like something to climb with a couple of Sherpas and an oxygen tent. In fact, Adam thought he might need the tent until Goldreckt groaned and sat up, the imprint of the ball visible as a white circle on his red skin.

"Fucking beginner's luck," he said.

Adam and Goldreckt had been playing squash for the last ten years, ever since Goldreckt introduced him to the sport when Adam was a summer associate at Cranberry, Boggs & Pickel. Goldreckt was fifty pounds lighter back then, though still enormous, and he was drunk. Very drunk. It was almost certainly an accident of fate that Adam was the summer associate to whom Goldreckt started unburdening his soul. But there Adam was, in Goldreckt's private bathroom as the partner threw up a half dozen times, and in between each hurl he regaled the young law student with the story of how he'd sacrificed to make it to the top. Months spent sleeping in his office, wearing the same clothes, eating cold food—and not because work kept him, but simply because he had no better place to go.

Yes, the firm was one of New York's biggest, with offices in twelve cities across the world, specializing in the kind of high-stakes litigation and corporate deals that justified billable rates above one thousand dollars an hour for top partners. And, yes, Goldreckt's specialty was the most lucrative of all: leveraged buyouts and institutional mergers and acquisitions. Big hospitals buying each other; big corporations buying small countries; big pension funds dumping their obligations and leaving senior citizens begging their children for help paying their bills. But all that money still didn't buy the man love.

It ended up being one of the only times Adam saw the inside of Goldreckt's bathroom, unlocked with a special key and off limits to associates, reserved for Howell alone so he could defecate in private. Even the cleaning woman, Adam later discovered, could only enter after signing a nondisclosure agreement. But that night, Adam was thrust into Goldreckt's inner circle, forced to listen to the man go on about why he had become a lawyer. In high school he was a champion player of Dungeons and Dragons and Strat-O-Matic Baseball ("on a board, not a video screen," he insisted). In college, the fraternities paid him not to rush. He went to law school because it was a way to maintain his baseball card collection without worrying about getting a job. But in law school, he told Adam, something finally clicked. The coolness of legal argument while bodies lay bleeding on the ground. The pure transactional value of human enterprise and behavior. He graduated at the top of his class, won every prize his law school could offer, and despite his lowly pedigree and social awkwardness, was hired by one of the best firms in the city at a time it needed more bodies in a booming market. He was so good at what he did, and so trusted by clients, that before long the partners had no choice but to ask him to join them.

When Goldreckt sobered up, Adam was still there, washing his tie that had been splattered in the line of fire. He helped the partner back to his office and onto his sofa, then found a blanket shoved in a closet filled with clothing and unpaired shoes. He covered as much of the man as he could, then tiptoed out of the room under cover of darkness and the earth-rumbling sound of Goldreckt's snores.

From then on, Adam was the man's confidant. Goldreckt would call him late at night while Adam was studying at Harvard and regale him with tales of personal woe and professional triumph. His need to be loved was so obvious and childlike that Adam couldn't help feeling sorry for him. Sorrow became pity, and pity became—not friendship, exactly, but an understanding, a symbiotic relationship where Goldreckt got a willing listener and Adam got an education. So when it came time to weigh the firm's job offer, Adam reasoned he could do worse than working at one of the most prestigious law firms in New York City for a partner who trusted and relied upon him.

Until the day Adam betrayed him by walking into his office and asking to quit. "This life's not for me," Adam explained.

"It's not for anyone," Goldreckt replied.

But Adam's decision was about more than just the typical complaints of a law firm associate: the long, unpredictable hours, the mind-numbing work, and the lack of the tiniest bit of control over one's life. It was the sudden realization, while he listened to a colleague as she walked a client through the proper procedure for minimizing its obligations to fund a health plan for its employees, that he was flying too close to the sun. The line between what the law permitted and what lawyers advocated for was sometimes so faint that it was easily blurred. By staying at the firm he risked becoming part of the machinery that encouraged line-blurring. Already he could see how the older attorneys ignored the lines entirely, their only boundaries whatever was necessary to achieve results. Advocacy became expediency, and expediency became the new norm. It was as close to his own father's life as he ever wanted to get.

So he decided to leave. He always had an intellectual passion for the academic life, and as a law professor he could advocate against the kind of expediency that turned lawyers into enablers. To get there, however, he needed Goldreckt's help.

The only job more difficult to land than a job teaching law was a job teaching law in New York City. Lawyers were leaving (or getting booted from) their firms in droves, and law school seemed a kinder, gentler place to land. Teaching salaries were decent; summers were free; and the students never aged. After three long hours of wheedling, pleading, and eating (because Goldreckt had to), the partner finally agreed to put in a good word with Dean Clopp at Goldreckt's alma mater, Manhattan Law School. The school owed Goldreckt—many millions, in fact—and his word carried the weight of his bank account. Adam knew it was a third-tier school, but he was also realistic: without a PhD or any publications to his name, it was slim pickings in the job market. And, he reasoned, once he had a foothold, he could write his way up the academic food chain.

In return, Goldreckt demanded an additional five hundred billable hours over Adam's assigned target of three thousand, and a promise to help him with recruiting from MLS.

"Tall," he insisted. "Slim hips. Breasts like melons."

"I don't think that's legal," said Adam.

"It's illegal now to have big breasts?"

"Wouldn't you rather hire someone who's competent?"

"Competent I've got." Goldreckt made a shooing motion with his hands. "Clopp sends me their grades. But the dean wouldn't know a hottie if she sat on his face. That's where you'll come in."

Goldreckt wanted facts and—most important—figures. His partners were giving him a harder and harder time leaving a slot open for an MLS student. In the good old days—back when Adam was hired—Goldreckt would never have needed to make a case to extend someone an offer. The firm hired as many as ninety summer associates a year, threw them lavish parties at the partners' country clubs (the ones that allowed minorities), and took them on cruises up the Hudson. But the work had soured and so had the lawyers. These days the parties were gone, replaced by discount vouchers to Broadway shows and free admission to the Transit Museum. Financial constraints also limited the number of summer associates the firm could hire. Now, fifty was a reach, thirty-five even better, and those who did not earn their keep wouldn't be invited back.

It was a battlefield out there, and Goldreckt was fighting a rearguard action against the other members of the hiring committee: Steve Spivey, a specialist in foreign mining leases, who helped multinational corporations strip the mineral resources from third world countries; Mike Weirhammer, who practiced admiralty law, a subspecialty so obscure its practitioners still wore wigs; Ursula Font, the only female partner at the firm, although technically she had failed the firm's mandatory chromosome test; and Cepeda Wilkins, who, two years earlier, tried to stab Goldreckt with a ballpoint pen but it didn't penetrate the polyester blend of his suit. All of these men, and the one woman, attended first-tier schools, and they would stop at nothing to keep the firm's bloodlines pure. At their hourly rate, as Steve Spivey put it, clients wanted more than "Schmuck, Putz, and Dreck."

Even with the proper pedigree, the partners rejected anyone who was too needy, clingy, or closely resembled an ex-spouse, ex-girlfriend, or, in Ursula Font's case, two ex-children she had fathered and then legally disowned in a precedent-setting legal dispute. They kicked to the curb anyone they thought might be pregnant, unvaccinated, or need medical care that could increase health insurance premiums or require paid leave under federal or state law. There was no such thing as a perfect summer associate, but the partners held fast to a Platonic ideal. Each championed his own favorite; each refused to see the virtues in another's top choice. Mostly they fought over perceived miniscule differences between their alma maters, with Weirhammer, from NYU, maintaining that Columbia grads were spineless and weak-willed, and Spivey, from Harvard, arguing that Yale grads were godless Communists. Font and Wilkins, who were in the same class at Stanford, claimed the elite Northeast schools were just part of a liberal conspiracy designed to hide their intellectual failings.

Goldreckt reminded Adam of his promise after they had showered and were dressing in the locker room. Adam did his best to avoid looking at Goldreckt's backside, but he couldn't help marveling at the size of the man's underwear, which was an engineering miracle on the scale of the Suez Canal. For a large man, however, he was incredibly dainty in his grooming habits, and took a good twenty minutes to apply various unguents to regions of his body that Adam wished he didn't know existed. Then, when Goldreckt had finished, he applied enough cologne to set off the fire alarm, which brought several staff members running in a futile attempt to silence the din.

Adam lowered his head and followed Goldreckt into the club canteen where the partner ordered himself a calorie-busting "Coffee No-No," which, as far as Adam could see, consisted of several drops of coffee, a heap of sugar, and a thirty-two ounce dollop of whipped cream. Adam ordered a bottle of vitamin juice, which had neither vitamins nor juice, but was a syrupy concoction that tasted like green chalk. They sat at a table overlooking one of the squash courts where a young woman was thrashing a man who looked old enough to be her father. With each shot he returned, she drove the ball into the opposite corner and sent him flying.

"So, can you do it?" Goldreckt asked. "Can you do this for me?"

Adam realized that the alarm had drowned out Goldreckt's question. Now he was waiting for an answer, and looking like a schoolboy about to receive his grades.

"I'm not sure," said Adam, stalling for time.

"Not sure?!" roared Goldreckt. "After everything I've done for you?" The big man's face reddened and Adam worried he might burst a blood vessel. Then his lower lip quivered, and he said in a voice so quiet Adam could only make it out by reading his lips. "Please?"

On the squash court the woman jammed an elbow into the man's gut as he lunged for the ball. It could have been accident, but it looked purposeful to Adam. The man stumbled, staggered, then crashed head first into the wall while the woman pumped her fist triumphantly.

"Okay," said Adam, not sure what he had just agreed to.

"Thank you," said Goldreckt. He looked, at that moment, like the little boy he must have once been. Bright-eyed and rosy-cheeked. Stubby little fingers and teeth. Milk breath. "Her name," he said, "is Ann Marie."

Adam didn't recognize the name. But whomever she was, the student clearly had the partner's number. His eyelashes fluttered as if he might start crying, and Adam had to turn away to save both of them the embarrassment. When he looked back down at the squash court the man was on the ground again while the woman stepped calmly around him and ricocheted the ball into his head. Point. Game. Match.

Oink

daily specials

long beach oysters
sandy (hurricane-inspired) brine, crispy pancetta, hypodermic tuile $16.00

hamptons-raised rabbit
shiitake and red wine reduction, tompkins square greens, persimmon soil $18.00

lower east side poached squirrel
acorn puree, pigeon feathers, "homeless foam" $32.00

hudson river trout
guanciale, hibiscus broth, subway "rat"atouille $34.00

pig roast (for two)
pineapple stuffing, carrots and figs, lardo crema $78.00

vegetable risotto
mushroom, beetroot, rutabaga, piglet snout $29.00

pork rind tiramisu
lady fingers, espresso, bacon grease $11.00

bacon-shell cannoli
butterscotch chips, ricotta, pork trotter ice cream $12.00

Cash only.

Oink
106A East 6th Street, in the basement
New York, NY
(no phone)

8

Love and Other Drugs

ADAM UNSCREWED THE TOP FROM the container of hair product and examined it closely. It had been so long since he last used it that the gel had hardened into a solid mass. He sniffed it, checking if it had gone rancid (could hair gel go rancid?), then ran the container under hot water to loosen the goop. He caught a palmful as it streamed out, and massaged it into his hair. It wasn't until he put on deodorant that he realized he had confused the two products, and now had spiky underarm hair and his scalp smelled like "Fresh Breeze." He climbed back into the shower and rinsed himself clean, then started all over again.

It had taken him a few days after their last meeting to get the courage to ask Laura out again. Even so, he did it over email, afraid of face-to-face rejection. He spent more time crafting the note than he had preparing for that day's class, but it was worth it. She said yes. And now, here he was, buttoning his only pair of not-jeans-but-not-business-casual pants, tucking in the brand new Banana Republic shirt his brother, Sam—always better at luring the ladies, although not necessarily the right ones—picked out for him online, and giving himself one last look in the mirror before heading out to meet Laura at Oink, a month-old, no-reservations, farm-to-table bistro in the East Village that he had read about in *New York* magazine. "A surprisingly romantic vibe," the review concluded, "perfect for first dates that you hope might lead to more. And save room for the bacon-shell cannoli for dessert."

The line was already out the door when Adam arrived, twenty minutes early. He meant to get there sooner but, as usual, the MTA had forgotten people lived in Brooklyn. The F train was under construction and replaced by a shuttle bus, so he walked to Atlantic Avenue and caught an N train. The N was making local R stops, until it stalled at Canal Street and the conductor told everyone to get off. Adam, quickly becoming drenched in sweat, walked through the station to catch a 6 train, took that to Astor Place and, finally, arrived at the restaurant. Next time he swore not to be such a cheapskate and splurge on a cab.

By the time Laura arrived, the estimated wait time had fallen to just over an hour. Adam surreptitiously popped a mint when he saw Laura approach. She was wearing a simple but sexy black dress, a book in her hand. She greeted him with a hug that felt too brotherly, but then gave him a quick peck on the lips as if to make up for it.

"I put our name down, but they claim it's still an hour," he said. "Apparently three different improvisational comedy teams sat down to eat at the same time, and so they're really backed up."

"It's okay," said Laura. "It's a beautiful night. I don't mind the wait. Besides, they have a bar."

Before long they had squeezed their way between a young couple arguing over who was more "emotionally available" and two bankers complaining about the high cost of doggy daycare. "That doesn't even include the Christmas bonus!" barked one. The bartender, a young woman who looked about sixteen years old and six feet tall, brought them their drinks—a margarita for Laura and a Scotch for Adam. Laura raised her glass and proposed a toast.

"To Manhattan Law School."

"Home of the brave."

"But not the free," quipped Laura.

Adam admired the relaxed way Laura held her glass and took a healthy sip of her drink. It was a welcome difference from the pinched imbibing of Jane Van Dyke, who drank modestly and never lost control.

"So what's a nice boy like you doing in a place like Gowanus?" she asked.

"Got on the F and just kept going."

"Funny guy, I'm being serious here. How'd you end up at Manhattan Law School?"

Adam quickly recited the story he'd told countless times before—to family, to friends, to colleagues who thought he'd lost his mind—although he skipped the part about avoiding his father's fate. Work at the law firm was making him crazy. The hours were too much to bear. He was good at it, but didn't care about the clients. Helping big corporations get bigger had no meaning, and since that was what he did all day (and night), it felt as if his life had no meaning. Looking around the firm, he could see his future: the older, divorced, burned-out partners whose kids ignored them and ex-spouses who hated them. Adam knew it was not for him.

"And now here you are," Laura concluded.

"Yes, I am," said Adam, with a twinge of sadness.

"It's not that bad," said Laura, misinterpreting Adam's melancholy for regret about the school where they both taught. "I have friends who've ended up in all sorts of places. Nebraska, Montana, a law and economics class at a community college in South Dakota."

"I hear the rents are cheap in South Dakota."

"There's a reason for that," said Laura.

"Listen to you—such a New York snob."

"If I were a New York snob I wouldn't be teaching in Gowanus."

"Why are you teaching here, anyway? You must have had lots of other options."

Before Laura could respond, a table opened up, and Adam's name was called. They followed the hostess to a cozy corner where, once seated, each ordered another drink. Adam felt the alcohol relax him, and listened as Laura shared her own carefully edited biography.

"They made me an offer I couldn't refuse," she said. "I was finishing a two-year clerkship and it seemed like a good way to stall. I didn't want to go to a big firm, but I didn't want to go to Iowa, either." She shrugged. "Okay, guilty. I am a New York snob."

"So where does Berkeley fit into the picture?"

"Maybe I'm done stalling."

"That would be a pretty dramatic move. All the way across the country. Isn't Columbia hiring? NYU? Or even Harvard?"

"Even Harvard! Listen to you. Let's just settle for Harvard."

Adam blushed. In his zeal over Laura's job opportunities, he felt like he had recklessly proclaimed his undying love.

Laura, however, appeared not to notice. "You know those jobs don't come calling," she continued. "It's more competitive than it has ever been. Too many lawyers; too few opportunities; and everyone who's working is looking for an exit strategy."

"But you're a rock star," Adam insisted. "You practically won the National Book Award."

"Please. That was four years ago." She crooked her neck and did her best imitation: "What have you done for me, lately?"

"Janet Jackson, circa 1986."

"Very good."

"Thank you."

"Anyway, sometimes a fresh start is needed. Someplace new. Without the baggage."

"You've got baggage?"

"We've all got baggage," Laura answered a little more seriously than Adam expected.

Adam's own baggage, he reflected, was neatly packed away at his father's death, although his mother periodically hauled it out for special family occasions.

The waiter arrived to inform them about the specials: a Hamptons-raised rabbit braised in a shiitake and red wine reduction, Long Beach oysters stirred in a hurricane brine, and an authentic Lower East Side poached squirrel with an acorn purée, garnished with pigeon feathers and a "homeless foam." They both ordered something more mundane—salmon for Laura, the trout for Adam—and after the waiter left the conversation turned to lighter subjects. High school sweethearts, college roommates, favorite movies and cartoon characters, books they'd read, worst New York City subway adventures, boxers or briefs.

After a few more drinks, Laura repeatedly touched Adam's hand for emphasis while she was telling a story, and somewhere in the middle of the tale Adam's fingers entwined with hers and held the hand there. Their legs brushed beneath the table and, having found each other, stayed. Soon, Adam was feeling a steady pressure on his thigh that radiated warmth through his pelvis. When Laura began to stroke his arm with her free hand, Adam quickly flagged down the waiter for the check. He paid with cash, leaving an outrageous tip because he was too impatient to wait for change, and they stumbled outside onto the street. Soon they were kissing in the back seat of a fifteen-minute, thirty-dollar taxi ride to Laura's apartment.

Adam had just swiped his credit card through the fare meter when he noticed Laura staring at a young vagrant sitting on the front stoop of her brownstone. In the harsh glare of the street-lights he looked awful. His face shone with several days of accumulated sweat. His hair was matted and mashed. And his clothing appeared to have been rolled in grease, dusted with soot, and wiped clean with a pizza slice.

As they got out of the cab the kid rose and motioned toward them.

"Careful," said Adam to Laura. In college one of his room-mates had been attacked by a homeless man brandishing a set of keys, and in the scuffle he received a slash across the face that required thirty stitches to close. The only weapon Adam had was his red Pilot G2 pen, which he raised now in self-defense.

"It's okay," said Laura. "I know him."

"You know him?" Adam was about to lecture her on the dangers of befriending psychotic homeless people.

"What are you doing here, Gary?" she asked.

"You said I should call if I needed help."

"Yes," Laura said tentatively.

"But I only had your office number."

"I see."

"I found your address on the Internet. It was easy. You really should do something about that."

"Gary, this is my home. It's Saturday night."

"But I need to talk."

"Now?" She looked to Adam for help.

"What's going on?" Adam interjected. He recognized the kid now as the student they passed on the street after their lunch date, and who nearly tripped him in the stairwell. He looked as if he'd lost twenty pounds—and half his hair.

"I'm going through a bad time," said Gary. His hands shook from four espressos and some pills he'd found in a law school wastebasket.

"Maybe you should talk to someone," said Adam. "Else," he added.

"What is it, Gary?" asked Laura.

"I'm sorry, Professor. I didn't mean to ruin a special night." He looked from Adam to Laura as if it had just dawned on him that Laura wasn't alone.

"It's okay. What do you need to talk about?"

"Can I come inside and use the bathroom?"

"No, Gary. That's a line you can't cross."

Gary fidgeted on the stairs. The street was relatively quiet, but the noises of city life surrounded them: cars honking, music drifting from a nearby club, laughter, shouts, a bell. Normal people having fun on a normal weekend night.

Gary unzipped his fly and began to urinate on the sidewalk.

"Gary!" said Laura.

"It's bigger when I'm sober."

Adam made a move to stop him but then thought better of it. Instead, the two of them stood there awkwardly while Gary finished his business.

"Sorry," he said. "When you gotta go, you gotta go."

"Speaking of going," said Adam.

But Gary sat back down on the stoop. Then he put his head in his hands and moaned. After a couple of minutes, when he hadn't stopped, Laura looked over at Adam with a worried expression on her face. Neither of them needed a suicidal student on their hands—especially on a full stomach. She went to Gary and sat down next to him. "Talk to me," she said.

So Gary did. He told her his story about Ann Marie—at least the expurgated version—and Laura listened politely. He was not the first young man she knew to be distracted by heartache and loss. But he was the craziest.

"Listen to me, Gary," Laura said when he was done, as calmly as she could. "Everyone has his heart broken. This is a normal part of life. People treat each other terribly, and they hurt each other. Some days we feel like we can't go on. But life goes on. We go on." She regarded him intently. He seemed to be listening, but he could have been hearing the radio transmitter in his head. "Do you understand what I'm saying?"

"I think so." Gary looked up at Adam. "Do you?"

"Me?" said Adam.

"Not him," Laura interrupted. "I'm not talking about him. He's a good man. I wouldn't be here with him if he wasn't."

"But you said—"

"Go home, Gary. Think about what we just discussed. This, too, shall pass."

Gary sat there for a minute, considering. Then he heaved himself to his feet. "What's the reading for tomorrow?"

"Tomorrow is Sunday."

"Oh, yeah." A semblance of a smile cracked his lips, which looked chapped and painful. "Okay. Well, thanks for talking to me. I really appreciate it." He held out his hand and Laura shook it, then he came around and offered it to Adam, as well. Adam hesitated, but over Gary's shoulder he saw Laura silently urging him to do it. So he took Gary's hand and gripped it. The hand was surprisingly firm, rigid and warm, not at all what

Adam expected. It was the handshake of a CEO or a law firm partner.

"Have a good night," Gary said like a normal person. Then he turned, waved once, and walked off into the night.

Adam and Laura watched him go until his back was clearly out of sight.

"Wow. What was that?" asked Adam.

"Poor kid. I feel sorry for him," said Laura.

"I feel sorry for you."

"I'll be okay," said Laura. "Nothing some good sex won't cure."

Adam gulped. "I'll try my best."

"No heartbreak, right?"

"No."

Then she took his hand and led him upstairs.

VIDEO: Associates at top Wall Street firm toss HUNDREDS OF LEFTOVER SANDWICHES in the trash...
Tax Partner takes vacation... OR DOES HE?

LAWYERS BUY NEW CHAIRS
DJUDGE REPORT

REPORT: CB&P associate sleeping with rival firm partner...

Sensitive information stolen...

Top firm management issues new directive on paper clips...

Will not tolerate excessive use without prior permission...

UPDATE: Still no cream cheese for Friday bagels at D&L...

Associates to form committee next week...

Which associate is vacationing in Argentina?

ABA: Profits at some firms up, others down...

Over 2,000 reams of paper wasted in aborted deposition...

Over 2,000 reams of paper wasted in aborted deposition...

Mind-reading robots taking over law firms nationwide...

App turns smartphone into automatic client billing system...

HP&V scales back bonuses...

Seven associates expected to leave IN A HUFF!

VIDEO: Lawyers using the restroom-- without washing their hands

Which firm's bathrooms don't even have sinks???

REPORT: Summer Associate Bled For 33 Minutes Before Help Arrived In Paper Cutter Accident...

Summer associates sort through garbage in search of tossed receipt...

9

A Kick in the
Kidney Pie

ADAM IGNORED THE BLINKING RED light on his living room phone when he returned to his apartment. He was probably the last person in New York City with a landline, and no one of any importance ever left him a message anyway. The phone was included in the cable and Internet bundle he was forced to purchase even though he didn't need one hundred eighty television channels or another telephone. But if he wanted the high-speed Internet connection and ESPN, there was no choice but to buy it all. Like the reading assignments he gave his students, the phone was a superfluous irrelevancy.

He puttered around his one-bedroom for half an hour, blowing dust bunnies into the corners, shifting dirty dishes in the sink, and figuring out whether he had enough clean socks to get through the week without doing laundry. He swapped an old photo of his parents with one of him whitewater rafting in Colorado with Sam. His brother no longer had the time, and Adam no longer had the money, but the trip brought back happy memories.

Finally, out of mindless things with which to distract himself from thinking about Laura, he picked up the phone and listened to the message.

At first, he didn't recognize the name. The voice, however, was unforgettable. High-pitched, reedy, a British accent by way of Rochester, New York. He said his name was Campbell Wiley, and it took Adam several minutes to realize this was the same Donald C. Wiley who sat next to him in first-year Contracts and Torts. They weren't exactly friends, but shared a bond common to POWs, reformed alcoholics, and former cult members.

Campbell, f/k/a Donald, had not survived to graduation. He abandoned Harvard after their first year and went back to journalism, his undergraduate major. Over the years, Adam had spotted his byline in a steady climb up the newspaper ladder: *The Rochester Daily, The Great Lakes Gazette, The Huffington Post, Newsday*, and, finally, The Gray Lady herself, *The New York Times*. There was a scandal in his background, Adam recalled, a reason he had abandoned journalism and gone to law school in the first place. Something about burning a source while on his college paper at Dartmouth, a member of the administration whom Donald outed after promising him confidentiality. The details were fuzzy, but Adam recalled Donald gleefully repeating Janet Malcolm's famous line over a couple of beers after their last final exam: "Every journalist . . . is a kind of confidence man, preying on people's vanity, ignorance, or loneliness, gaining their trust, and betraying them without remorse."

It was curiosity rather than a death wish that motivated Adam to return Donald's call, but it would have the same effect. Donald represented the road not taken, and Adam wondered where it had led. Although they ended up in different places, perhaps they hadn't traveled as far as he once expected.

"Hey, old chum," said Donald when Adam reached him.

"How are you, Donald? Long time, no speak."

"It's Campbell now. I'm called Campbell."

"I heard that on your message. Didn't know who you were at first."

"Same bloke I've always been."

"So what do I owe the pleasure?"

"I thought we could meet for a pint."

"A pint?"

"There's a terrific pub not far from you. Used to be a crack den."

"How do you know where I live?"

"I'm a journalist, Adam," Donald laughed. "You free in an hour?"

They made arrangements to meet at the Spotted Lout, overlooking the Brooklyn-Queens Expressway. The Lout, as it was known among the locals, served warm beer and kidney pies, and had a loyal following among the British expat crowd. It was rumored Prince Harry got naked in a back booth once, although older patrons swore it was Hugh Grant.

When Adam walked in, the jukebox was playing the Sex Pistols' *God Save the Queen*. He ordered a Guinness from a comely bartender and watched her pour while he waited for Donald. The bar looked to be about two miles long and carved from an ancient oak. The wall behind it was filled with amber liquids, most of which Adam assumed were whiskey, but could easily have been gasoline. Two men about his age were having a vigorous argument about Manchester United while next to them a young mother was breast-feeding her baby and drinking a beer.

D. Campbell Wiley was about five-foot seven, stocky, with a thatch of black hair. He was wearing a blue pea coat and tan boots that made him three inches taller when Adam spotted him at the door. He waved, then came over to the bar.

"Hello old boy," he said and nodded approvingly at Adam's Guinness. "I'll have one as well," he instructed the bartender, with a wink.

"Good to see you Don . . . uh, Campbell," said Adam.

"You too, old chap."

As Adam recalled, Donald had not been happy at law school almost from the day he arrived. He missed the "rough and tumble" of the real world, as he had called it, and disliked the "pinhead professors" whose heads were in the clouds.

"Congratulations," said Adam. "I've been reading your articles in the *Times*."

"Thanks, mate. Congratulations to you, too. Got out of the rat race."

"Out of the rat race and into the rat business," said Adam.

"Ha! Bloody good! Must be challenging."

"Definitely. Especially at a place like Manhattan Law."

"No kidding. Not like when we were in law school."

"You went to law school?"

"Funny, mate." Donald's beer arrived, and he lifted his glass in a mock salute. "We can't all sell our souls; otherwise, there would be nobody left to sin."

"Touché. I'll remember that."

Donald signaled the bartender for two more beers, although he had barely sipped the first. "So what are your students like?" he asked.

"Oh, they're a mixed lot," said Adam cautiously.

"How so?"

"The dumb, and the dumber."

Donald slapped the bar. "Toots! You're hilarious!"

Adam suddenly regretted belittling his students, even as a joke, so he added, "Actually, there are some very bright ones."

"Really?"

"Sure. I've been impressed."

"So you're not giving out A's just to satisfy the curve?"

"No, of course not."

Donald quickly jerked his head, distracted by something to his right.

"Blimey, take a look at that," he said.

The mother had finished nursing her baby and now one of her breasts, full and firm, was partially exposed. Adam turned, then looked quickly away.

"Mama! Give me some milk," said Donald.

"It's nice that she feels comfortable nursing in public."

"I'm all for it," said Donald. "Let's pass a law."

"Actually, there is a law."

"Even better!"

The two men arguing about Manchester United stopped talking for a moment and looked their way. It occurred to Adam that the nursing mother might be married to one of them. He broke out into a nervous sweat, and steered the conversation onto safer ground. "So what's new in your life? Married? Kids?"

"Nah. I was married, but it only lasted about six months," Donald said, as he took the final gulp of his beer.

"What happened?"

"Thought I was in love. Turns out it was the whiskey." He laughed. "How about you?"

"Still single. Haven't met the right person yet."

"What about that Jane girl? From law school?"

"Van Dyke. Didn't work out."

"Sorry to hear that. Terrific knockers on her."

As Donald prattled, Adam questioned why the hell he had agreed to meet him in the first place—and, more importantly, what Donald wanted from him. How long would he have to stay before it was polite to leave? He was not-so-subtly checking his watch when Donald said, "I'm writing an article about law schools."

Adam's ears perked up. "Something I should read?"

"You know, how they're just a giant Ponzi scheme."

"Well, not all of them."

"Not all, true. But ones like Manhattan Law." He held Adam's gaze.

"It depends," Adam said carefully. "For some students they can be a good deal. We offer a lot of financial aid."

"I'm sure," said Donald.

"And our best students get good jobs," Adam added, although he had seen no proof of it yet.

"That's not what I'm hearing."

"What are you hearing?"

"There are rumors about Manhattan Law."

"Like what?"

Donald shrugged as if he didn't pay much attention to rumors. "Rumors about students buying grades."

"That's ridiculous," said Adam.

"And still not getting jobs, to boot!"

"I don't believe it."

Donald's tiny eyes drilled into Adam like black lasers, and Adam squirmed under his gaze. In the back of his mind he recalled Laura's comment about not telling anyone what really went on. Was this what she meant? Impossible. He refused to believe that about Manhattan Law School, or about her.

"You've got some angry, ripped-off students on your hands," Donald said.

Somehow Adam had finished his second beer, although he didn't remember drinking it. He signaled the bartender for a third.

"You haven't heard anything?" Donald pressed.

Adam recalled once, at his law firm's summer outing, an associate stripped down to a bikini and went for a swim in the pool. Two days later a popular legal website reported she had been skinny dipping with a partner. It took an entire year to dispel the rumor, and there were still people who referred to the firm's Trusts & Estates practice as the T & A practice. The point was that stories quickly took on a life of their own, morphing into far more interesting and sordid tales, especially among lawyers who loved nothing like a good scandal. Adam told himself it must be like that.

"Where did you get these reports?" he asked.

"You know a journalist can't reveal his sources." Donald gave him a sweet smile that made Adam feel sick.

"Well, they're not true, and I wouldn't make such a serious accusation if I were you."

"Is that some kind of threat?"

Adam hadn't intended to sound menacing, but he felt defensive and protective of Laura, if no one else. He was also a little bit tipsy—three beers on an empty stomach had gone right to his head. "Not a threat. Just a caution. I'd hate to see you ruin someone's career on the say-so of a couple of frustrated students."

"That's why I'm talking to you, old friend."

"Like I've said, I've never heard of it."

"Pity. You'll keep your eyes and ears open though? For your old Torts mate?"

"Sure." Adam would be damned before he told Donald anything, even if there were any truth to the rumors, which he hoped there wasn't. All he wanted was to get the hell out of the pub and away from the faux-Brit as quickly as possible. He signaled to the bartender and asked her for the check.

"Now there's a piece of work," said Donald, after the bartender delivered their bill.

Adam pulled out a twenty to pay for his share.

"We should leave her a little more, don't you think?" said Donald.

Adam looked at the bill, looked at the twenty, then looked at Donald. He realized the guy expected him to pay for their drinks.

"I thought we would split it," he said.

"Come on, mate. You're the one with all the money." He laughed.

"Not anymore," Adam said weakly. But Donald had left him in an impossible situation. Either he was a tight-fisted jerk or a gullible rube. He pulled another twenty out of his pocket and laid it on the bar. Then he stood.

"You taking a cab back?" Donald asked.

"I think I'll walk," Adam lied. He didn't want to get stuck in a cab with Donald. "How about you?"

Donald stared wolfishly at the bartender who was just picking up Adam's money. "Nah. I think I'll stay for a few more rounds."

The bartender counted out the change and laid it back on the bar.

"Keep it," Donald said to her.

She smiled and dipped down to pick up Adam's change, the white crescents of her cleavage shining like twinned moons. "Thank you," she said to Donald in a lilting accent.

"You English?" asked Donald.

"Irish," she said.

"You've got beautiful eyes."

When Adam walked out the door Donald was leaning in to the bar, his head practically nestled between the bartender's breasts. The bartender was laughing as if he were the funniest man in the world instead of a cheap, slime-ball, low-life journalist.

The door slammed shut and a foul gust of diesel fumes blew in from the expressway. Adam zipped up his jacket and walked quickly toward home.

PROFILE READER REVIEWS

Bar Bar

15 South Canal, Brooklyn, NY 11217
nr. Old Tire Alley See Map | Subway Directions
No phone → Send to Phone

* **Reader Rating:** 0 out of 10 | 54 Reviews | Write a Review
* **Scene:** Filthy Dock Worker, Toxic Bar Food, Classic NY, Infested,
  Hipster, Swank

Map Rate & Review

Profile

Down a dark, rat-filled alley, near one of the country's
poorest law schools is Bar Bar, a former hangout for
homeless canal workers and now a dive that even taxi
drivers are frightened to approach. The highlight, if
there is one, is the Wall of Shame, a bulletin board
featuring thousands of rejection letters from law firms
across the nation, addressed to the Manhattan Law
School students who drown their sorrows in the "ultra-
strong drinks" served up by the untrained bartenders
and wait staff. Don't forget to check out the bathroom,
where you'll likely find someone vomiting up some of
Bar Bar's famous incendiary chicken wings, slathered
in a sauce made with scotch bonnet peppers, store-
brand ketchup, and a generous helping of canal water.

10

Money for Nothing; Drinks for Free

STACI FORTUNATO LIVED IN THE one high-rise apartment building in Gowanus that wasn't infested with rats, lice, bedbugs, or all three. A building that was far too expensive for a student, but located in far too unappealing a location for anyone else. It had been designed by a famous Italian architect who thought Gowanus was a charming up-and-coming neighborhood in southern Manhattan rather than a trash heap on a toxic canal. As a result, the building stood out like a raised middle finger among sore thumbs, calling attention to itself and telling its neighbors to go screw themselves. The developer went bankrupt in the middle of construction when the scope of the architect's plans were revealed, and a Saudi bank bought the rights at a fire sale. It converted the top two floors to penthouse suites, reserved for a Prince who never set foot inside, but whose relatives often used the lobby as a soccer field or a place to tether their goats.

Staci's apartment had sweeping views of lower Manhattan, blurred only by the fumes that wafted from the crematorium across the street. Her father bought the apartment when Staci started law school. It was the perfect residence for his beloved daughter, and an occasional refuge when his wife locked him out of their house. He wanted to buy something in Manhattan, but Staci was both logistically and philosophically opposed to the public transportation system, and licensed cabs refused to travel to Gowanus. Normally, she would never have deigned to live in a borough without a Prada boutique, but she visited the apartment on a day when the setting sun cast a golden glow off the building's soft marble and the green-tinted windows shimmered iridescently in the fading light like newly printed hundred dollar bills. Also, that day the goats were at the slaughterhouse.

The doormen loved Staci—as older men always did—and greeted her effusively each time she entered the lobby. After all, she was one of the few residents who didn't eat trash and shed all over the carpet. They held the door for her, and gave her boyfriends the evil eye. Once they even banished an ardent suitor who tried to carry a very drunk Staci into the elevator. The building's superintendent escorted her to her apartment instead, and made sure she had brushed her teeth before shutting the lights and double locking the door behind him. She had that effect on people: solicitude, followed by heavy security precautions.

Now, as she stepped out of the shower and dropped her towel, she padded across the cherry floors without a care as to who could see her through the floor to ceiling windows. She threw open the double doors of her walk-in closet and scrutinized the shelves for the perfect outfit. On the left were tops and jeans—stacked from the darkest black to the most faded blue—while the right wall was entirely shoes. Directly in front were four drawers of lingerie and leggings, and one drawer devoted entirely to contraceptive devices. She settled on a conservative thong and matching bra, along with black tights and a top that barely covered her bottom and couldn't possibly keep her warm. A pair of black boots with a stiletto heel added three inches to her petite frame. Hair extensions added another six to her locks. In just ninety minutes, she was dressed.

It took another hour to pluck, tweeze, polish, and apply her makeup. She was fastidious about giving her skin exactly the right shine: too much and she looked like Joan Rivers, too little and she wouldn't glow in the dark. Finding the right perfume—her own blend of Marc Jacobs Daisy and a glass of Kendall-Jackson Chardonnay—and carefully misting herself took another thirty minutes. Finally, she spent another quarter of an hour scrunching her face in front of the mirror to be certain no lines showed and her foundation didn't crack. All in all, it was 10 PM by the time she was ready to leave.

In the lobby, her shoes clacked over the granite tile, distracting the men (and the goats). She smiled at all and none of them, and ran a hand along the curve of her thigh to smooth her body-hugging leggings. One of the men—a Saudi diplomat wanted for tax evasion—lifted a hand to call her over, but she ignored him. Ever since watching *Lord of the Rings*, she had something against people from the Middle East.

Fernando, the doorman on duty, greeted her with a kiss. He felt about Staci the way a man would feel about his own adopted stepdaughter—if that man were in prison for incest. He scolded her for not being properly dressed for the elements, and insisted she wait inside while he hailed a cab. When he returned, his face was flushed and a jet black Lincoln Continental idled by the curb.

Her destination was less than a half mile from her apartment, but Staci did not believe in walking. Especially not in heels that carried a warning label from the American Society of Podiatrists. The limo driver was not pleased by the short fare, but he brightened when Staci adjusted her top and gave him a better glimpse of her breasts. She tipped him generously, but only because she was bad at math.

Bar Bar was the watering hole for the law school's serious drinkers, those who couldn't afford a more expensive prescription drug addiction or whose dealers were out of town. Founded in 1867 to provide sustenance for workers dredging the Gowanus Canal, its rise and fall followed the history of that ill-fated waterway. By World War One it was one of the most popular bars in the region, and men spilled onto the street through its saloon-style doors both day and night. But with the building of the nearby expressway and construction of the F subway line, the bar sank into disuse. Although the canal usually smelled worse, there were nights when the back of the bar rivaled it. Different proprietors tried their hand at everything from darts to karaoke to cockfighting, but the bar didn't turn a profit until the latest owner renamed it and constructed a Wall of Shame on which he invited students from the neighboring law school to paper their law firm rejection letters. The Wall now had over thirty thousand papers, on which patrons scrawled graffiti. It had recently been featured in the Styles section of the Sunday *New York Times* ("Dear [Your Name Here]/ Local bar puts a face to the rejection").

Staci greeted the bouncer with a double air kiss. She had been in law school only three months, but already she felt like a regular. Nearly everyone at the bar was either a student or a recent unemployed alum with nowhere else to go. Each year a new class claimed Bar Bar for itself, the way a group of tourists glom onto a tour guide or a John falls for a prostitute, confusing business for affection. Bar Bar cared for the students about as much as Manhattan Law School did—it just offered more for the money.

Staci's friends were gathered at a table in the rear. The boys were sharing a pitcher and Samantha was drinking a Manhattan on the rocks. Sam was dressed like a retro chic punk rocker with clip-on safety pins and temporary tattoos. She was scared of needles, and had only one permanent tattoo: a jet coming in for a landing on her pubis. She whooped when she saw Staci, and gave her a wet kiss on the lips.

"Girlfriend!" she shrieked.

"You're drunk," said Staci.

"And beautiful!"

Staci took a sip of Samantha's Manhattan, but the bourbon twisted through her gut like a trapped opossum. She was a wine drinker, normally. She refused to drink beer because it reminded her of frat basements and keg parties, wasted hours she preferred to forget. She looked around for someone to buy her a real cocktail, but the boys were engaged in a loud argument about the Jets and she couldn't get their attention.

Frustrated, and slightly annoyed by the drunken Samantha, she stomped off to the bar to buy herself a vodka and Red Bull.

She carried no cash, but was well-armed with her father's credit cards, some of which he knew she had. As she pushed her way to the front, she ignored the young men who stared at her hungrily as if she were a baby seal waiting to be clubbed.

The bartender, a giant with a shaved head, attended to her immediately, ignoring her classmates who clamored for another round at the far end.

"Here you go, sweetheart," he said as he set down her glass of amber and ice. "That'll be twelve dollars."

Staci withdrew the black AmEx from her ostrich skin wallet.

"No credit cards," said the giant, pointing to a huge sign behind the bar that said Cash, Grass, or Ass—Nobody Drinks for Free.

Staci blinked uncomprehendingly. "Is that new?"

"No."

"But . . . . then how do I pay for it?"

"You know those green pieces of paper? With the picture of Alexander Hamilton?"

"I don't have any cash," said Staci, pronouncing "cash" as if it were "herpes."

The bartender withdrew the drink from the counter. "Sorry. No tickey, no laundry." Although he could have made an exception and given it to Staci on the house, he hated her. Truly, he hated everyone in the place: the spoiled, unjustly entitled Manhattan Law School students who rarely tipped, hardly paid, and looked mostly awful (Staci being the exception). His real passion was the drums, but his thrash metal band was stuck in litigation with their manager who had impounded their equipment. The law was killing him—all day and all night.

"Nooooo!" Staci wailed.

As he lifted the drink to spill it into the sink, the undersized man standing next to Staci slapped a twenty on the bar.

"Drink's on me," said Asher Herman.

Staci turned just as the Jets scored a touchdown. A roar from the crowd, and the blue light from the television screen cut the hollows of Asher's face like the sun glinting off a glacier. He had never looked more rugged or attractive, and never would again. Staci cozied up against him. "I'll have two, then," she said.

"Make it three," said Asher, feeling expansive as he slapped down another twenty.

The bartender frowned, but mixed up two more cocktails.

Staci took her vodkas and raised a glass to Asher. "I love a man with cash."

"I'll drink to that," said Asher. He clinked her glass and grinned like a dervish.

At that moment the Jets converted the extra point, and John Tarantula, Asher's friend and fellow editor, shouted "Score!"

"Keep it in your pants," said Staci, who thought he was talking about Asher. It took more than two drinks to get to her end zone.

Asher quickly explained John was talking about the Jets. "He gets excited."

"I can't help it," said John, wiping away tears.

"We don't let him out of the *Law Review* office except on game day."

Staci stopped. "You're on the *Law Review*?"

"We both are," said Asher. "I'm the Editor in Chief. The most important one."

The *Law Review* writing competition, Staci knew, was judged by students. It was supposedly anonymous, but already she'd heard rumors of favoritism and preferential treatment. Like any student-run organization, it was easily corrupted.

Staci smiled flirtatiously at Asher, and shook her hair loose. "I heard you guys get the best jobs."

"No one gets better," said Asher truthfully.

"And there's a writing competition where you pick the new editors."

Asher hesitated. "Uh, that's one way we do it."

"Is there another?" Staci leaned in close so that her breasts were practically rubbing against Asher's shirt.

Asher looked to John, but John's attention had returned to the Jets who were now being beaten back on defense. The *Law Review*'s rules were quite strict, and Asher knew them. But he had never stood next to someone as attractive and good-smelling as Staci, and the pheromones played havoc with his neurons.

"Can I trust you?" asked Asher.

"Of course you can trust me. Don't I look trustable?" She gave him her best trustworthy look: eyes lowered, lips pouting, thumb hooked inside her waistband and fingers splayed beneath.

He lowered his voice. "There's Pay for an A."

"Pay for an A?"

Asher could have sucked Staci's ear, he was that close. As he whispered the details, his lips brushed the whorled ridges that guarded entry to the deeper parts of Staci's brain. It sent a chill down her back, not because of the physical contact, but because his words were so naughty, delicious, and utterly corrupting.

"So that's how it works," he concluded.

"And all you have to do is invite me?"

"I'm the Editor in Chief." He sounded offended.

"Then I accept your invitation."

"I think there's a vote, too," Asher stammered. "At the end of your first year."

"I thought you said you were the Editor in Chief?"

"I am."

"Then you just voted." She gave him a quick peck near his lips, but it was enough to send his circulatory system into overdrive, shutting down his brain and shunting his blood to his nethers.

Asher ordered another round, and three drinks became five which soon became nine. The jukebox spun through a selection of tunes about love, loss, and late nights wasted on quixotic pursuits. In a dark corner, someone lit his torts casebook on fire, and the smell of burning paper mingled with stale beer and expensive perfume. Conversations rose and fell, the noise punctuated by a shout or a burst of laughter. At midnight, Staci's friends left without her. Samantha murmured a cautionary word into her ear. "Loser."

But Staci ignored her. She knew what she wanted; it was her friends who would go begging for jobs. Hard work and diligence were nothing if you couldn't find the ways around them. Those were the lessons her life had taught her. Law school perplexed her at first with its emphasis on actual reading and writing, but she knew she would figure it out. She always did.

The warmth of the alcohol suffused her, making her extremities tingle and her adrenaline flow. She wanted to jump Asher's bones, dig in her spurs, ride him until he barked. By now she was sitting in his lap and stroking his four-day-old stubble while he struggled to remain upright on the bar stool.

"Take me home," she whispered.

"I have roommates," said Asher.

"I don't."

That was how Asher found himself playing twenty questions with Fernando, who eyed him with suspicion and scorn.

"It's fine, Fernando," Staci reassured him. "It's only for the night."

Fernando hated to see another man with Staci—especially one as young and sexually inadequate as Asher—but unless she was blind drunk or passed out there was little he could do. Instead, he shrugged and then, when Staci wasn't looking, caught Asher's eye and drew a finger across his throat.

"Nice guy," said Asher when they were safely in the elevator.

"Ah, he's a sweetheart. He just doesn't like men, that's all."

Staci pulled Asher down the hall and kicked open her door with the heel of her boot. They fell into the room and onto the couch in a tangle of clothing and undergarments, their body parts bumping and knocking into and against each other. Asher was neither well-endowed nor particularly sober, but he managed to do his part. Staci didn't see supernovas, but the occasional comet that streaked across her vision kept her from falling asleep beneath him.

In the morning, Staci called her father to tell him the good news. It took a little arm-twisting to get him to cough up the money, but he capitulated when she threatened to date a Mexican.

"I thought I already paid your goddamned tuition," he complained.

"You did, Daddy. This is an extra activities fee for *Law Review*."

"That's a hell of an activities fee."

"Hold on, Daddy. Manuel is calling me on the other line."

After that, things went smoothly, and when she met Asher again that night at Bar Bar she was a member of the club for which she had paid to be a member. There were drinks all around, and much good cheer, and even the bartender didn't mind when Staci rubbed his bald head for luck. No genie appeared, but fortune shined on the few. Of which she now was one.

WIKIPEDIA

English
The Free Encyclopedia
5 027 000+ articles

Deutsch
Die freie Enzyklopädie
1 883 000+ Artikel

日本語
フリー百科事典
994 000+ 記事

Русский
Свободная энциклопедия
1 273 000+ статей

Español
La enciclopedia libre
1 218 000+ artículos

Français
L'encyclopédie libre
1 703 000+ articles

Italiano
L'enciclopedia libera
1 240 000+ voci

Português
A enciclopédia livre
896 000+ artigos

中文
自由的百科全书
850 000+ 條目

Polski
Wolna encyklopedia
1 147 000+ haseł

Howell Goldreckt (born 1956) is a partner and member of the executive board of Cranberry, Boggs & Pickel LLP, one of American Lawyer's "Top 50 Firms Whose Names Start With The Letter C" and known for its handling of many top mergers and acquisitions. Goldreckt started at the firm as an associate and moved up the ranks to partner after the Mass Jumping of 1991, when thirteen top attorneys at the firm all committed suicide on the same day, one week before a special prosecutor revealed a series of irregularities in the firm's accounting records. The firm has since paid restitution to the government and the chairman emeritus is no longer under house arrest.

Howell Jefferson Goldreckt	
Personal details	
Born	March 17, 1956
	Albany, New York, United States
Spouse(s)	Angie Goldreckt (1981-1982), Tiffanni Goldreckt (1990-1994), Sunshine Spice Goldreckt (2000-2000)
Alma mater	Manhattan Law School
Profession	Lawyer

CB&P is known for its stringent hiring practices, accepting only the very top students at some of the nation's best law schools. Goldreckt leads the firm's hiring committee, as well as its bathroom committee, which manages entry and exit privileges for the office's twenty-three restrooms.

In his spare time, Goldreckt enjoys fine dining, cigars, and bird watching. He and his second wife, Tiffanni Goldreckt, starred in a reality television pilot for the A&E network that was not picked up to series, titled "M&A, T&A." (Tiffanni was later a contestant in Season 7 of Survivor, forced to leave the show during its fourth episode after an emergency medical evacuation following an incident with one of her breast implants.)

Goldreckt splits his time between Bedford, New York and midtown Manhattan.

11

If It Quacks Like a Duck

THE STEAKHOUSE WAS WHERE MEN died and went to heaven (literally—there was a defibrillator mounted by the bathroom): red brocade and draperies, waitresses whose décolletage left little to the imagination, hushed conversation punctuated by uproarious laughter, a humidor and cellar devoted to red wine, single malts, and Cubans.

Howell Goldreckt was already seated when Ann Marie arrived. She saw him waving down the waiter and ordering another cocktail even as he drained the one he had in his hands. He was an enormous man, nearly as wide as he was tall, and she could hear his booming martini order across the restaurant. When the maitre d' asked if she was waiting for someone, she just pointed at Goldreckt, and he nodded sagely.

"Ah, yes. My sympathies."

Ann Marie smiled politely. Not counting her callback interview lunch with a group of lifeless associates at Goldreckt's firm, her only two expensive restaurant meals were in her hometown of Buffalo, New York. One followed her high school graduation (with her father and sister), and the other coincided with the loss of her virginity (with her first serious boyfriend, who, unlike her father, let her order dessert). Although Goldreckt frightened her, the maitre d' frightened her even more. She dreaded saying something that would indicate she was an outsider in this world of privilege and money, or betray her disbelief she belonged here. Silence always served her well in these situations. It was better to keep your mouth shut and be thought a fool, her father was fond of saying, than open it and prove everyone correct. Ann Marie was not a fool.

The maitre d' guided her through the narrow aisles to her table. The hubbub and harrumphing ceased momentarily as she followed him, and a reverential hush fell over the restaurant. Ann Marie was unaware of the effect that her physical presence in a simple navy dress and black shawl had on the male population, but Goldreckt looked up from his drink and nearly choked as he watched her approach.

"Mr. Goldreckt," she said, and extended her hand politely.

"Howie, please," said Goldreckt as he wiped his palm against his trousers before grasping Ann Marie's cool, delicate, and dry fingers.

Ann Marie nodded demurely, but she couldn't possibly bring herself to call Goldreckt by his first name. Not here; not ever. She waited while the maitre d' pulled her chair out, then ushered her into the seat. The waiter hurried over to ask if she wanted something to drink, and she flitted over the wine menu for several minutes before settling on a glass of reasonably priced California Chardonnay. Goldreckt ordered another martini.

The waiter scooted off to the bar, and an awkward silence settled upon the table.

"Well," said Ann Marie. "How are you?"

"Excellent."

"That's excellent," Ann Marie responded.

"Never been more excellent," Goldreckt confirmed.

Ann Marie hadn't known what to expect when she got Goldreckt's voicemail. The rumor was the firm had begun to extend summer associate offers, but when she returned his call he didn't say anything about it. Would he invite her to a fancy restaurant just to tell her there was no job for her? A simple phone call or letter would be cheaper, and a lot less discomfiting. Yet here they were: Ann Marie waiting for the axe; Goldreckt waiting for his drink.

She knew the odds. Despite her GPA, her letters of recommendation, her good looks, and her work habits, Goldreckt's firm had a pattern of taking just one summer associate from Manhattan Law School each year. Although Ann Marie was confident in her own skills, she knew there were others who had outperformed her, students with more exalted *Law Review* titles, or cozier relationships with some of the professors. She expected the worst, and was prepared for it. Unlike most of her classmates, she did not believe the world owed her something. She worked for what she achieved, and knew that there would always be those who worked harder.

Ann Marie gulped her wine when it arrived. It tasted acrid, like grapes soaked in gasoline. Goldreckt's martini, meanwhile, appeared to have been pure ethanol: it fueled his conversation and sent him sputtering on about his latest deal—the acquisition of a health-care plan by the largest private operator of prisons in the United States, who proposed to replace nonessential medical personnel with low-level felons. Ann Marie nodded politely, and tried to follow the thread of the conversation, but she would have been confused by the intricate legal details even if she weren't distracted and already buzzed as a result of an empty stomach and generally low tolerance for alcohol. Goldreckt's deals tended toward the arcane and barely legal, skirting administrative regulations and venturing into a statutory no-man's land.

"So when the EPA rolled around we told them it was Chinese fireworks—nothing a little topsoil removal wouldn't fix—and the dopes believed us!" Goldreckt exploded with laughter, and Ann Marie followed as best she could.

More war stories followed, the theme of which was Goldreckt as a cunning and cutthroat deal-maker. Pity the fool who mistook the blood on his tie for ketchup. Goldreckt ground him up for hamburger.

The waiter returned to take their order. Goldreckt ordered the biggest steak on the menu with a side of creamed spinach and a baked potato. To maintain his body at fighting weight, he required a minimum of four thousand calories a day. Ann Marie chose the red snapper. Goldreckt insisted they split a dozen oysters and also ordered a Caesar salad as a concession to healthy eating. "Hold the lettuce," he added.

It took the waiter a moment to realize Goldreckt was joking. Then he forced a chuckle, and gave Ann Marie a painful smile.

"My ex-wife thought I was going to have a heart attack before I turned forty," said Goldreckt. "Joke's on her for taking the lump sum!"

Ann Marie felt a pang of compassion for the aforementioned Mrs. Goldreckt, whom she imagined folding towels at a tanning salon where she worked part-time to supplement her meager remaining funds. Goldreckt couldn't have been an easy husband, and he certainly wouldn't be a generous ex. When Ann Marie married, she intended to be able to support herself. It was not the only reason she went to law school, but having a career that would allow her not to worry about next month's rent payment was certainly a priority—and if it meant suffering through dinner with Howell Goldreckt, she would endure it.

Meanwhile, the partner prattled on. He had plans to renovate his home in Bedford, and it was important that Ann Marie know the details. The architect had feminine notions of style against which Goldreckt struggled. Not that he knew anything about style; but he knew what he didn't like: cupolas. The contractors and craftsmen were in cahoots with the supply houses, and everyone was in thrall to the local zoning board. Goldreckt fought them all relentlessly, and would beat them back like barbarians at the gate.

There was a slight lull in the conversation as Goldreckt drained the last of his martini, but then the waiter returned with the oysters, and Goldreckt spent the next ten minutes trying to cajole Ann Marie into eating one. He finally succeeded, although Ann Marie struggled for air as it went down.

"Oysters are an aphrodisiac," Goldreckt noted.

"Maybe if you're an octopus," said Ann Marie, as the color gradually returned to her face.

"I've never met an octopus who liked oysters," said Goldreckt.

"Have you met a lot of octopuses?"

"Octopi," Goldreckt corrected her.

"Pizza pie," Ann Marie giggled. She was, she realized, a little drunk. It was a pleasant feeling, like wrapping her brain in a fuzzy blanket. Most of the time she was so damned serious, reading and studying as if her life depended on it, which it probably did. She was determined to pay back her father's miserly contribution to her education, and even do some good in the world—although exactly what that good would be she still did not know. Getting drunk was not part of her plan.

The waiter refilled her wine, which she didn't recall ordering. Goldreckt had stopped talking and, to her surprise, she was telling a story about the dog her sorority adopted. A little mutt they named Chet, after one of the girl's ex-boyfriends. The college threatened to fine them if they kept him, so the women took turns hiding Chet in their room. They couldn't bear to let the dog go, even though he was never housetrained, chewed their boots, and howled when they tried to sleep late. One day, after receiving their third warning letter from the college provost, one of the sisters "accidentally" let Chet outside, and he promptly ran away, never to be heard from again. Although they were heartbroken at first, the girls quickly realized they were better off without the dog. His absence was a blessing, and they soon forgot all about him.

Ann Marie had told the story before, but this time as she was talking she realized it was a metaphor for her relationship with Gary. The mewling, weeping, and soiling of sheets. The threats and provocations. The open window through which Gary jumped that required a night at Methodist Hospital but no lasting injury. Unlike the dog, however, she couldn't just remove Gary's collar and hope he would go away. He was permanent, like a bad tattoo.

Yet somehow she had managed to survive her first year of law school, and even to ace her final exams (it helped that she broke up with Gary right before they began). She made *Law Review*, got an internship with a local judge in Buffalo for the summer, and was one of a handful of students to land an interview with the few firms that hired from MLS. By the time of Goldreckt's phone call, she had managed to put the craziness of that year behind her.

Now the future speared an untouched oyster from her plate. "Are you going to eat that?" asked Goldreckt. It was down his gullet before she could respond.

"Please, help yourself," said Ann Marie. The wine had emboldened her, but Goldreckt missed the sarcasm.

"Some weekend I'll take you to the shore. Best oysters in the world."

That should have been her first warning, but Ann Marie was so inured to men making passes and inappropriate remarks that she had developed a survival mechanism known as Selective Defensive Deafness. It enabled her to put up with men like Goldreckt. Like a trauma victim, certain synapses simply refused to fire, leaving her in blissful ignorance of boorish behavior. It was how Ann Marie ended up with Gary. She listened to his tales of woe until the wee hours of the morning, then slept with him because it seemed like the kindest thing to do. Fixing the mistake took most of the ensuing year and all the antipathy she could muster.

Goldreckt, on the other hand, was so used to women batting, slapping, and spitting at him, that he immediately assumed the absence of hostility was an invitation. Ann Marie owed him one, after all, even if she didn't know it. Thanks to his help she had jumped to the front of the line. Now he would extract his pound of flesh.

"We went there last summer after my pool party," said Goldreckt.

Ann Marie nodded smartly, as if Goldreckt's social life were the most interesting thing in the world to her.

"For the associates," he added.

Her ears buzzed. Was he making her an offer? Had she heard correctly? Although she was bad with innuendo, she was pretty good at logical reasoning and had scored in the ninety-third percentile on that section of the LSAT. She came to law school on one of MLS's few merit scholarships, and passed up a place at Fordham to secure it. Since then, Ann Marie had lived up to her promise as a bright light of her class. She was a pleaser, and drawn to men who needed saving—from themselves, their wives, their lives. They, in turn, were mesmerized by her preternatural calm, her sweetness, and her hourglass figure.

Now Goldreckt sat before her, panting like a puppy. There was lust, but abject need, as well. For all his wealth and bluster, Goldreckt was a lonely, lonely man. In his secret heart he was still the fat boy with no friends. He had bought his ex-wives' affection (in one case, literally), and regularly paid for companionship, yet Ann Marie treated him with genuine kindness, which he had never experienced. She couldn't help it—the emotion was hard-wired in her personality—but for Goldreckt it was a revelation. Until then his work and personal life had been an endless series of transactions. For Ann Marie, however, he would have sacrificed anything—if only she would say the word.

Ann Marie felt that power, and it was better than oysters.

"Why Mr. Goldreckt," she said coyly, "is that an offer on the table?"

"Howie, please."

Ann Marie's mouth formed the syllable, but the best she could manage was, "How can I ever thank you?"

"So, you accept?"

"Yes!" If Goldreckt had tried to kiss her at that moment, Ann Marie might have complied. Fortunately, for her, he did not. All she could think about was calling her father to tell him the good news. He had encouraged her to go to Fordham, even if it meant she had to mortgage her future. He was cheap, but not stupid. He had read up on Manhattan Law School, and claimed it was a racket, a pyramid scheme that took students' money and left them floundering. She might get a degree, but she wouldn't have a job. But she couldn't bear the thought of all of those loans, debt that would take decades to pay off. And now she had a job—a good one for the summer—that, if she played it right and worked hard, would fill her pockets, sharpen her mind, and brighten her future.

"This calls for a celebration," Goldreckt insisted. He called the waiter over and ordered a bottle of expensive champagne. He touched Ann Marie's hand when he raised his glass and she didn't flinch. The champagne was excellent, dry with a hint of citrus. Goldreckt gulped his down in one swig.

It was a night to remember, although Ann Marie would have trouble recalling specifics the next day. At one point in the evening she could have sworn Goldreckt started quacking like a duck, but she chalked it up to a hallucination. For the most part, he was a gentleman, and Ann Marie was disarmed and enchanted. They left the restaurant together, and he hailed her a cab, making sure her seatbelt was fastened before he shut the door. When the cab sped up the avenue she turned around to see the partner standing in the middle of the street without his shoes or socks, dancing what looked like a waltz with an imaginary partner as the maître d' and several waiters tried to usher him back inside.

MANHATTAN LAW SCHOOL COURSE EVALUASION FORM

COURSE NAME: Torts   INSTRUCTOR: Prof. Wright

Why did you enrole in this? Requirement - no choice

STUDENT SELF-EVALUASION
How many hours did you spend on this course each week? (Include read, write, study, ect.) 0.5

1. Did you come to class prepared?
   - ____ Always
   - ____ Usually
   - ✓ Sometimes
   - ____ Never

2. Did you work to best of your potential in this class?
   - ____ Always
   - ____ Usually
   - ✓ Sometimes
   - ____ Never

COURSE EVALUASION
1. What were strongest aspects of this course?

Professor did not take attendance. Person in front of me took good notes so I knew answers when called on. Sometimes there was food left over in room from previous event.

2. What changes or improvements would you reccommend?

Please fix leaky ceiling in lecture hall! Wi-fi not always working and download speeds generally slow. Insufficient number of power outlets. Casebook was expensive, so I did not buy it. Reading assignments were too long. I do not understand what torts is. ~~because torts~~

3. Do you have any coments about instructor?

Did not like his shirts. He needs haircut. Did not seem interested in the material. Would prefer attractive, female professor in future.

4. Would you reccommend this class / this instructor?

____ yes   ✓ no   ____ maybe

PLEASE EXPLAN: Torts should not be required class because it is not interesting.

12

Cat Scratch Fever

T HE GRADES ARRIVED WITHOUT WARNING, stuck between bar exam review brochures ("never too early!"), loan refinancing solicitations ("never too late!"), and stale Christmas fruitcake courtesy of the Manhattan Law School Christian Fellowship. The school had accepted that email was here to stay, but grades were still delivered in hard copy, inside transparent white envelopes that turned the purest members of the student body into criminals, unable to resist sneaking a peek inside the boxes of their friends, or, more often, their enemies.

Despite the liberal curve and the scourge of grade inflation, there were still more C's than A's, more dissatisfied customers than happy ones. The grades seemed random and unjustified, an unfair and inaccurate representation of a student's worth, as disconnected a reflection on the ability to practice law as a law school degree itself. Each year the Student Governance Counsel proposed switching to an honors/pass/fail system ("just like Yale!"), but there was too much resistance from the faculty and members of the *Law Review* who, after all, had a lot invested in letter grades.

Staci carefully stepped over a student who was sleeping in the mail room and searched for her box. She had only been to this corner of the basement once before, when a friend left her a dozen pills of Adderall hidden inside the handle of a plastic gavel. She found her mailbox stuffed with credit card offers and invitations to open houses from student legal organizations, intramural sports teams, and obscure religious sects. Stuck to the inside of the box, taped closed—not even sealed—she found the envelope and quickly opened it. Straight A's, just as Asher had promised. But then she blinked and rubbed her eyes, and one of the letters fattened and turned on her like a high school frenemy. She shook the page, but the grade was still there. She threw it to the ground, stomped on it, then picked it up once more. But there it was, albeit smudged and splotched with brown mashed cockroach. Professor Wright had given her a C– in Torts.

She kicked the sleeping student. He rolled over and blinked at her. "Mom?" he asked.

"Shut up, jerkoff," she said.

"Name's Gary," he said, then went back to bed.

Staci ignored him. How could Professor Wright do this? She paid good money for those grades. It was more than unfair; it was practically criminal. Her father would be furious, although she had no intention of telling him. He had already mortgaged a good part of her sisters' inheritance to send her to law school, and though she felt some guilt for it, she had no desire to pay them back.

It was 2:45 on a Friday afternoon. The new semester had barely begun. The registrar had surely left already. The administrative offices were probably locked for the weekend. And who could she complain to anyway? Who would hear her plea for equality in dishonesty, justice for the corrupt? No, she would have to do this herself. She withdrew her rhinestone-studded compact from her purse and touched up her makeup, then tightened her shit-kicking boots. With one last look at her grade for inspiration, she went right for the man himself, straight to Professor Wright's office.

It took some time, however, to find it. For security reasons, there was no directory that listed office numbers. Staci had also thrown away the class syllabus on which Professor Wright detailed his office hours and location. Plus, the office was in an obscure part of the building that could only be accessed by going to the fifth floor and then walking down three flights, which Staci discovered when she asked directions from a janitor who was looking for cleaning supplies suitable for huffing.

Professor Wright was packing a leather satchel with the Torts casebook and a thick stack of articles when Staci banged on his partially open door, then stomped into the office.

"Can I come in?" It wasn't a question.

"Make yourself at home," he said, although sarcasm was lost on her.

Now that she was actually inside Professor Wright's office, her resolve wavered. She had never been in a professor's office before—at least not for an academic reason—and was surprised by how spartan and shabby it looked. Professor Wright's desk was crammed into one corner, between a heating duct and a large rat trap. With no bookshelves, his papers and books were piled on the floor. A single light bulb swung from a wire in the ceiling. All in all, it resembled a cell on Rikers Island—at least from what Staci had seen on *Law & Order*.

"How can I help you, Ms. Fortunato?" Professor Wright asked.

"I just got your grade. My grade," she corrected herself.

Professor Wright sighed, as if he had hoped to avoid this conversation. He seemed to be judging the distance to the door to see if he had enough room to escape.

"I'm sorry. But there's a strict curve, and I don't set the numbers. Your performance on the exam—"

"Yes, but we had a deal."

"A deal?"

"You were supposed to give me an A."

Wright cocked his head. "I don't remember making that deal. Like I said, your performance on the exam—"

"With the *Law Review*. Pay for an A, you know?"

Staci could have sworn she heard Professor Wright gasp, but she decided it must have been a burp, which was just plain rude.

"Are you saying you expected to pay for a higher grade?"

"Duh. I paid for an A. And it wasn't cheap," said Staci.

"Is this common?"

Staci hesitated. Asher assured her all the professors knew about the system, and everyone had signed on. But Professor Wright sounded like he had never heard of it, and he did look a little confused. He was new, Staci reminded herself. Perhaps he just didn't understand the details.

"First-years don't participate. Usually," Staci explained.

"But everyone else does?"

"Well, most everyone. I don't know. I assume so. I mean, I assumed you knew."

Professor Wright shook his head. "I had heard some rumors, but . . . ." his voice trailed off.

"Oh shit. I'm sorry I said anything. Forget about it." Staci took one step backward toward the door. "Fuck. Sorry about the 's' word," she added.

"Wait," said Professor Wright. "Who told you about it?"

"My, uh, boyfriend." Soon-to-be-ex-boyfriend, she thought. "He's on *Law Review.*"

"And the professors. You said everyone participated?"

"I don't know. Don't you have faculty meetings about this kind of stuff?" Now Staci was nervous, and her palms and neck began to sweat. She hated her own perspiration, almost as much as she hated body hair, and now she was grossing herself out.

"Did everyone else give you an A?"

Staci nodded.

"And you studied the same for their exams?"

"Of course."

The tiny room was making Staci claustrophobic, and Professor Wright was staring at her as if she had forgotten to tweeze her eyebrows.

"Anyway, Prof, I gotta run," she said. "Sorry about everything. Really."

She bolted out of his office without looking back. By the time she reached Asher's building, three blocks away, she was red-faced and winded. Her breath fogged in the winter air, or maybe it was the smoke from her nostrils. The building was squat and wide, and resembled a fortress. It had been built for low-income housing, but was repossessed by the city for housing code and drug violations, then sold to the law school for a box of pencil erasers and an assumption of debt. The school's housing clinic quickly got the violations dismissed, then locked out the low-income tenants and dumped their possessions along the bank of the canal. The building had no lobby or doorman, and the front door was made of reinforced steel and bulletproof glass. It was yawning open on two broken hinges when Staci shoved through it with the heel of her palm. Inside it smelled like stuffed-crust pizza, old condoms, and socks. Asher's apartment was on the top floor, a five-flight haul, and Staci took the stairs two at a time, her little legs churning like an Olympic hurdler. One floor below the landing she encountered Asher's roommate, a Mormon who had gotten off track on the way to his mission and remained in Gowanus.

"Hi, Staci," he said brightly.

"Fuck you, Hal," she said as she sprinted past him.

Asher was sitting on his Craigslist couch watching SportsCenter and eating Lucky Charms straight from the box. His feet were propped up on the empty Con Ed cable spool they used as a table, next to the carton of milk and surrounded by burning candles that smelled like cheap aftershave. On his iPod, a rapper spat out angry rhymes about privileged white kids. He waved broadly when he saw Staci and motioned her inside.

"Heyyyyyy babe." He removed his headphones and handed her the box of cereal.

"I got a fucking C minus!" she said.

"Wha?" said Asher.

"C minus. In Professor Fucking Wright's Fucking Torts class."

"Wow. That sucks."

She advanced on him like a matador. "You said it was Pay for an A. I paid. I want my A!"

"But you got a C minus."

"No shit, Sherlock. And I paid for an A."

Asher's brain worked slowly, even in the best of circumstances. Now he gradually put it together like a Contracts hypo-
thetical: Student S pays four professors to give her an A; three
accept, but the fourth declines. Does she have a cause of action?
"It's a unilateral contract," he explained. "It's not enforceable
because there's no meeting of the minds."

"What the fuck are you talking about?"

"Wright is new. He probably doesn't know about the system
yet."

"He doesn't!"

"See. I told you." Satisfied, Asher pulled a jug of milk from
beside the couch and took a gulp.

"But what about my money?"

Asher shrugged. "You still got three A's, right? Have some
milk." He offered her the container.

"I paid for four A's."

"You're lucky you got three."

"What the fuck does that mean?"

Later, Asher would regret his choice of words. Perhaps, if he'd
been more politic, things would have turned out differently. But
he suffered from the illusion that being handed something was the
same thing as earning it.

"Come on Staci. You're not the brightest bulb in the socket.
You know that."

"Who's talking about bulbs?"

"In a normal semester you'd be lucky to get four C's," he
continued. "We gave you a gift."

"I paid you!"

"We don't usually let first-years buy in. We did it as a favor
to me." He winked.

Staci looked around for something to throw at him. The TV
was far too big; the box of cereal too small. Then she saw the cat,
scratching the plastic legs of the TV stand. She grabbed it with
both hands and flung it before Asher had time to react. The cat,
however, was quicker. It pirouetted in mid-flight and extended its
claws, landing on Asher's face and digging in before it fell to the

table, knocked over the container of milk, then landed feet first on the carpet where it began to lap up the milk.

"Ow! Shit! The fucking cat!" yelled Asher.

"Serves you right," said Staci, but a little less sharply. She loved cats even less than dogs, and only slightly above goats, but she hadn't meant to scare it.

"I'm bleeding," said Asher. Three ragged lines ran down his face like war paint.

"Oh, baby, I'm sorry. Let me see." Staci tucked in next to Asher on the couch.

"It hurts," Asher whined.

"Poor baby." Staci examined the wound, then said, "You should get that cat checked for rabies."

"Really?"

"Yeah. This cut looks a little infected."

Asher bolted upright on the couch. "You think so?"

"No, you idiot," said Staci. "You can't get rabies from a fucking house cat."

"But, you said. . . ."

"And you believed me. Which makes you the dumb bulb."

Asher nodded knowingly. "I get it. You're just mad because I said that thing about the C's."

"And you're so smart? You've been buying your grades for the past two years."

"I'm the Editor in Chief of the *Law Review*."

"Really? Who'd you blow to get that job?"

"I'm sorry, okay? I'll talk to Professor Wright about the grade."

"Like that's going to change anything."

"It's not right."

"No. Fuck the grade. And fuck you and your pricks on *Law Review*. Strutting around like you earned it. Well, you know what? You didn't earn shit. You may have paid for it, but you don't deserve it."

"What's the difference? An A is an A. No one cares how you got it."

"Maybe that's why you don't have a job. Because people know you don't deserve it."

"I don't have a job because our school sucks."

"No, you suck."

"Whatever." Asher touched the wound on his face. He missed and poked himself in the eye instead. "Dammit," he said.

"Loser," said Staci.

But if he was a loser, what did that make her? A loser's girl-friend who couldn't even buy an A. It would be wrong to call the moment an epiphany, but something shifted, and a slight crack of self-awareness shined a light through the opacity of her narcissism. In the shadows, she could see her better half.

"Do you smell something?" she asked.

"Toast?"

"Like someone burned it."

"Must be Hal."

"No. Mormons can't eat toast."

"I'll check."

Asher rose from the couch, but it was too late. The smoke was beneath them and then all around them, billowing from the carpet where the milk container had knocked over the candles. A lick of flame rose from the sparkling fibers of flammable polyester. The cat clawed at the front door trying to escape. Staci saw her life pass before her eyes, the regrets and missed opportunities, the lies, and unexamined possibilities. But then she realized it wasn't her life, or it didn't need to be. So she pushed past Asher, opened the door, and left that life behind.

Brooklyn Heights Farmers Market and Vegan Craft Fair

THIS SATURDAY 10 AM
until the Republicans chase us away

Featuring

Peanutless Peanut Butterless Spread
Candy-Free Candy Apples
Parsnip Scarecrows
Joanne the Lesbian Psychic
Hemp Stroller Covers
Twelve Lactation Stations
Cage-Free Pumpkins

WE WILL ALSO BE AUCTIONING OFF ORPHANS FOR CHARITY

13

Invasion of the Body Snatchers

ADAM AWOKE IN A RAY of light. It bathed his face in a golden glow and flitted across his eyelids like a beckoning promise. The blankets around his body were warm and the pillow beneath his head was soft. In the air was the scent of lavender, and outside there were real birds chirping near the open window. He rolled to his side, and reached for the woman lying next to him.

Laura.

He had been spending nights at her apartment, even though his was closer to school and classes were back in session after Christmas break. Hers, however, was better decorated, cleaner, and didn't need mouse traps. It also had Laura.

He trailed his fingers over the smooth skin of her back, a cocoa color that faded to pale tan below her waist. Her hair fanned across one shoulder, a wavy brown-black that kinked and curled as it fell. She sighed in her sleep but didn't move. He rested his hand at the base of her neck, the narrow points of her shoulder blades climbing on either side. He could feel the rise and fall of her breathing, the gentle ridges of her spine. Laura was a championship sleeper, he had learned; it took two alarm clocks and her dog, Monk—a German shepherd/retriever mix—to get her awake.

His previous girlfriend, the aforementioned Jane Van Dyke, was an insomniac and a closet bulimic. Usually both at once. He would awake in the middle of the night to find the bed empty and the lights on in the bathroom, Jane kneeling on the ground, alternately vomiting and typing on her laptop, which was perched on the edge of the sink. When she was in full neurotic mode she subsisted on Cheetos, Twizzlers, Halls cough drops, and Diet Barq's Root Beer, and could go for days without a real meal. In fact, most of the women he dated were hyperactive overachievers who thought they could outsmart the digestive process. Somehow Laura managed to get the hyperachievement without the overactivity, a skill she attributed to yoga, psychotherapy, and a daily multivitamin, but which Adam believed was heredity, self-confidence, and sufficient rest. She was born with the gene for quality sleep.

Monk greeted him as he slipped out from the blankets and tiptoed to the bath. The dog waited patiently while Adam did his business, then followed him into the tiny galley kitchen.

"Okay," said Adam, knowing what Monk wanted. "But coffee, first."

Laura was a bit of a coffee snob, and her espresso machine and French press sat next to a ceramic jar of beans and a dual-burr grinder. The setup intimidated him, and he had yet to make himself a fresh cup in the morning. Instead, he found the thermos with yesterday's brew and reheated a cup in the microwave. Then, cup in hand, he grabbed a coat from the closet and leashed up Monk for the walk outside.

The coat was ridiculously short—Laura's Burberry rain poncho—but it covered his ratty, old Harvard Law T-shirt and hid the fact he was still in his boxers. Although he looked like a flasher, at least he wouldn't be arrested—as long as he kept the coat closed.

Adam would have preferred a walk along the promenade that went beneath the Brooklyn Bridge, but Monk pulled him in the opposite direction toward his favorite spot, a tiny patch of grass the city insisted on calling a "park." Monk circled around until he found a spot to his liking, then squatted on his haunches. What did dogs smell, Adam wondered, that made one location preferable to any other? Dogs were so particular about where they made their mark, and yet it all looked the same to Adam, one bit of dirty city indistinguishable from another. It was, perhaps, the same thing dogs wondered about humans.

Monk finished, and Adam fished in his pockets for something to pick up his droppings. He had forgotten a plastic baggie, and his sense of civic duty compelled him to clean up the waste—that, or fear of being arrested. He didn't want to be a snarky "Law Professor Above the Law" headline on Gawker. He looked around for something to cover his hands, and spotted several newspapers lying atop a garbage can. He grabbed the top one and tore off the first page. There, below the fold, was an article by D. Campbell Wiley about the implosion of yet another Wall Street law firm. Adam wrapped the article around the dog feces and tossed them both in the trash.

When he got back to the apartment, Laura was still sleeping. He reheated another cup of coffee and sat down at the kitchen table. The birds chirped, but now he could hear the grinding gears of a garbage truck backing into the alley behind Laura's apartment. It beeped loudly in an octave designed to attract raccoons and drive humans crazy. As far as he could tell, city employees worked from 4 in the morning until daybreak, unless they were working on the street outside his classroom window, in which case they worked on Mondays, Wednesdays, and Fridays, from 10 until 10:50.

Adam got up and slammed the window shut.

He wished that student—Staci Fortunato—had never said a word. Why couldn't she go home, pout, drink it off, lie to her parents? She could rant on a message board, tweet his name in infamy; he wouldn't have cared. Instead, she had to spill the beans.

In truth, the clues had been there all along: the subcommittee meetings behind closed doors, the jokes about "expense accounts" and "donation dinners," Jasper Jeffries's new BMW 535i. If students were paying for grades, it would explain a lot of things.

Yet he had no proof. An untrustworthy pseudo-journalist and an angry student did not constitute guilt beyond a reasonable doubt. They weren't even a preponderance of the evidence. He had no documents, no photographs, no surreptitious recordings. Instead, he had suspicions. Even in the court of public opinion that wouldn't do.

He peered over at the bedroom where Laura rested peacefully. How deep did the lies go? He couldn't believe she was involved, but he couldn't believe she wasn't. Her warning from months earlier rang with an eerie clarity: *They don't need to know what goes on here.* Nights they had lain together, Laura's head resting on his chest, telling each other everything. Or, now it seemed, nothing.

Monk nuzzled his foot. He bent down and petted the dog absentmindedly while gazing out over the living room. Laura's apartment was small but elegant, with expensive kitchen appliances and designer furniture. That espresso machine was no joke. Her bathroom was tiled in Italian ceramics, and the paint in her bedroom had been hand-detailed by a local artisan. Now he wondered how she could afford these luxuries on a professor's salary.

He rose and walked to her bookshelves. There were the usual rows of shamans and sophists—Hobbes, Mill, Marx, Locke, Rousseau, Descartes, Kant, Hume, Gramsci, Foucault, Derrida. Beneath them, the serious nonfiction, biographies, and histories. Then the novels and short-story collections, the books of poetry and art history, and finally the paperbacks and popular works of fiction. He poked around in them, removing one from the shelf and rifling its pages, then returning it and pulling out its neighbor. He wasn't even sure what he was looking for. An account ledger? A black book with names, dates, and receipts? A wire-transfer record or a stack of bills stashed in a hollowed-out novel?

"What are you doing?"

He jumped as if burned by a hot poker. "Me?" he asked, as if she might be talking to Monk.

"Are you looking for pictures of old boyfriends? There are probably a few of them in there." Laura was in a nightshirt and boxers, her hair still gathered at one shoulder, her bare legs muscular and brown.

"No. I was just trying to find something to read."

"Then why do you look so guilty?"

"I don't."

"You can't see your own face."

She was a tough prosecutor. And he was an even worse liar.

"Laura." He hesitated. "A student came to me."

"Okay. But her photo's definitely not in my bookcase."

"I know."

Laura shook out her hair. "Should I be jealous?"

"She told me something."

"Something about what?"

"The system. Pay for an A. She thought she had bought a better grade."

He expected Laura to deny it. Or laugh. Or plead ignorance. Instead, she sighed and said, "Well, now you know."

"It's not true, is it?"

"Of course it's true. I warned you."

"But how could they . . . ? How could you . . . ?"

"Sell out?"

"Yes. And take such a huge risk."

"There are all kinds of risks."

"Laura. It's crazy."

"No, what's crazy is the system that rips these kids off in the first place. I didn't lie to them about law school or their future. I'm just their professor. I teach, do my research, and keep my head down."

"Even if you forget the ethical issues," said Adam, "you could get caught. Disbarred."

"I think you're exaggerating."

"Students are paying for their grades. That's bribery. Fraud. Larceny."

"This is a private institution." She pulled her shirt tight; her arms wrapped around like a straitjacket. "The government can't regulate a strictly private transaction."

"Prostitution is a private transaction, but it's illegal. So is murder for hire."

"Now you're comparing it to murder?"

"If anyone learned about it, the whole school would blow up," Adam warned. "It would be a huge scandal."

"Maybe. But no one's going to find out."

"How can you be so sure?"

"Because it's been going on for years and no one has found out yet. And, really, is it so different from what happens elsewhere? You hear all the time about professors grading exams by tossing them down the stairs or giving them to their kids to read."

"Those are just rumors. Urban myths."

"There's a random element to grading even in the best of circumstances. You know that."

"Randomness is not the same thing as fraud. You're screwing with our students' lives. They work hard for those grades."

Laura raised one eyebrow at him. "How are they harmed? The ones who deserve good grades still get good grades. It's just that there aren't very many of them."

"You screw with the grading curve and hurt the students who don't get A's. Not all of them are useless or corrupt. The ones who aren't deserve better."

"It's too late to change things." Laura bent down to pet Monk. "There's nothing we can do. We're here, and this is how it works."

"No."

"Come on, it's not worth getting upset over."

Adam wheeled on her. "Not worth it? This is how people's lives are ruined. Trust me, I know what I'm talking about. You can't sit around and close your eyes to it."

"What do you want me to do? File a grievance? Write an op-ed? Call the fire department? Adam, my hands aren't clean. And I don't intend to ruin my career by exposing myself."

"It doesn't have to be that way."

"Maybe not. But it will."

"Laura. Listen."

Laura straightened. "You listen, Adam. Do you really want to lose your teaching job? For what? Some students who treat you like hired help and couldn't get jobs anyway? You're a nice guy, and I like you very much. You're cute, and you're not bad in bed. But don't be naïve. This isn't some abstract debate about Aristotelian ethics. It's the nasty rough and tumble of the real world."

He couldn't believe what he was hearing. Beautiful, clever Laura. With whom he thought things might work out. "What you're giving up is more than just your career."

"I'll be the judge of that, thank you."

"Well, I'm not going to have anything to do with it."

"If you want to keep teaching here, you'll have to."

"Never. And I couldn't be involved with anyone who is."

Laura's eyes did not waver. "You know what you're saying?"

"I do," said Adam.

He felt like he had taken a punch and fallen down a flight of stairs. His teeth hurt, and he was bruised and aching. But he was still standing, and not afraid where his next step would lead.

"So you're saying we're done?"

"Is there anything else to say?"

The words hung between them like a guillotine. Then Laura turned and shut the bedroom door behind her.

He packed his few things and gathered his books. He unplugged his phone and shut off his laptop. And all the way down the hall he could hear Monk barking in vain.

HEALTH SERVICES RELEASE OF LIABILITY

YOU MUST SIGN BEFORE THE STAFF WILL SEE YOU

Student Name:_____

Medical Problem (Circle One/All):
- Panic Attack
- Professor Attack
- Cafeteria Poisoning
- Fell in Canal
- Loose Bowel/Obstructed Bowel
- Didn't Do the Reading
- Need Medical Excuse to Miss Exam
- Failed Suicide Attempt
- Successful Suicide Attempt
- Other (_____)

In consideration of being seen by our medical staff, I, the undersigned:

1. The risk of injury from allowing your medical staff to treat me is significant, including the potential for permanent paralysis and death.

2. **I VOLUNTARILY AND FREELY ASSUME ALL SUCH RISKS**, both known and unknown, **EVEN IF ARISING FROM THE NEGLIGENCE OF MANHATTAN LAW SCHOOL OR ITS EMPLOYEES/CONTRACTORS** and assume full responsibility for my health services visit.

3. I grant and convey to Manhattan Law School all rights in and to all photographic images and/or video and/or audio recordings made of me during this visit to be used for publicity or any other purpose, including by our affiliated Internet side business, SickLawStudentsUndressed.com, in all media in perpetuity throughout the known and unknown universe.

4. I will notify the health services office if I have any preexisting medical conditions. I understand you are unable to treat any preexisting medical conditions in this office. A preexisting medical condition is defined as a medical condition that existed before I entered this office.

5. I understand that the health services office is staffed by financial aid students who have taken an online first aid course and have access to a medical textbook published in 1936.

X_____

Student's Signature   Age   Date

14

The Bernie Madoff Bypass

THE EDITORS WERE IN A panic. They'd gotten a Snapchat from Asher telling them to meet at the office, along with a photo of his bloodied head and the cryptic command, "BURN IT ALL!" Although Asher was prone to hyperbole, the scratches on his face looked real, and the fear made his eyes—already lopsided—skew like a Dali nightmare.

Willow Summer was already in the office, hard at work. Not on articles, of course. She'd been nominated to handle the most important job—recruiting. Pay for an A wasn't as simple as it sounded. The faculty couldn't just advertise that grades were for sale. Instead, each current *Law Review* member was permitted to invite one new student onto *Law Review* at the end of every year. Willow was tasked with scanning through the financial aid statements of the first-year class to weed out students whose families were too poor to afford the added cost of *Law Review* membership. From the list that remained, she would strike troublemakers, hotheads, and do-gooders. Then, the editors would all go into the field and conduct in-depth interviews, probing for problem spots ("do you have trouble keeping a secret?") and running credit checks. On the last Saturday in April, the entire *Law*

Review (except for the Associate Editors) gathered to approve the selections with the assistance of Professor Rodriguez. The writing competition that followed was a complete sham, as fake as the school's hiring statistics, but necessary to preserve the illusion of merit.

"What's going on?" asked Raya Kurdle, who arrived breathless in black Lycra. She had been interrupted in the middle of her jog along the canal just before she would have passed out from the fumes.

"I don't know," said Willow. "He looked freaked."

"That's the way he always looks," said John Tarantula, who followed Raya into the office and nearly decapitated himself on a book shelf because his gaze was fixed on Raya's ass.

"Yeah, but there was blood."

"He cut himself shaving," said John.

"He doesn't shave his forehead," said Raya.

"How do you know?"

Charlie Spires arrived, martini shaker in hand. "Anyone have vermouth?" he asked.

"This is serious, Charlie!" said Willow.

"That's why I'm drinking."

Meanwhile, the object of their concern was only several hundred feet away, filling out paperwork in the basement of the law school. Asher had never been to the student health center before. As far as he knew, no one had. Rumor was that a few years earlier Prof. Ogden Templeton, born 1906, had died there, and the nurse, afraid she would be blamed, simply threw him in a file cabinet and pretended it never happened. At least that would explain the smell of formaldehyde that pervaded the place. But Asher's health plan didn't cover doctor's visits or emergency rooms, and Asher—face scratched, fingers singed—was desperate, so into the bowels of Manhattan Law School he descended.

In the cold, empty waiting room, he was convinced he was dying. His life unspooled before his eyes like the damaged print of an old movie. The regrets, the lost chances, the phone number of that runway model—or perhaps she'd said "runaway model"—

he'd accidentally left in his pants before he washed them. In high school he had wanted to be an actor. Then his voice changed (late puberty, but that was another story) and he decided to become a radio deejay. After the university shut down his college station for broadcasting the answers to a chemistry exam, he turned to modern interpretive dance. Yet somehow he ended up here, on the banks of the Gowanus. How did it all go so wrong?

Asher's existential musings were interrupted by Nurse Brinda ☺—or so read her nametag—who called him into the examining room.

"How are we today?" she asked. "Quite a nasty boo-boo we have there."

"I think I might have rabies," said Asher.

"Where did Professor Hotchkins bite us?"

"He didn't bite me."

"Are we a student at the law school?"

"Is there a doctor I could see instead?"

"Open your mouth so we can draw some blood."

"Actually, I think I'm feeling a little better."

He tried to get up from the exam table. Brinda pushed him back down.

"You stay here. We'll be right back with some gauze for your wounds. We're not allergic to gauze, are we?"

"I'm not. Are you?"

Brinda laughed. As soon as she left the room, Asher grabbed his backpack and ran for the door.

"Come back here!" she yelled. "We haven't tested for a hernia yet!"

Asher kept running.

Although the *Law Review* office was also in the basement, it was in a different section than the nurse's office. To get there required going to the fifth floor, crossing through the Bernie Madoff bypass, then ducking through a small ventilation tunnel before heading back down another stairwell. By the time Asher arrived he was panting, out of breath, and still bleeding from the cat scratches. His hair was matted and clumped, and he was sweating like a pipe in August.

"He's not wearing deodorant!" Willow shrieked.

"What the fuck happened to you, dude?" asked John.

Asher collapsed in a chair. "Water," he managed.

Charlie brought him a bottle of water from a stash he had stolen off a Poland Spring truck earlier in the week. Asher gulped it down, and then burped loudly.

"Staci," he said. "She screwed us."

"Who's Staci?" asked Raya.

"The chick he's been screwing," said Charlie.

"That's gross."

Charlie shrugged. "I don't know; I think she's kind of hot."

"What happened?" asked John.

Asher told them about Staci's grade and her confrontation with Professor Wright.

"Professor Wright scratched you?" asked Willow.

"Not him. The cat."

"Your cat scratched you? Why? And why do you look all . . . burned?"

"Aren't you listening?" Asher was getting agitated. "Staci told Professor Wright everything."

"So what?" said Charlie. "What can Wright do?"

"He could tell Dean Clopp."

"The Dean knows," replied Charlie. Everyone knows."

"No. I don't think he does. Professor Jeffries said he didn't."

"How is that possible? He's the Dean."

"Have you seen him lately? At 1L orientation they had to pretape his remarks so he could lip-sync them."

"I heard he pooped on the floor of the library," said Raya.

"That wasn't him," Charlie admitted.

John pulled up a chair and perched on the back of it, resting his feet on the cushion. "You've got to go talk to Wright," he said to Asher.

"Me? Why me?"

"Because you fucked this up."

"But it wasn't me! It was Staci."

All four editors gave him a long silent look. "Enough said," said Raya.

Asher hung his head. A drop of sweat rolled off the end of his nose. His scratches stung and his hair itched. He regretted the primal urges that made him want to impress Staci. He should have let her chart her own course through the law school's capricious grading system. But now, of course, it was too late.

The school kept professors' home addresses in the same hidden, password-protected directory as it stored information about the school's legal settlements, health code violations, and data concerning the cancer cluster centered around the student cafeteria. Within a few minutes, Willow had cracked the code ("password123") and printed Professor Wright's address on a slip of paper. "It's a twenty-minute walk," she said.

"I'll expense a cab."

"Not a chance," said Raya. "You're not using the slush fund because you're too lazy to walk."

So he walked.

The neighborhood around the law school was barren and bereft. But as he got closer to Professor Wright's neighborhood, the streets came alive with people: young mothers pushing strollers, kids running home from school, hipsters carrying messenger bags weighed down with Kerouac and David Foster Wallace. Asher gaped openly. It had been so long since he had seen a real person that he forgot they existed. Kids, for example—who knew they were so small? And babies—they couldn't even walk! In his bewildered state he nearly collided with a stroller.

"Watch your fucking self!" the mother yelled at him.

"Fucker!" said the father, glaring over his Warby Parker frames.

"Sorry! Sorry," said Asher. He backed away and banged right into a scrawny guy carrying a guitar and an espresso.

"Fucking dude!" said the guy.

"My bad," said Asher.

"You don't look too good, dude."

"I know. A cat scratched me."

"You should have that checked out. Dude could have rabies."

"Very funny."

"I'm not kidding. Buddy of mine got scratched by a feral hamster and got hepatitis C. I'm telling you, that shit's serious."

Asher scrambled away as fast as he could.

"It's your life, dude!" the guy yelled after him.

Asher was pale and shaken when he arrived at the front stoop of Professor Wright's brownstone in Cobble Hill. The day had started badly and was about to get worse—he had a feeling. He wasn't a moral person, but the wrongness of what he was doing struck him at that moment. It was bad to buy grades, and worse to threaten faculty about it. Yet he was swept up in a system that led him slowly, inexorably, to this point of no return. He blamed society.

He rang Professor Wright's doorbell. No answer. He waited, then rang again, a little longer this time. Still no answer. He rang a third time for a good minute until the ringer sputtered and died.

Relieved, he was about to turn and go home when he heard the clomp of footsteps behind the door. He considered running, but the street was long and wide open and Professor Wright would surely see him before he got very far. Instead, he stood frozen on the stoop like a statue to stupidity.

"Yes?" Professor Wright opened the door. He was dressed in jeans and a white T-shirt. His brown hair curled down around his ears, and he had two days of stubble.

"Professor Wright, I'm Asher Herman."

"Am I supposed to know you?"

"Asher Herman. Editor in Chief of the *Law Review*."

"You realize you're bleeding?"

"Yeah, a cat scratched me."

"I think you broke my doorbell."

"Sorry. I didn't know you were home."

"I was writing. I don't like to be interrupted."

"Yes. Well. I'm here on a very important matter."

"If it's got to do with the *Law Review*, I haven't written anything for it. And if I did—if you need to talk to me—I have office hours."

"I'm sure you do," Asher interjected. "But this is a matter that's outside regular office hours."

"Like I said, I'm trying to do some writing. Do you think you could send me an email?"

"It's about Staci Fortunato."

"What about Staci?"

"It's about her grade."

Professor Wright's face darkened. "I've already talked to Staci about her grade."

"I know. And I don't think you understand the system."

"Oh, I understand it quite well."

Asher peered over Professor Wright's shoulder. He could see through to the kitchen: white and black tiled walls, a loaf of bread on the counter, a jar of pickles beside it. "Do you mind if I come in?" He felt exposed standing on the stoop, and he suddenly had a craving for pickles.

Wright opened his door wider, and motioned for Asher to come inside.

"Thank you for inviting me in," said Asher.

"I didn't invite you. You invited yourself."

"Well, thanks for opening the door, at least."

Wright nodded. Standing inside, Asher noticed that the apartment could use a coat of paint. There was a large crack running along one wall and a chunk of plaster was missing from the ceiling.

"I know you're new and all," Asher began. "But there's a system in place; it's been around forever. It works a certain way and everyone knows how it works. They're supposed to tell you—the other professors? There was like an orientation or something."

"There wasn't an orientation. But I know how it works."

"Then you should know that Staci was supposed to get an A."

"Staci got the grade she deserved based on her performance on the exam."

"But she paid for an A."

Professor Wright stared at him. Asher had never been this close to a professor before. He could see the hair follicles on Wright's unshaven face and a small scar above his left eye. There was a loose thread on the neck of his T-shirt where it rubbed against his throat. When Wright exhaled Asher could smell the pickles on his breath.

"No one pays for an A," Professor Wright said.

"You don't understand. She did."

"No, you don't understand. No one in my class pays for an A, a B, or otherwise. Paying for grades is wrong. Didn't your parents teach you that?"

Asher shifted uncomfortably. "My parents had... flexible morals. Besides, everyone does it. And it looks like you could use the money."

"Of course I could use the money, but if all I wanted was money, I'd be a partner at a law firm. Believe it or not, I became a professor because I wanted to teach students, not become rich. Although when I meet students like you I wonder why I'm in this business at all."

"I'm sorry we couldn't all go to Harvard."

"Even at Harvard students work for their grades."

"That's because they're at Harvard. We have to buy our grades because our degrees are worthless."

Professor Wright grimaced. "I think it's time for you to leave." He opened the door and gestured outside.

Asher stood his ground. He decided to try a different tactic. "Come on, Staci's exam couldn't have been that bad. Maybe you can reconsider?"

"If she'd written an A exam, I would have given her an A."

"We both know she couldn't do that."

Wright shook his head sadly. "You realize you're just hurting the students who least deserve to be hurt, don't you? The ones who actually deserve their A's. By perpetuating this scam you're debasing everyone's grades and telling the world you can't hack it as a law student. That's something, I think, you don't want the world to find out."

"Why would the world care?"

"The people who matter will care."

"Who's going to tell them?"

"The law may not always tell us how to act. But that doesn't mean you should sit idly and watch a crime happen. Maybe it's too late for you to learn this—although I hope not." Then he took Asher by the elbow. "Now please get out of here."

Asher stumbled as Professor Wright dragged him from the apartment. The guy was stronger than he looked. Asher caught himself from falling on the outside railing, then turned just in time to have the heavy wooden door slam shut in his face.

"I was leaving anyway!" he shouted.

He descended the stairs and found a patch of sidewalk that looked relatively free of dog feces. Then he sank to the ground. He sat there with his head in his hands trying to remember what the world was like before he decided to go to law school. When he looked up, it had started to rain.

BerkeleyLaw
UNIVERSITY OF CALIFORNIA

Boalt Hall

FACULTY DINING HALL
LUNCH MENU
FEBRUARY 21-27

Sunday 2/21	Monday 2/22	Tuesday 2/23	Weds. 2/24
Our traditional Sunday brunch, featuring buckwheat waffles made from our own homegrown buckwheat.	Cafeteria closed to commemorate Liberation Day in Denmark, celebrating the end of the German occupation.	Pesticide-free market greens, dressed with local olive oil and Meyer lemon, topped with organic walnuts.	California artichoke mousse on whole wheat crostini with a drizzle of bear urine vinegar, harvested from local bears.
Organic maple syrup harvested from the maple trees behind the moot courtroom.	Instead, there will be a selection of Danish pastries delivered to each faculty member's home.	Sunflower seed raviolini, in an heirloom tomato sauce studded with fresh figs.	Smoked tofu salad with herb medley carefully picked from the cracks between the stones outside the law library.
Egg white omelet, with eggs from Heidi and Sassafras, our "chickens of the week."	Please donate any uneaten pastries to our organic food bank, serving local homeless, organic families.	Chocolate hemp cake, made exclusively from hemp grown by Viola Jackson, assistant sous pastry chef.	Apple multi-racial gender-neutral dessert* topped with hand-churned blueberry ice cream.
Fresh fruit cobbler, fruit to be determined by what naturally falls from the trees on Saturday.	If you are willing to host a homeless, organic family for dinner, please e-mail the office of organic food services.	Red wine donated by Prof. Tarnson from the batch produced by his Wine Law class this past winter.	*This dish used to be known as an Apple Brown Betty, but we have chosen to use a less offensive name.
Thursday 2/25	**Friday 2/26**	**Saturday 2/27**	
Edible flower salad, to be eaten while blindfolded in order to symbolize unfair flower-picking practices in Latin America.	Cafeteria closed to celebrate birthday of Otis, the tallest tree on the Berkeley campus.	Tree bark and foraged mushroom appetizer, served on plates designed by residents of a local senior center.	**DID YOU KNOW?** *Our faculty dining hall utensils are made entirely from acorns.*
Macaroni and "cheese," with the cheese made from an emulsion of aloe and cactus pollen.	In tribute to Otis, please don't eat any leaves today.	Butternut squash soup, garnished with the tears of abused children being helped by our pro bono legal clinic.	**DID YOU KNOW?** *8 cents of every dollar we collect at the dining hall goes to help save sick plants.*
Multigrain bread, baked in an authentic clay oven, designed from plans found drawn on the walls of a local cave.	And, like all days, please don't eat any meat.	Fair-trade nut and seed burger, served with organic ketchup and an onion jam made by prisoners.	**DID YOU KNOW?** *Gluten-free options are always available in the pantry, open to faculty on the honor system 24/7.*
Cookie dough dessert, each serving shaped to look like a bust of Oliver Wendell Holmes.	Also, please avoid dairy, since Otis is vegan.	Vanilla cupcakes with red beans, sesame tofu cream, and local grasshopper feces.	**DID YOU KNOW?** *This menu is 100% edible and an excellent source of fiber.*

15

A Dump with a View

IT WASN'T FLEEING, EXACTLY. No one had chased her or driven her out. And it wasn't retreating because that implied being beaten and running away. Yes, they had fought. Yes, it was over. But as Laura stepped off the plane at San Francisco International Airport, she allowed herself a faint glimmer of optimism about the future. The clear blue skies, the lift in the breeze, the moist Pacific air. In the distance the hills sparkled and shined, while wildflowers bloomed in the sunlit valleys below. It was winter in New York, but in San Francisco the season glowed.

She had not been looking for another job although, in truth, it was never far from her mind. But she was always too busy to update her resume, attend the job fairs, or gather her thoughts for a faculty presentation. When a former classmate and friend was appointed Dean at Berkeley in August, however, the second person she called was Laura. (The first was her agent at the Speakers Bureau to tell him to increase her fee.) Rosalind Minsky had been the student graduation speaker at Yale, a Supreme Court clerk, and the youngest tenured professor at Boalt Hall. Fiercely intelligent, opinionated, and sober, she was everything Dean Clopp was not. Since then, she and Laura had traded messages, emails, and updates about their lives, until Rosie finally prevailed upon Laura to pay a visit.

Now, as her cab swooped down the steep inclines of the city, Laura felt the vertiginous thrill of new beginnings. Maybe she really could start again, leave the failed promises behind her. Manhattan Law School had trapped her—not just the system that corrupted and changed her, but New York City and all it signified: home, family, and, sadly, Adam.

She hadn't told him about the interview, or even the trip West. Since their fight in her apartment they had not spoken. He avoided her in the cafeteria, and she never saw him in the halls or on the street. One time she called him after blocking her number, but she hung up after the first ring. She had too much pride to ask for forgiveness, and every time she almost did she got angry at Adam for even making her consider it. It was easy to play the scold without a stake in the game; but once vested, what did he expect her to do? And at what cost?

Her arrival at the hotel forced her mind in other directions. The doorman helped her from the cab, then insisted on carrying her single small bag. In the lobby he transferred it to a bell boy who escorted her to the reception desk. An Asian woman with cheekbones like razor blades checked her in, and informed her she had been upgraded to a deluxe suite and all charges were prepaid— even the minibar. It was a far cry from her interview at MLS where the finance department refused to reimburse her for the cab fare downtown and the cafeteria manager sent her a bill for lunch.

In her room there were flowers and a gift basket with Ghirardelli chocolate and two bottles of Napa Valley Pinot, along with a welcoming note from Rosie. Outside she could see the bay from her window and, in the distance, the Golden Gate bridge. She ordered room service, then took a shower, liberally applying all the gels and creams the hotel helpfully provided. The food arrived, and she curled up in the king-sized bed with a good book and a glass of the Pinot. Twenty-one minutes later she was asleep.

The next morning she violated a city ordinance by taking another shower and using two towels to dry off. Then she ran the blow-dryer and the coffee maker at the same time. Emboldened by her lawlessness, she flushed the reusable tissues down the toilet. She laughed to herself thinking how Adam might view her environmental mischief, then felt a keen urge for his presence. But she pushed it aside as she hustled out the door.

Her two student escorts were waiting for her in the lobby, more Ghirardelli chocolate in hand. Both were blond and wind-tanned from outdoor activities Laura could only imagine. The boy took her bag while the girl took her elbow and guided her to their car—a wheatgrass green Prius. She laughed when Laura asked if they were a couple, the toss of her head indicating she was too post-millennial to be "coupled" with anyone for more than a weekend.

"Did you have a good trip?" asked the boy, whose first name was Kennedy ("after the President, not the Justice").

"Very nice," said Laura.

"What did you do with your carbon offsets?" asked the girl.

"I, uh, gave them to Greenpeace," Laura lied.

"They do good work," said Kennedy.

"Puh-leez," said the girl.

"Remember *In re Trans-Atlantic Cable Litigation?*"

"Hello? Rainbow Warrior?"

While they bickered, Laura marveled at their quickness and breadth of their knowledge. Most of all, she marveled at their desire to argue about anything except Mets versus Yankees, Kanye versus Jay-Z, vodka versus tequila. She had nearly forgotten law students cared about things other than getting a job, getting stoned, and getting laid, not necessarily in that order. Of course, the students at Berkeley had real prospects, which freed them to debate the kind of topics they would never encounter in the real world. Her students did not.

The law school sat inland, near the entrance to the main university campus, surrounded by low-slung buildings with red Spanish tile roofs draped by vines and bordered by grasses. The sun burned through the remnants of morning fog and tendrils of light shot through the mist. To Laura, it felt as if she were in

JEREMY BLACHMAN and CAMERON STRACHER

another country, one where grime and rudeness were banned by treaty. When she stepped from the car it was like stepping onto the yellow brick road—if Dorothy were braless and the Tin Man sported muttonchops.

Rosie met her at the entrance. She smiled widely as Laura approached.

"Laura!" she cooed. "So good to see you."

They hugged and exchanged air kisses. Rosie was not wearing deodorant, Laura noticed. Her brown hair was also unruly and longer than in law school, cascading over her shoulders in a snarl of curls. She had the weather-beaten look that seemed to be a status symbol in the Bay Area—a sign of second homes, summer vacations, and leisure activities—and her bare arms were sinewy and muscular like a rower's. She also had something in her hair—not quite a flower—an herb, perhaps. Cilantro? Parsley? Organic, for sure.

"Come, come," Rosie gestured after they unclenched. The students followed but she shooed them away. Instead, they stood at a respectful distance and said polite goodbyes to Laura, then waved as she walked down the hallway. "Students," sniffed Rosie. "Who needs them?" She grinned, which could have meant she was joking, although Laura suspected she wasn't.

As Laura recalled, in law school Rosie had been a bit of a snob. She was two years older than most of their classmates (a congressional internship), and acted as if that made her the smartest girl in the room. She had edited Laura's law review Note, and was obsessive over the use of the "em" and "en" dashes. She took personal offense at improper italicization, and nothing made her angrier than incorrect use of the semicolon. Several times Laura's draft was returned with a red circle around the offending mark and the word "punctuation!" written beside it.

These things came back to Laura as they walked past the sparkling student cafeteria. It actually smelled good—unlike the one at MLS that reeked of backed-up sewage and dead cats. Here Laura could smell fresh bread, the tang of citrus, and hints of the field where the grass fed cows had lived good lives before being turned into cracked pepper bresaola for the evening meal. An espresso machine hissed noisily while a woman wearing a long cardigan and a beret expertly foamed milk. Two students waited patiently for their coffees, and they were neither underdressed nor visibly tattooed. No one was dressed like a hooker, stripper, or minor league baseball player.

Laura and Rosie whooshed upstairs in a clean silver elevator that didn't shudder or suddenly drop half a floor, and the doors opened without the need of the Fire Department or the jaws of life. Stepping out, Laura admired the modern artwork in the hallway—pastel landscapes in angular patterns that reminded her of Richard Diebenkorn—carefully hung without duct tape or thumb tacks. There were no holes in the wall where the Building Department had drilled to determine whether the structure should be condemned, and no bait stations in the corners for rats.

As they walked, Rosie explained their schedule. First stop was a casual coffee with a handful of younger colleagues. Informal, nonevaluative, get the blood flowing. Then a series of meetings with tenured faculty. Three to four at a time, polite, but more rigorous. They would want to know about her work, and would ask pointed questions, probing both her intellect and her politics. "Hint," said Rosie. "Karl Marx is too conservative for these people." Then it was on to her faculty presentation, where she would be expected to present a paper in progress to the room and entertain questions for forty-five minutes. Finally, a glass of wine back in Rosie's office, where they could debrief, decompress, and compare notes for the day.

"Easy enough?" asked Rosie.

"I think I'll go back and take a nap now."

"You're a superstar!" said Rosie. "Nothing to worry about. Anyone gives you trouble just remind them you got the Wootfried prize for Civil Procedure at Yale."

"That gets 'em every time."

Rosie looked at her seriously for a moment. "Your first book practically won the National Book Award. You have written more articles than anyone else I know our age. And you're gorgeous. Who can resist you?"

Laura smiled, but suddenly she felt like a fraud. What would the editors at the Yale University Press say if they knew about Pay for an A? Her academic reputation would disappear down the toilet as quickly as her recycled tissues earlier that morning. That was why she needed to give this job interview her best shot. She would put three thousand miles between herself and New York, and would worry later about her mother, her apartment, Monk, Adam.

Rosie left her in a cozy conference room with a bright-eyed group of dweebs. There were seven—four men and three women—and she quickly forgot everyone's name. In fact, two were so androgynous she forgot their gender. All of them munched happily on sugared beignets with rhubarb dipping sauce and chatted eagerly about eco-feminism and trans-race theory. Laura could do post-Modernism with the best of them, and had even read Foucault in the original French (after which she had a headache that lasted through the winter), so the hour passed quickly, albeit nonlinearly.

Then it was on to meet the more established faculty. They were an intimidating group that included one rejected Supreme Court nominee (too liberal), two retired federal appellate judges (too old), and a former Junior Deputy Assistant Attorney General (too many titles). All had their own views on Laura's appointment to the faculty, which were directly proportional to Laura's admiration of them. So they probed and prodded for compliments, which Laura dutifully delivered, leaving them flattered and impressed with her acumen.

At lunch she sat with the two genderless professors she had met that morning and learned that they were, in fact, transgendered. Having tired of gender studies, the legal academy had recently turned to transgender studies, spawning articles like "Penis 2.0: Civil Rights, Transgenderism, and the Law" and "Transgender Theory: What We Talk About When We Talk About Hermaphrodites." They were joined at the table by a coterie of associate deans and even a couple of nonacademic staff, one of whom was either wearing some kind of indigenous outfit with a headdress or was on her way to a costume party. No one gave the woman a second look; she was just another colorful light in a vibrant palette that wasn't white-washed and gray-haired. It would be a relief, Laura thought, not to be the poster girl for diversity.

For her presentation to the entire faculty, Laura had chosen carefully: a modest work in progress with impeccable support. No risks here. She crafted a solid thesis that built off established foundations rather than tearing them down. The point was not to blow anyone away with her cogitations, but to present herself as a solid and reliable colleague. Like so many faculty candidates, once she had the job she could go off the reservation. But she was still nervous. She hadn't done a job talk since she was first hired by MLS, and there she had won them over by breathing.

She needn't have worried. No one was really listening; they were just waiting to demonstrate their superior intelligence. As soon as Laura finished, the questions began—which weren't really questions but soliloquies with inflections tacked to the end. "The Fourteenth Amendment transmogrified a loose coalition of diverse political philosophies into a monolithic uniformity, don't you agree?" Or "The jurisdictional limits of the federal courts instantiate the Constitution's driving ethos toward restraint and limitation, haven't you found?" Laura just had to nod and say, "That's a good question," before the speaker went off on his own frolic and detour that left her glassy-eyed and dazed. By the time the presentation concluded, her feet had gone numb from standing at the podium and her face felt like it might crack from the smile frozen on her lips.

Rosie saved her. She pulled her away from the yammering throng who continued to pontificate, each on his own soap box, and pushed her unapologetically out of the room. "Otherwise, they'll never shut up," she explained.

Laura protested feebly that she was enjoying the monologues—everyone was so smart and articulate—but she did have a plane to catch and all that freshly roasted coffee had left her desperately in need of a restroom.

"No excuses needed," said Rosie, as she led Laura to her office. "You know how we love to talk."

Laura smiled, but a spasm of guilt cut through her. She told herself she wasn't betraying Manhattan Law School by leaving; she was saving herself. Yet she felt like a traitor, nonetheless. The ship was sinking, and she was leaving the rats to drown.

Rosie's office was a modern suite, with three desks and a small conference table in an outer reception area, and then an inner sanctum that glowed with a greenish light. Everything was stainless steel and redwood, burnished and polished to a dull sheen. It reminded Laura of a partner's office at a corporate law firm. The two secretaries who snapped to attention when they entered made her feel underdressed. One handed Rosie a stack of message slips while the other handed her a bound report. Rosie dismissed them and ushered Laura into her office.

"You realize this is all a formality," she said when they were seated.

"Your office?"

"Your visit. The presentation. If you want the job, it's yours. Say the word."

"You can do that?"

Rosie laughed. Deep and husky like a smoker. "Honey, I do what I want."

Laura didn't doubt it. Despite the unruly hair and peasant skirt, there was a regality to Rosie that she carried wherever she went, a liberal entitlement to fine Merlot, unpasteurized cheese, and gluten-free biscuits. The whole school stank of it. These people weren't going somewhere; they had already arrived, and the school merely stamped its approval on their foreheads.

"So, what do you say?" asked Rosie.

"It's a big move," said Laura.

"It's the right move. Now. For your career. You can't keep teaching at that toxic dump—no offense."

Laura shook her head. "Manhattan Law School is a dump," she agreed. "But it's my dump."

"Maybe it's time to find a new dump."

Maybe it was, thought Laura. A dump with a view.

Rosie smiled at her. Her Cheshire cat grin expanded and Laura felt herself being drawn inside. It was dark in there, and confusing. Laura reached out to steady herself but she was falling, falling, falling. Where would she land?

Staci Fortunato—Torts/Prof. Wright

(cont'd from prev. page)

and if the court follows the holding in *Westbrook v. American Telephone and Telegraph (1974)*, it has no choice but to rule for Plaintiff and hold the telephone company responsible for the broken equipment. It is like when the screen on my iPhone cracked and I could not read my texts and missed my friend Kayla's party. It definitely should be on the phone company to compensate me for that, even though the screen only cracked because I accidentally stepped on it with my new boots. Which are awesome, by the way. If you have a special lady someone in your life and you need a gift for her, definitely a good choice. I can hook you up with a 20% off coupon if you want, just text me.

5.   I think the answer to this question is yes. I wish I could tell you all of the cases that also support that position, but I don't really remember their names. I do remember there's the one with the dog, though. I pictured the dog as a little cockapoo, although I'm not sure if that's really what she was. I wish the casebooks came with pictures—does the teacher's edition?

Pictures make things so much easier to remember. There was also that one with the malfunctioning escalator. I know that one because when I went to buy the boots, the escalator at the mall was broken and I had to take the stairs. Can I sue someone for that?

Oh, and the case with the guy and the stuff. I think his name was John something. I pictured him looking like my ex-boyfriend Tony. I don't know why, I just figured he looked like a Tony. Do I get partial credit for knowing something about the cases even if I don't know their names? One of them was Silverman or something religious like that. He was the plaintiff, right? Or was he the defendant? Damn, there are so many cases.

6.   On my Contracts exam, we're allowed to skip one of the questions. We only have to answer 4 out of 5. So I think I'll skip this one, and you can just count my best one, twice. Ok?

16

solitaire

ADAM WAS STARING ABSENTLY AT his computer screen when he heard a knock on his office door. It was a quiet afternoon, and he was distracted. School had resumed from its short February break, but teaching was the furthest thing from his mind. For weeks he had been trying to forget Laura, hoping desperately that the Pay for an A scandal was something far less awful than it seemed. He had even started running, a sport he hated, nearly killing himself on the frozen Cobble Hill sidewalks. For the hour of diversion, however, it was worth the risk to life and limb. But the more he tried to put it out of his mind, the heavier it weighed upon him. No amount of effort could loosen the burden.

Maybe he'd misunderstood. Maybe it was limited to a few students and a handful of professors who were making some extra tutoring money on the side. Maybe Asher and the rest of the *Law Review* were creating something out of nothing. It wouldn't be the first time lawyers had overreacted. Theirs was a profession of exaggerators and dissemblers.

So maybe it was like that, Adam thought. And then came the knock. And his hopes evaporated like the milk in the faculty cafeteria.

"Hello?"

The door creaked open, and the unmistakable bald head of Professor David Wheeler poked through the opening.

"May I come in." It wasn't a question.

"Sure, David. Sit down."

The last time a professor had knocked on Adam's door, it was Professor Harding looking for the men's room. Adam was hoping Wheeler wouldn't repeat Harding's mistake and use the corner of his office as a toilet.

Wheeler swung open the door to reveal Rick Rodriguez and Jasper Jeffries standing right behind him. Adam knew right away this wasn't going to be fun.

"I'm not sure I have enough seats for all of you," he joked.

"Maybe you should yield your chair to tenured faculty," answered Jeffries, dead serious. Without thinking, Adam stood. Jeffries clomped behind the desk and collapsed in the seat, testing the chair's structural integrity. Adam tried to recall the last thing he had been working on, and hoped he remembered to save it. From the way his forearms rested on Adam's keyboard, it appeared Jeffries was intent on destroying it.

"We can see you're busy," said Wheeler, flicking some leftover lunch from his shirt onto the carpeted floor, "so we'll get right to the point."

"Please do," said Adam, bracing himself.

"We've heard that you've been deviating from the grading curve. Not your fault, really. You weren't properly informed of the way grading works here. We take full responsibility for the oversight, of course. We just want to clear the problem up, and make sure something like this doesn't happen again."

"I'm not sure I know what you're talking about, David," replied Adam, trying not to say more than necessary.

"Exactly. That's good. Very good. You see there's a special curve here at MLS that I don't think you were effectively briefed on. A lot of professors pick it up on their own, but sometimes we have to spell it out a little more clearly." He coughed and scratched a suspicious black mole on the side of his head. "We have . . . let's call it an arrangement. We're able to supplement our earnings, so to speak, in exchange for a willingness to be a little more flexible with our grading than we might otherwise be inclined. Nothing crazy. Just trying to do our students a service as they go out into the world. It's a shame when talented young lawyers don't get jobs. We make it a little bit easier for them. They make it a little bit easier for us. You understand what I'm saying?"

"I understand what I think you might be saying."

"Good. Very good. It's not something you really have to worry much about until you start teaching upper-class electives—that's why you didn't know about it—but there is one small problem that has arisen this year."

"And what's that?"

"Staci Fortunato."

"What about Ms. Fortunato?"

"My colleagues and I took a look at her midterm exam," interjected Jeffries, as he leaned forward on Adam's chair, making disturbing cracking sounds as he did. "We think you were too harsh. You didn't take the curve into consideration. We believe it was an A paper, nothing less."

"I believe you're mistaken," answered Adam.

"No," said Jeffries. "We are not."

"It's completely understandable given the circumstances," added Wheeler. "You're not used to the caliber of work here. Maybe you're holding them to a Harvard standard."

"Some changes in perception will have to be made," said Jeffries.

"For the institution."

Adam felt a rush of anger like a tropical storm descending. It swirled around him, violent purples and reds blackening his vision. He swam up through the darkness, taking several deep breaths before he spoke again.

"Can we cut the crap?" he asked.

The three professors stared him down. Or tried to. Like many academics, each suffered from a mild form of autism, so the staring consisted of their eyes focusing intently on Adam's ears and chin.

"I know all about what's going on here," Adam continued. "The grade-buying, the pay-offs, the violations of every rule in the faculty handbook. It's unethical and surely illegal. And it's not something I will have anything to do with."

Now it was Rodriguez who spoke, in his high-pitched faux Latino-inflected English that he saved for true histrionics. "You want to discuss ethics?" asked Rodriguez. "Let's discuss ethics. How ethical is a system that teaches students to do a job that doesn't exist?"

"I see," said Adam. "It's the system's fault."

"Yes," said Rodriguez. "It is. When students are not getting what the system promises, that is the system's fault."

"And the remedy is cheating?"

"Not cheating. Modifying. Redirecting. Repairing."

He let the words hang in the air for a moment as if they were snowflakes.

"We don't promise jobs," he continued, "We promise grades. And that's what we deliver."

"You're veritable saints."

"We like to think so."

"What about the others?"

"What others?"

"The ones who don't pay for good grades."

Rodriguez shrugged, but Wheeler answered for him. "They're no worse off than they would otherwise be. We don't lie to them."

"Not telling the truth is lying."

"Not telling the truth is an omission. There is no affirmative misrepresentation; no *mens rea*."

Adam shook his head. "I don't buy it. If the system doesn't work, you fix it. You don't corrupt it further. You're running a criminal organization here."

"And you're part of it."

"Never."

Rodriguez clucked disapprovingly. "Don't be naïve, Wright. Either you're with us, or you're nothing."

"Or, here's another option: I turn you in."

"You wouldn't," said Jeffries. "It would put your own career at risk. Can you imagine what your association with the law school would mean to your future? No other school would touch you, and good luck getting your law firm job back." He reclined in Adam's chair and wiped the sweat from his hands on the armrests. "No. We're all in this together," he said contentedly. "One happy family."

"Not me."

Jeffries pushed himself forward. "Don't be a troublemaker," he said. "The new ones often are, but they come around."

"And if I don't?"

"The Promotions and Tenure Committee doesn't look favorably on troublemakers."

"You see, we want to help you," said Wheeler. "But first you have to help yourself."

Adam wished he was taping their conversation. His phone, however, was on his desk, next to Jeffries' elbow, out of reach. It would be, instead, his word against the rest of the faculty. One crazy conspiracy theorist against the sober hordes. And even if he made himself heard, then what? What would be the point? Jeffries was right: speaking up would ruin his career. He would be damaged goods, tainted by scandal, and carrying the poisonous whiff of impropriety. Even that might have been acceptable at one time, his cross to bear, if not for Laura. They hadn't spoken since he walked out of her apartment, but she was always present. His brutal runs were testament to that, if nothing else, and still easier than missing her.

"Shall we take another look at Ms. Fortunato's exam?" asked Wheeler.

Adam sighed. "I'll take another look, but I'm not promising anything."

"Of course. We understand."

"And I'm not accepting money from anyone."

"That's your prerogative."

Maybe in the light of a new day, with another read, Staci Fortunato's unfortunate exam would look a little better. Maybe he had read it too quickly, didn't notice the subtleties, the incisive analysis buried between the ramblings, misstatements, and simplistic, third-grade analysis. But he knew that exams, like cheap wine, rarely improved with age. Instead, imperfections became more glaring, flaws less fixable, and the whole construct exposed as shaky and unsustainable.

"Now, if you don't mind," said Adam, motioning toward his computer. "I'd like to get back to my work."

"Suit yourself." Jeffries stood, and motioned to Rodriguez and Wheeler. "Come, gentlemen. Our business here is done."

"Remember," said Wheeler, as he followed Jeffries. "We're all on the same side."

"Are we?" asked Adam.

"Of course. You went to Harvard, didn't you?"

Then the three of them turned and left his office.

Adam sat back down at his desk and regarded his computer screen. Jeffries had destroyed his work, as he feared. The neat rows of reds and blacks were mangled, and the ordered numbers in disarray. Adam tried moving the cards back to their proper positions, but it was too late. The damage was done; his game of solitaire ruined. The Jack of Spades sat atop the King of Diamonds, his one-eyed smirk welcoming cheaters, liars, crooks, and con men.

Adam leaned back in his chair, and it creaked ominously, like a dying man's last wheeze. He straightened, and placed both hands back on his desk. But it took several minutes before the chair steadied, and the feeling of uneasiness stayed with him the rest of the day.

New York Bar Association

Law Schools in the 21st Century	
Track 1	Recruiting New Customers
Track 2	Outsourcing Legal Education
Track 3	New Uses for Buildings
Track 4	Maintaining Illusions of Prestige

DAY 1 AGENDA

8:00 AM—4:00 PM	Registration			
9:00 AM—10:30 AM	Opening Ceremonies Keynote Address: Henry Steele, Getting out While the Getting Is Good (Grand Ballroom)			
10:45 AM—12:00 PM	Telling Millennials What They Want to Hear (North Hall)	Finding Adjunct Faculty in the Third World (South Hall)	Renting Mock Courtrooms (East Hall)	Strategies for Gaming the Rankings (West Hall)
12:00 PM—1:30 PM	Lunch Break			
1:30 PM—3:00 PM	What Is Facebook? (North Hall)	A Cable Modem Education with a Dial-up Connection (South Hall)	Is Your Septic System up to the Task? (East Hall)	Employment Statistics Unmasked (West Hall)
3:15 PM—5:00 PM	Afternoon Workshops			

DAY 2 AGENDA

8:00 AM—4:00 PM	Registration			
8:00 AM—9:00 AM	Continental Breakfast			
9:00 AM—10:30 AM	Ceremonial Induction of New Dues-Paying Attorneys			
10:45 AM—12:00 PM	Finding Stock Photos That Work! (North Hall)	Do You Really Need Faculty? (South Hall)	The Shelf Life of Shelving (East Hall)	Seducing Reporters 101: Making Your Agenda Theirs (West Hall)
12:00 PM—1:30 PM	Lunch Break			
1:30 PM—3:00 PM	New Names for Student Loans (North Hall)	Seminars That Teach Themselves (South Hall)	Building Services You Don't Need (East Hall)	Does Money Buy Power? (West Hall)
3:15 PM—5:00 PM	Closing Ceremonies			

17

Grades, Gold, and Steele

EAN CLOPP RETURNED TO HIS office holding his usual post-lunch beverage, a glass of whiskey mixed with vanilla Ensure. He took several healthy sips before he spied the brown-skinned woman sitting in his favorite wing chair by the window. She was young and attractive, but that was no excuse for slacking off on the job, and he told her so. There was still dust visible on the mantel.

"I am not the cleaning woman," Laura said. "And I have an appointment. Your secretary told me to sit here."

"Wait a minute," said Clopp, a vague recollection coming back to him. "Shouldn't you be in class?"

"I don't have a class right now."

"When I went to law school, class was sixty hours a week, the reading took another sixty, and, if you were lucky, you had a few hours left for drinking."

"I'm not a student. I'm a professor."

"A law professor? Here?"

"That's correct."

"I highly doubt that."

"I've been teaching here for nearly a decade."

Clopp shook his head. Sometimes the pace of social change was dizzying. First, the right to vote. Now, this. Heaven knew what the liberals would concoct next.

"Well, then I don't want to keep you." Clopp looked at his watch. "Besides, I have another appointment." He motioned for Laura to go. She remained seated.

"I came to tell you I'm leaving."

"Please do."

"I got an offer from Berkeley."

"Surely you can find work closer to home."

"Dean Clopp, do you understand what I'm saying? I am a tenured member of your faculty, and I'm here to tell you I've accepted a job offer from Boalt Hall."

The dean took another sip of his whiskey Ensure and fixed Laura with his most inquisitorial glare, although with his burly belly and bushy white beard he didn't intimidate anyone except children who were frightened of Santa Claus.

"My dear, you've given yourself away. First, you said Berkeley, but now it's Boalt Hall."

"Boalt is the law school at Berkeley."

"So you say."

Laura grimaced. "I'll be leaving at the end of the semester, as soon as I turn in my grades. We both know what we're doing here can't go on indefinitely. Eventually the truth will come out, and when that happens, I don't want to be around."

"Then off with you." He shooed Laura out of the chair with his foot, spilling half of his drink in the process.

"Dean Clopp!" Laura stood. "You'll put an end to this business, if you know what's good for you."

"I have no idea what you're talking about. Business has never been better. Applications are down, but we keep dropping our standards so matriculations are up. Jeffries explained it to me."

"It won't end well."

"For you, perhaps," said Clopp as he nudged her to the door.

At the threshold, Laura made one last grab at the jamb. "Please," she said, "think about what I said. There are good people being hurt by a bad system. You can change things here." Her eyes held the dean's, and Clopp noticed the dark shadows below her lids. He made a mental note to speak to Health Services about the drugs they were dispensing to students. Then, he kicked her in the heels and closed the door behind her.

Satisfied that he was finally alone, Clopp went back to his desk and plunked himself in his swivel chair. He spun around to stare out the window at his unobstructed view of the canal while he finished his drink in peace.

Unlike everyone else at the school, Clopp happened to enjoy being situated on a toxic tort site. It gave him a sense of adventure, a bit of the Wild West. When he was teaching at Fordham several centuries ago, the worst thing that had ever happened was someone stole the bust of William Rehnquist he kept in his office. Here, his skin could flake off and blood might seep out of his pores from some waterborne plague that thrived in the sewage-infested canal. It was almost as exciting as a talking picture—in full Technicolor.

He swiveled back to his desk and lifted the thick dossier his assistant had prepared for his next appointment. It was the first real work Clopp had given her in six months, and she tackled it with enthusiasm. Henry Steele had made his fortune from the failures of the educational system, and his net worth was now at over five hundred million dollars. He had started with a small tutoring business that charged parents by the hour to help their underperforming children get B's. This grew into a larger tutoring service that helped the formerly-satisfied-with-B students get A's. It was an easy move from tutoring into test-taking services, for high school and college at first, and then subsidiaries focusing on medicine, law, business, and podiatry.

The passage of charter school laws gave Steele an opportunity to move into elementary education. Soon, Steele Educational Enterprises, Inc., was running eight public schools in New York State, and fifty others across the country. With the Internet came "distance learning," and the addition of two online colleges and a graduate program in finance. But Steele had a bigger plan: he wanted to transform higher education and run it like a for-profit corporation, answerable not to students and their parents but to shareholders and investment banks. He wanted, in short, to ruin it.

He quickly found that the college market was saturated, with little room for a new player. Medical schools required too much capital investment, while business schools required too little. Steele needed barriers to entry, students held captive by a regulated monopoly and lured by false promises of wealth and status. What he needed was a law school.

The dean ignored most of these details, focusing instead on the ones that really mattered, like net profits. When he was first introduced to Steele by Associate Dean Jeffries at a Bar Association seminar entitled "Getting Out While the Getting Is Good," Clopp was surprised to learn how profitable even a failing law school could be. Since then, he had come to see the inadequate services, shabby facilities maintenance, and rote course materials as pure financial wizardry on his part. He wasn't a neglectful and absent dean with a penchant for drinking himself into a stupor, but the leader of hidden economic gem about to be polished for the world to see.

After a brief nap, Clopp was awakened by his assistant just in time to welcome the educational visionary into the office. Henry Steele greeted him with a smile whitened to one shade shy of blinding and a handshake firmed up with the help of a personal hand trainer. He wore a crisp gray suit with a lavender tie, and his salt-and-pepper hair bristled like a porcupine. He inquired after Clopp's wife, the son who worked for the SEC, the married daughter with the two girls in Chappaqua, and the Filipino cleaning lady whom Clopp had deported when she asked for a raise. Clopp loved a good conversation about himself, and regaled Steele with tales of his darling granddaughters using names that were almost the ones that belonged to them.

"Sit, sit," said Clopp, after he had displayed one photo of a toothless grandchild playing the recorder, and another of a horse which Clopp confused for the child's nanny.

Clopp's office furniture was banged and dinged, and looked as if it hadn't been dusted since the Pleistocene era. His shelves were disarrayed and disorganized, with mountains of documents, piles of books, and the occasional empty liquor bottle that tumbled to the floor. In short, he didn't inspire confidence so much as the need for a good vacuuming.

Steele sat in the chair recently vacated by Professor Stapleton. He folded his manicured hands in front of him and waited. Time was on his side. Clopp and men like him were a dying breed. Guardians of a more genteel era, where no one sought to question the value of the services they provided. Now they needed to get out before they were trampled—or throttled.

"You've developed a number of impressive programs," said Clopp. "But tell me: Why law?"

Forty million dollars in yearly tuition revenue, Steele might have said, amortized and securitized into AAA bonds yielding a steady six percent. Instead he said, "A keen desire to shape and improve the future of our legal system."

"Excellent, excellent," said Clopp, who could smell money from twenty blocks away, although he could no longer keep the denominations straight.

"You have a fine institution here, and a valuable investment asset."

"We do fairly well for ourselves," agreed Clopp.

"But you could do better."

"A man can always do better." Clopp tried to wink, but his right eye got stuck, so he squinted at Steele like a pirate instead.

Steele explained that the law school was an attractive opportunity for investors looking for a steady and reliable stream of cash. But the spigot couldn't run forever. The school had leveraged its Superfund credits to pay for professors, chairs, and free popcorn at every other faculty meeting. Already, applications had dropped precipitously. Eventually, the banks would get wise. And then what? What would happen to the older faculty past the age of retirement, burning through their TIAA-CREF accounts? What would happen to Clopp, if pneumonia didn't strike him first?

That was where Steele came in.

Clopp no longer had a full deck, but he understood the need for an exit strategy. There were only so many papers Jasper Jeffries could sign for him, only so many speeches he could lip sync. It was only a matter of time before the law school's Board of Trustees removed him. He needed to make sure he didn't lose his long-term care plan at the Scottsdale Home for the Doddering, and he wanted his wife to have enough to last the rest of her days. So he listened to Steele's plan with growing interest. The law school couldn't survive its staggering debt load, constant tuition increases, and pathetic career opportunities without a bailout. The consultants had made that clear. At some point students—or their more sensible parents—would scream uncle. Clopp needed to go while the going was good. One step ahead of the angry and vindictive masses.

That cleaning woman had the right idea, Clopp concluded. Why change things when you could leave them behind? Start afresh in another country without an extradition treaty.

As for the students, who needed them? The ones who weren't criminals or certifiably psychotic were brain dead, oblivious, or overindulged. Their manners were tragedies, and their clothing wasn't much better. Clopp hated them. If only Steele could design a program that eliminated students altogether, that deposited their parents' checks directly and cut out the middle man. He had no love for his fellow faculty members, either. Although he had checked out long ago from the true administrative responsibilities of running a law school, and no longer taught any classes, he was still required to preside over faculty meetings and hobnob at social functions with his colleagues. They bored him to tears when he understood them, and put him to sleep otherwise. The law had not been an academic pursuit when he started teaching, and he never felt comfortable with the long German words and fancy French theorists.

All was not well in higher education, and at Manhattan Law School in particular. Clopp knew this, although he couldn't quite finger the reason. Perhaps it was the extra money that appeared in his bank account every few months, or the inability of *Law Review* editors to spell "Manhattan" correctly on their resumes, or the angry messages (dutifully transcribed by his assistant) from parents. In any event, ignorance was bliss—until it became a RICO violation.

Clopp took Steele's hand—at least what he thought was his hand but turned out to be his elbow—and shook hard. "Here's to doing better," he said.

"I'll drink to that," said Steele.

"It's five o'clock somewhere."

Clopp refilled his glass and poured another whiskey for Steele. Then the two men toasted each other and poured another. Several hours later, Steele slipped quietly out of Clopp's office, leaving the dean asleep on the floor, curled up like a baby with his thumb in his mouth.

WHO'S WHO

IN AMERICAN EDUCATION
SOUTHEAST NEW YORK ED.
1983

DAVID WHEELER
ROGER TANEY PROF. OF
CONSTITUTIONAL LAW,
MANHATTAN LAW SCHOOL

From his modern, wood-paneled office overlooking the rapidly up-and-coming Gowanus Canal area of Brooklyn, David Wheeler has it all. At six foot four, two hundred fifty pounds, he's an imposing figure, even without his toupee. Recently named co-chairman of the technology committee, Wheeler successfully led a three-year capital campaign for Manhattan Law School to purchase its very own computer. "I guarantee we'll still be using this machine thirty years from now," he said at a press conference, dressed in a distinguished brown flannel suit, his mustache feathering out from his face like the wings of a bird. With consulting gigs around the world -- the governments of East Germany, Czechoslovakia, Yugoslavia, Burma, and Zaire have all employed his services -- he is poised to be an influential constitution-shaper for decades to come.

18

Dropping the ꟻ Bomb

WHEN THE CALL CAME FROM *The New York Times,* Asher Herman was taking a nap. This was not an unusual occurrence for the *Law Review* Editor in Chief. Having spent much of the last few months interviewing unsuccessfully for law firm jobs, as well as trying to get back into Staci's pants, he was tired. With a few dozen resumes out there, and a handful of interviews still on the calendar, he wasn't finished, but he was losing hope.

"Hello?" he slurred into the phone.

"I'm sorry, is this Asher Herman?" said a vaguely British-sounding voice at the other end of the line.

"Are you from Allen & Avery?" said Asher, trying to remember the name of the best British law firm he could. He hoped that even if it wasn't them, whoever was on the line would be impressed that it could have been, and bump his application to a higher priority.

"Allen & Overy," said the caller.

"You are?" asked a shocked Asher, now shooting up from his couch and wiping ash from face, as if the caller could see him through the headset. The apartment was soot-stained and smelled of burned plastic since the fire, but the couch was mostly intact though charred and blackened.

"No. I was just correcting you. You said Allen & Avery. The firm is Allen & Overy. But, no, I'm not from there. I'm from *The New York Times*. D. Campbell Wiley. Friends call me Wills."

"Wills?"

"Yes. Nickname. Like it?"

"Okay. Wills."

"I'm writing an article about law schools and grading, and I'm wondering if you would have a few minutes to talk with me."

"Uh . . ."

"Specifically, it's about the grading at Manhattan Law School. The *Law Review*, the write-on competition, the fact that students are allegedly buying their grades, and, as Editor in Chief of the *Law Review*, you're the one managing the entire scheme."

Asher turned a ghostly shade of white and, operating entirely on instinct, hurled his phone out the open window of his fifth-floor walkup. After a beat, he realized that was probably not the smartest thing to do. He found it about ten minutes later in the gutter, screen cracked, battery already stolen by someone who clearly knew more than he did about how to jailbreak an iPhone. Asher swallowed hard, put the remnants of the phone in his pocket, and took off for campus.

He found Professor Rodriguez in his office, his shirt untucked and his door half open. Rodriguez regarded him with alarm, then his eyes quickly dropped back to his computer monitor.

"Professor—" Asher interrupted.

Rodriguez sighed. "If you're going to show up at my door unannounced, at least be someone else."

"Excuse me?"

"Never mind. I assume you're here because of the *Times*?"

"Yes. Did they call you?"

"D. Campbell Wiley. I've done some research."

Asher could see now that Rodriguez's computer monitor showed Wiley's Facebook page, and the image on the screen was a shirtless vacation picture of the pasty white reporter. Rodriguez saw him looking.

"It's important to know who we're dealing with. I've already called David, and we're meeting in ten minutes."

Rodriguez was talking about Professor Wheeler, whom he had reached on his cell phone in the middle of recording a lecture for his online course about *Star Wars* and long-arm jurisdiction. It was Wheeler's thesis that by transporting Luke Skywalker from Tatooine, Han Solo should have reasonably expected to be hauled into court on that planet.

Asher followed Rodriguez through the back hallways of the law school. The two professors had arranged to meet away from the prying ears of the school's IT department, which had inadvertently connected the school's phone system to the loudspeakers in the lobby—leading to a host of embarrassing public revelations whenever a professor accidentally hit the pound sign on his handset.

Instead, they met at the law school bookstore, although it took Wheeler twenty minutes to find it. While he waited, Rodriguez regaled Asher with the last time someone had inquired about the grading system: several years earlier a reality television crew had spent a week with a *Law Review* editor filming a program where six young nymphomaniacs shared a beach house with six Orthodox Jews. The show—called "That's Not Kosher!"—never made it past the pilot, but the crew had filmed the student skipping his final exams, which led to phone calls from network fact checkers, followed by letters from the law school's attorneys, followed by the excision of the offending segment (and the student). It was then that the professors came up with their emergency plan.

Wheeler finally arrived, carrying a light saber.

Rodriguez grabbed the toy from Wheeler's hand. "Where were you?"

"Sorry. I got lost. Was the bookstore always here?"

"Since the '60s, David."

"Who buys books anymore anyway?" Then he looked at Asher. "Who are you?"

Asher extended his hand. "Asher Herman. Editor in Chief of the *Law Review*."

Wheeler grabbed his light saber back from Rodriguez. "It's not what it seems," he said to Asher.

"It seems like a toy from *Star Wars*," Asher said.

"Well, it's not."

Asher didn't think much of Wheeler's *Star Wars*–themed teaching—none of the students did—and his distance learning program was known to be a serious gut. But now the entire future value of his considerable law school investment rested in the portly professor's hands. "What are we going to do?" he asked.

"Ed Con Five," said Wheeler.

Rodriguez nodded. "Let's inform Jasper."

Associate Dean Jeffries' office was on the law school's top floor. Although it was designated the "penthouse," it was better known as the "flophouse." The roof leaked regularly and the windows were prime targets for pigeon droppings. To save money, the ventilation system and the elevator stopped one floor below, and the only access was a set of metal stairs that had never passed inspection. Nevertheless, because the floor was situated furthest from the classrooms—and, therefore, students—it was prime real estate, and Jeffries occupied the corner office.

"I've never liked the *Times*," said Jeffries, when Rodriguez had finished talking. "Although that Maureen Dowd isn't bad looking."

"She speaks like a mouse on helium," said Wheeler.

"You don't have to speak with her," said Jeffries.

Asher couldn't believe professors would talk about a Pulitzer Prize-winning journalist the same way he and his buddies talked about women they met at a bar, but it was liberating to know that men were jerks no matter their age or education. It was simply a matter of hardwiring in the DNA. He couldn't wait to explain it to Staci.

"Never mind that," said Rodriguez. "We've trained for this eventuality, and it's time to put our training into action."

What the professors had planned would require work—lots of it—the old-fashioned kind. Late nights burning the candle in the library, stacks of books piled high before them (although they'd have to find some first). Greasy chicken, M&Ms, and burned deli coffee. But there was no alternative. They could hide, but they couldn't run—at least not forever. The professors knew this moment would come, sooner or later, and the fact that they had covered up their scheme for so long was a testament to the rigor of their fraud and the willing stupidity of those around them. Law school had always been a shell game, with the nut moving quicker than the eye. As long as everyone was a winner, no one complained. But lately the list of losers had grown too large to hide and the pot of money too big to ignore. It was time to face the music.

The job, however, was too much for a few brave hearts to handle. It wouldn't take long for a nosy journalist to discover that *Law Review* editors spent their time copying and scanning articles already in print, rather than researching and writing them, and that the profits flowed to the faculty. They had evaded detection so far because the *Law Review* was not available in the legal databases and its website was coded so that it was unsearchable. But now, because Wiley might actually read an article (the first outsider to do so since a librarian at Pace with chronic insomnia used it to help her fall asleep in the mid-1980s), they had to cover their tracks. And that meant work.

The three professors divided the *Law Review* editors into six teams, each led by two faculty members who outlined one Article, two Notes, and four Case Comments. Regular classes were suspended for two weeks on the pretext of an Asian flu pandemic, and the school was shuttered to everyone except those in the know. Extra security guards were hired who stood sentry outside the law school's main entrance like SS officers. Food, beds, and portable showers were trucked into the basement where trusted administrative staff set up a FEMA-funded shelter. The toilets backed up from overuse and discarded pizza crusts, while a foul stench rose through the hallways like purulent socks. The teams worked round the clock in eight-hour shifts to create an entire year's paper trail of *Law Review* articles that no one—except D. Campbell Wiley—would ever see.

It was all hands on deck, steel balls to the floor, do or die, now or never, backs against the wall. Everyone was expected to give one hundred and ten percent, take no prisoners, and leave no stone unturned. There was no time for regrets, no "I" in team, and no crying in baseball. In this crucible, friendships were forged and old enmities forgotten. Swords became ploughshares, and ploughshares blossomed into footnotes.

That was how it came to be that Staci Fortunato found herself working on Asher's team, writing a section of an article Professor Rodriguez had outlined, entitled "The Conundrum of the Penumbra: Repealing the Ninth Amendment." She was the only first-year on the team—indeed, in the whole building—but like the others she had a vested interest in protecting the system from exposure. She hadn't exactly volunteered—in fact, Asher threatened to give her name to the *Times* if she didn't help—but she found she had a knack for legal argument, especially as outlined by Professor Rodriguez. Ever since her quasi-epiphany in Asher's burning apartment, Staci had been doing her reading for class and trying her best to keep up. Sometimes the Latin words overwhelmed her, and other times the sheer nonsense of disputes over widgets and peppercorns bored her to tears, but her efforts began to pay off. Professor Rodriguez praised her efforts when she turned in her section ten hours early, spell-checked, properly formatted, and reasonably coherent. Then he set her loose to write her own Case Comment which, once completed, he arranged to be published immediately in the bound volume the school had contracted for at great expense with an overnight printing company in Tulsa, Oklahoma. The first (and only) original work of scholarship ever published by students at Manhattan Law School.

D. Campbell Wiley was duly impressed. In fact, he spent most of his visit trying to get Staci's phone number. He practically ignored the cartons of newly minted *Law Review* issues, the manuscripts ready for cite-checking, the source documents piled high on the shelves. He interviewed Asher and the other top editors with one eye on Staci's quite visible décolletage. He blew off his lunch with his former law school classmate, Adam Wright, to brown-bag it with the students (which conveniently included Staci). When it was time to leave, he thanked each student personally, and slipped his card into Staci's outstretched hand. *You're so hot you should be illegal*, he wrote. *Call me.* Staci, who knew a dork when she saw one, tossed the card in the shredder after he left the building.

That night, to celebrate deceiving *The New York Times*, Professors Jeffries, Wheeler, and Rodriguez took the students to a popular Tapas bar for food and drink. Staci arrived in thigh-high black boots, black bolero, and an electric green brassiere, which nearly gave Asher another heart attack. Emboldened by their accomplishment, he cornered her at the bar.

"Buy you a drink?" he asked, although Staci had one and drinks were free, courtesy of the *Law Review*'s slush fund.

"I don't think so."

"That was good work you did," he said.

"It was more fun than I thought."

"I may have been wrong about you."

Staci smiled, just a bit. The bar was crowded with law students and Gowanus hipsters who had gotten lost on their way to Williamsburg. Wedged into a seat next to her was a classmate who looked familiar, although she couldn't place him. He wore a moth-eaten sweater and nursed a beer through a straw. Not everyone had his life served up to him on a silver platter, she thought. There was sadness, and madness, and people who were just plain lazy. But not her. Not anymore.

She turned back to Asher and stomped on his big toe with the pointed heel of her boot. Asher cried out in pain, a noise that was lost in the electronic throbbing from the restaurant's sound system, and grabbed at his injured foot. As he bent over, Staci kneed him in the groin. The lights flickered, and Asher went down for the count.

The boy on the bar stool, who had seen the whole thing, rocketed out of his seat.

"Stay," said Staci, pushing him back down. "Buy me a drink."

"But drinks are free tonight," said the boy.

"What's your name?"

"Gary Deranger." He was trembling slightly.

"Gary, I hope you're not a big loser."

"I'm not."

"Good. Because it's your lucky day."

And it was.

MR. GOLDRECKT INVITES YOU AND
A SUITABLY-GENDERED GUEST TO
HIS ANNUAL

SWIMMING PARTY

for members of the firm in good
standing, who do not have urgent
deadlines with which this gathering
would interfere

FOOD WILL BE SERVED
ALLERGIES PROHIBITED
There will not be games.

NO CHILDREN AT ALL
Please wear business attire.

The Paleskin Club
Sunday, July 25, 6:45 AM

19

All Men Are Socrates

FOR TWO WEEKS ADAM HID in his office and his apartment, venturing outside only when absolutely necessary for food or air. He left the law school after dark, and avoided human beings on the street. He made no phone calls, and returned only the most urgent emails and messages. It wasn't that Jeffries intimidated him, but he didn't trust himself not to do something foolish. He had grown up amid foolishness, and saw what it did to people, and swore he wouldn't make that same mistake.

One of the emails he returned was to Laura, after she left a half-dozen messages on his phone, culminating with the one that informed him she had accepted a job offer at Berkeley. ("I wish I didn't have to do this on voicemail," her recorded voice said, "but it's not like you're giving me other options"). He replied, simply: "Got your vm. Happy for you."

Of course he wasn't happy—anything but. When he read the email he felt the heart-crushing sickness of the high school valedictorian who watches the girl he has pined for waltz off with the football captain. All his diligence and moral uprightness ignored in favor of big pecs and good hair. True, it was his decision, but what choice did he have? Hadn't she forced him to choose between the right thing and her? Walking out her apartment door felt more like being pushed off a cliff than jumping into a pool. His bones still ached at the thought of landing.

Thus, it was with a sense of doom that he came to the realization he couldn't keep teaching at Manhattan Law School. Not after what he knew. Quitting was for cowards, but it was also the only way to survive. Jeffries was right: if he exposed Pay for an A, it would taint everyone and take them all down, Laura included. So, despite his noble pronouncements, he would have to slink out quietly with his head low, mouth shut, and fingers holding his nose. He had no choice. He cared too much for Laura to hurt her.

With nowhere else to turn, tail between his legs, he called Howell Goldreckt.

"If you're calling about Ann Marie," said the lawyer after his secretary left Adam on hold for fifteen minutes, "I nailed her."

"I'm very happy for both of you," said Adam. "I'm sure you'll make a lovely couple."

"No thanks to you."

Despite promising to feed inside information about the law student to Goldreckt, Adam had conveniently forgotten. Apparently, Goldreckt had not.

"Let me apologize at lunch."

"I don't have time for squash this week. I'm training a service dog."

"A what?"

"For my PTSD."

"Since when do you have posttraumatic stress disorder?"

"Since I learned they board first on airplanes."

"Bring the dog," Adam said. "I'll buy the martinis—for both of you."

If there was one thing Goldreckt couldn't resist, Adam knew, it was free alcohol. They made a date, and Adam promised to reserve Goldreckt's favorite table.

After Adam hung up his hands were clammy and his feet itched. There were other law firms where he might land, he knew, but getting a job at one of them could take months. Meanwhile, every day at Manhattan Law School he slipped deeper into the moral morass. If he was going to do nothing about Pay for an A, he needed to do nothing quickly.

For his lunch with Goldreckt, Adam dressed in a suit. Goldreckt hadn't seen him in one since he left the firm, and Adam didn't want to take any chances. Cranberry, Boggs & Pickel adhered to a strict dress code; no one dressed "business casual"—not on Fridays, not during the dot-com boom, not on Halloween or at Goldreckt's annual pool party in the Hamptons, never. The only exceptions were the firm's Scottish partner who wore his kilt on Hogmanay and the one Orthodox Jewish partner who wore his *yarmulke* to meetings until a client accused him of making fun of the Pope.

Adam was early, and the maître d' escorted him to the table with a look of pity. It was a look with which Adam was familiar, seen on the faces of messengers, secretaries, and older associates. Been there, taken that, worse for the wear. No one who worked for Goldreckt for more than six months survived without the scars. Adam was a veteran, and proud of his wounds, even if they disfigured him. At least with Goldreckt you knew what you were getting, he reasoned, and there was no doubting the man's talent or energy.

To fortify himself against the latter, Adam ordered a Scotch. The drink was harsh and burned the back of his throat, but it warmed his insides and filled him with a relaxed glow. Thusly prepared, he gently eased into the soft cushion of his chair.

A commotion at the door distracted him. He looked up and saw Goldreckt trying to shove a small poodle back into his briefcase while the maître d' and several waiters flitted around him offering assistance. The dog didn't want to go, but after much snarling and snapping—and the dog wasn't too happy either—Goldreckt succeeded in shoving the pooch inside. He flipped the latches shut, leaving just a tuft of hair sticking out from the side.

"Goddamn mutt," said Goldreckt when the maître d' sat him at the table.

Adam had never seen Goldreckt with a domesticated animal—at least not a living one. The partner explained that the firm wouldn't let him leave the dog alone in his office. It had already chewed up three pairs of his secretary's shoes and defecated twice in a conference room. Not unlike Goldreckt himself.

As if to protest the comparison, the dog began barking, his howls muffled slightly by the leather. Goldreckt kicked the bag, and the dog yelped, but then stopped. All around them people were shaking their heads and muttering, and Adam expected the arrival of PETA imminently.

"Is he getting enough air in there?" Adam asked.

"He'll be fine. The leather breathes for him."

The waiter arrived to take his cocktail order, and Goldreckt ordered the "usual," which was a gin martini in a glass big enough for a milkshake. "Doctor's orders," he said, indicating the glass. He took a healthy swallow and then placed both arms on the table. "So, let's get down to business. I know you're not wearing a suit to take me dancing, at least not that one."

The last time Adam had lunch with Goldreckt it was interrupted when the partner's third wife served him with divorce papers during appetizers. The ensuing fist fight made Page Six of the *Post*. Adam reasoned it couldn't be worse. He plunged ahead.

"I'd like to come back to the firm."

Goldreckt laughed. "I knew you'd come crawling back eventually. The money doesn't smell so bad once you've left it behind."

"It's not the money. I don't expect partnership track."

"The Socratic Method not as much fun as you had hoped?"

"It isn't that either."

"'All men are fools; Socrates is a man; all men are Socrates,'" Goldreckt recited.

"Not exactly," said Adam.

"Annoying bastard. No wonder they killed him." He signaled for another martini. "Make it a double," he instructed.

The waiter balked, but took the order and walked away muttering about lawyers and liver disease. Goldreckt continued. "You should know the law isn't a bunch of philosophers drinking bark.

It's plumbers kicking each other in the balls when the ref isn't looking."

When Goldreckt got going like this it was best to let him roll. He thrived on offending people, and to take the bait was only to encourage him to be more offensive. "I'm not defending the Socratic Method," Adam said, "but there's a place for making students question their assumptions."

"That's what wrong with you professors. You only care about the questions. Clients don't want questions. They want someone to ram their adversary up the ass. At least Socrates got that part right."

Now it was Adam's turn to order a second drink, which he did as soon as the waiter brought Goldreckt's martini in what appeared to be a flower vase. Perhaps he would become an alcoholic, Adam thought. If he was going to work for Goldreckt again, it might be for the best. A steady dulling of the senses leading to brain cell pickling and an early death.

"Anyway, it's all academic," said Adam, smiling slightly at his pun. "I'm done with teaching. I want to come back to the firm."

"That's not going to happen," said Goldreckt.

"Excuse me?"

"No refunds, returns, or exchanges."

Adam smiled wanly. Surely, Goldreckt was joking. It was all part of giving him a hard time and making him grovel. He deserved it. But in the end the economics worked in Goldreckt's favor: a senior attorney who didn't draw a partner's salary was billable gold for any law firm. Or so Adam thought.

"You don't need to decide right now," he said. "Take it back to the partnership. Bring it up for a vote."

"I've already voted for everyone."

"I understand you were angry when I left, but I'm willing to admit I made a mistake. You know I can do the work, and you know it will be done right."

"I had a little chat with Associate Dean Jeffries after you called me. Just in case you had something like this in mind. It seems you've gotten your panties in a twist over the school's grading curve. Not a good idea to cause trouble your first year in a new job. Jeffries and I discussed it, and we decided the best thing for everyone was to let you get a little more experience before you made rash decisions."

"You know about Pay for an A?"

"Of course I do. You think I want to hire idiots?" His laugh was loud enough to leave a stunned silence throughout the restaurant in its wake. "Each recruiting season Jeffries gives me a list of the *Law Review* editors who didn't pay for their A's. Then I hire the prettiest ones."

Adam tried to process what he had just been told. It sounded like the school's proudest alumni was saying he knew the school sold grades like black market pharmaceuticals. But that couldn't be right. For all his flaws, Goldreckt was a meritocrat. He believed in giving the just what they deserved, and despised the elites who rigged the game. At least that's what he claimed. But here he was acting like any other insider, stealing from the poor to keep everything for the rich.

"If you know about Pay for an A, how can you let it continue?" Adam realized he was raising his voice when a waiter approached their table and asked if everything was okay. Goldreckt waved him away. When he left, Adam lowered his voice and hissed, "Don't you care the school is misrepresenting students' qualifications based on their grades?"

"I've never met a law student whose grades weren't a misrepresentation."

"That's not true. Grades aren't perfect, I know. But there are students on *Law Review* who can't even do basic legal research. How do you think employers feel about Manhattan Law School when they hire one of them?"

"Who cares?" Goldreckt belched.

"You should. Isn't that why you give so much money to the school?"

"I give money so I can get the good students." He cackled.

"But there won't be any good students left if this continues."

"There will always be at least one. Jeffries promised me."

It was a cynical and mercenary attitude, but Adam didn't doubt it was true. The law school could limp along for years, relying on financial aid or a poor sense of direction to lure a few top candidates to Gowanus. And, as long as Goldreckt kept the charade alive by hiring a lucky (and comely) few, the rest would follow like lemmings.

But there was one thing that didn't make sense to Adam. "If you don't care about the school's reputation," he asked, "then why do you care if I leave?"

"Can't trust you. You're a goddamn pussy. If word leaks out, then there really won't be any good students left. The damn accreditors will shut the school down."

Adam shook his head sadly. "I'm not going to cause trouble. I've already sold out. I just want to leave quietly and get my old job back."

"Sorry. I promised Jeffries."

"Promised him you wouldn't hire me?"

"Promised him no one would hire you."

"That's ridiculous. You can't stop me from finding another job somewhere else."

"But I can, Adam. And I will."

Goldreckt put the flower vase to his mouth and gulped. His gullet bobbed like a snake's, and a driblet of gin ran down his tie. "But we're still on for squash next week," he added, then drank the remainder.

Adam watched in horror, realizing that he was just a small mammal trapped in that snake's mouth, struggling to breathe as the life was slowly crushed out of him. His cries for mercy swallowed whole.

Pasta, 2002.
Good with sauce.
Remember—must cook first

20

Bologna Dreams

THE TWO-WEEK SHUTDOWN TO FAKE the *Law Review*'s archives had finally given Dean Clopp a chance to finish the scrapbook of his trip to Italy nearly a decade and a half earlier. Over time he'd stuffed all the photos, menus, and magazine clippings between the pages, and sorted everything into a rough chronological order, but it wasn't until he was able to carve out an uninterrupted stretch that he could make real progress on pasting his final selections into place. "Risotto or ricotta?" he asked himself, debating the merits of a meal they'd eaten in Bologna with Giuseppe Borgese, the Dean of the Faculty of Law, and his wife. He was just about to glue a photo of the couple into the book when the phone rang.

"Pick it up, Millicent. It's interrupting my work," he yelled, using the name of his long-deceased first wife. When the phone rang for a second and then a third time, Clopp threw the photo to the floor where it adhered permanently to the carpet and shuffled over to the receiver himself.

"This better be important," he barked.

"It's Henry Steele," said the voice on the other end of the line. "My lawyers have done their due diligence, and we're ready to make an offer."

"An offer for what? Who is this, and what are you trying to sell me? I'm on that do-not-call list, you know. I'm aware of my rights."

"It's Henry Steele," the voice said, this time slower, and louder. "We met a few weeks ago, in your office. I was the one looking to buy Manhattan Law School."

"Ah! Why didn't you say so? No need to be so secretive about it. We've been expecting to hear from you." Clopp put his hand on the mouthpiece, and shouted to the empty room, "Millicent, it's him!"

"Yes, well, I just wanted to touch base," Steele continued, "and let you know I'll be sending some papers over for your review. You can have your lawyers take a look at them."

"I am a lawyer, Mr. Steele."

"Yes, of course, but I meant the legal department. At the school. The people who read the contracts."

"Those are our students. Send the papers over by courier."

"I can have them emailed, if that would be easier."

"This is the twenty-first century, Mr. Steele. Mail will take days. Courier, please, at your expense."

After he hung up the phone, Clopp marveled at the archaic ways of communication among the younger generation. Instead of using a modern invention like the telephone, they wrote illiterate messages on tiny typewriters with their thumbs. Instead of scrapbooks, they took "Snapchats" that barely lasted for more than ten seconds. The students on *Law Review* didn't even know how to use the mimeograph machine that the law school had purchased in a bake sale from the church next door. He wondered what would become of them. Fortunately, however, that would no longer be his problem.

The courier arrived with the papers in forty-five minutes. Once Clopp found his glasses in the refrigerator and was able to read the numbers, they were staggering. He recalled that they had discussed how the deal would enable Clopp to retire, but Clopp figured that meant a hundred, maybe two hundred thousand dollars. Combined with his TIAA-CREF account, he thought it would be enough to buy a small apartment and live in Bologna a few months a year as long as he could wrangle a part-time teaching position and his wife kept her job at Nordstrom's. But if he was reading Steele's papers right—and there was a small chance he was—Clopp realized his share alone would be more than a million dollars. With that much money, he wouldn't have to teach, and his wife could find a job at any Italian department store she wanted.

Clopp immediately picked up the phone to call Jasper Jeffries. On the third try, he got the number right, and Jeffries picked up.

"What is it, Clopp?"

"How'd you know it was me?"

"For the millionth time, phones tell you who's calling now."

"Seems pointless. I could tell you just as easily myself."

"But I'd have to answer first."

"Why wouldn't you answer?"

"Because . . . . Never mind. Why did you call?"

"I've got some wonderful news. That man laid it on the table. And it's a big one."

"Excuse me?"

"You know, the man I told you about. The investor."

"Oh, thank God. I thought we had a really serious problem on our hands."

"Of course not. I told you everything would be fine. And now he's going to make us all rich. Well, most of us, anyway."

"Can you email me a copy of the offer?"

"I'm sure I can't."

"Can you at least read me the terms?" Jeffries asked.

After Clopp finished reading the one-page term sheet, the phone went silent. "Hello?" he asked. "Well, that was rude," he said to the phone. "He hung up on me."

Clopp had never liked Jeffries, but he tolerated him because he realized he could never manage the law school without him. In fact, there were days he couldn't find the faculty dining hall without Jeffries. But soon he would be rid of the man and his cronies—the homosexuals, libertarians, and federalists. In Italy, he would associate only with the pure of heart and simple of mind, and leave politics for the opera.

A light was blinking on his telephone, but when Clopp pressed the button, there was no one there. He made a mental note to get Millicent to have the phone replaced with something that functioned properly, without all the bleeps and squawks that distracted his callers when he tried to type a simple message using the keypad.

He returned to his scrapbook, and had just glued a piece of rigatoni from his favorite restaurant onto the page when he was interrupted by a banging at his door.

"Millicent!" he shouted. But the banging continued. The woman really had grown deaf and batty in her old age, he thought. In fact, the other day she insisted her name was not Millicent. He would have to talk to someone about her, if he could only remember whom.

He shuffled to the door and opened it to find Jeffries standing there, looking exasperated.

"Jasper! You hung up on me. That was very unprofessional."

"I didn't hang up on you. You hung up on me!"

"Now why would I do that?"

Jeffries rolled his eyes, but he took the purchase and sale agreement from Clopp's hands. As he read it, his eyes widened. When he was done, his bald head was sweating.

"We're rich!" he announced.

"Let's not park the car before the house."

"Horse. Cart before the horse."

"It's still subject to a faculty vote."

"It will pass unanimously."

"No hiding behind anonymity. We will vote in the open."

"Clopp . . . ." Jeffries shook his head.

"Yes?"

"Never mind." Jeffries went to Clopp's desk and opened the bottom drawer. He pulled out two glasses and a bottle of whiskey. "This calls for a celebration."

"That's where Millicent put the Scotch!"

Jeffries poured two glasses. "Here's to wealth and happiness," he said, raising his glass. "Ours."

Clopp was already imagining the faculty meeting where he would present Steele's proposal. He could picture it all in his head. Applause—a standing ovation, perhaps—and a whole spread of food. Yes, for this meeting they would have real food. Clopp decided they should go all out: sandwiches. Maybe even some of those wraps the kids were all talking about. Sure, there might be some questions about ethics, and the future of the school, but they'd crossed that line long ago. Who could argue with selling out to an educational robber baron when they'd already been selling out their students for years?

"I can't believe all Steele wants us to do is sell the school," said Jeffries, still flipping through the agreement. "I would have thought for this much money, I'd have to blow someone."

"Blow someone what?" asked Clopp.

"Blow someone's horn," Jeffries improvised.

"Toot, toot," said Clopp, which surprised both men, though for different reasons.

The only thing that made either man pause was a set of terms and conditions at the back—contingencies that needed to be met before the deal would go through. The faculty vote and approval of the Board of Trustees—but those would be mere formalities. An audit of the books, but Steele already knew the salient details. And a handful of other terms Clopp expected would cause no significant problems—an inspection of the building by an outside engineering firm (paid off to avoid water and soil sampling), a review of all employees' immigration status (which would cost them some legal writing instructors—but none who couldn't be replaced), and a morals clause that would void the deal if something occurred that would bring the school into "disrepute" before the end of the academic year—unlikely, given its reputation.

Clopp scheduled the faculty vote for Wednesday, the third day back from the Asian flu scare. The professors were not told in advance why they were required to gather in the Summer Associate on *Ally McBeal* moot court/gymnasium at noon sharp, but the Evite invitation insisted it was mandatory—for all but Professors Chang, Chen, Huang, and Lee who would be joining via video-conference, a final precaution against potential infection (Prof. Lee wasn't even Asian—he was eighth-generation American, from Charleston, South Carolina—a direct descendant of the famous Civil War general, but the school was taking no chances). Those who hadn't RSVP'd by Tuesday received a follow-up email threatening to block their access to Pinterest unless they confirmed attendance at the meeting. It was an empty threat—no one on the faculty used the website—but it sounded frightening, and few were technologically sophisticated enough to risk it.

The court room/gymnasium was one of the few well-maintained gathering places in the building, which is why Clopp chose it for his announcement. The Summer Associate was a law school alum, and although her acting career went nowhere, she inherited a multimillion dollar fortune from her father, who had invented plastic, and donated a portion of it to fund a performance/workout space at Manhattan Law School. One side of the room contained three sets of free weights, four Nautilus machines, and a half-dozen treadmills, while on the other side the chairs were arranged in a wide semicircle beneath paintings that depicted two landmark Supreme Court cases, *Dred Scott*, and *Bowers v. Hardwick*, both of which had since been overruled, to the dismay of some of the law school's more conservative alumni.

"Thank you for coming," boomed Dean Clopp, when everyone was seated. "You may wonder why we've gathered you here. We have some exciting news."

"We're finally shutting our doors?" yelled an elderly Professor Emeritus from the back.

"Actually, in a manner of speaking, we are." A few audible gasps were heard. "No reason to get alarmed. It's good news. We're entertaining a sale of the law school to a company called Steele Educational Enterprises."

"A nonprofit known for its charter school initiatives," added Jeffries, leaning in toward the microphone from his place at Clopp's side.

Rick Rodriguez stood up from his seat in the front row, pulled an index card from his pocket, and turned to his colleagues. "They did quite a profitable turnaround on a number of elementary schools in Connecticut, did they not." It was supposed to be a question—he was supposed to have rehearsed it—but it came out sounding like a statement.

David Wheeler followed, and pulled his card from his pocket as well. "And I hear the teachers made out like band-aids."

Jeffries cleared his throat. "You mean bandits."

Wheeler squinted, looked closer at his card. "Yes, I guess I do."

"Excellent points, gentlemen," said Clopp. "Steele has come in with a very generous offer. Tenured faculty will retain their positions, subject to certain revisions in their employment status, and receive bonuses of as much as one hundred thousand per year of service, up to a maximum of two million dollars."

A louder gasp this time, followed by a wave of chatter and then a crescendo of greed. Clopp's promises were vague, but that didn't prevent faculty members—who weren't very good at math anyway—from trying to run some quick calculations on their phones.

"I'll also be retiring," added Clopp. "Lucinda and I have long wanted to travel and spend more time in our beloved Bologna." Lucinda was the correct name of Clopp's secretary, and this caused some more gasps. Mostly, though, there was admiration—at least from the male faculty members—who elbowed each other enviously at their dean's good fortune. "You dog!" shouted a Tax professor.

"Thank you," said Clopp. "I'm sure a suitable replacement will be hired, and it should come as no surprise that I've recommended Jasper for the position."

"Let's all give Dean Clopp a round of applause for his years of service," said Jeffries, lifting his glass of triple-filtered water. There was no response from the crowd.

"It's been an honor and a privilege," Clopp said, over the silence. "And now, unless there are questions, it's time for tenured faculty to vote on the sale."

Adam Wright raised his hand from the back. As a nontenured member of the faculty, he would have little to gain from the deal, and in fact wouldn't even have a vote. Clopp reluctantly gestured at him, and he stood.

"Will Steele be making any substantive changes to the school's policies, such as our grading curve?" he asked.

"Sit down, jackass!" shouted Rick Rodriguez from across the room.

A few others added their own hoots and hisses, but Clopp raised his hand to silence them. "I'm sure there will be policy changes, but it would be premature to speculate."

"Will the faculty be involved in those changes?"

Clopp looked to Jeffries for help, who looked to David Wheeler. Wheeler raised his hand. "I move to close debate."

"Seconded," said Rodriguez.

"Objection," said a female voice from the left center of the room.

Heads swiveled as Laura Stapleton rose to her feet. She was dressed all in black, except for a red sash that held back her hair, and it made her a look like a samurai or a ninja. Her voice, however, was soft and sad.

"I think we all know the truth about our grading curve," she said. "Cutting off debate won't make the problem disappear."

"There's a motion on the floor," said Rodriguez.

"I'm embarrassed we've allowed it for so long," Laura continued. "No, embarrassed is the wrong word. Shamed. Humiliated. Horrified."

"Please, spare us the ethics lecture."

"But it's not too late to change things. Maybe we're being given a chance here to start again. Maybe this deal will give us the chance to put our house in order. But how will we know if we don't ask the hard questions? The ones we should have started asking years ago?"

"Point of order," Wheeler said loudly.

"Yes?" asked Clopp.

"As I recall Professor Stapleton has accepted a job offer from the University of California at Berkeley. Therefore, under Faculty Rule two point three dash 'a' small 'i,' she has divested herself of eligibility to vote or participate in debate."

"That's true," said Clopp.

"Her remarks, therefore, are a nullity, and should be stricken from the record."

"So struck."

"My motion is pending."

"All in favor?"

A rousing chorus of ayes shut down further discussion, and Clopp brought the deal to a vote. It passed, with only a handful of objections, and then the partying began, turning the courtroom/gymnasium into a spectacle worthy of an HBO series. Over sandwich wraps and boxes of wine, the faculty partied well into the afternoon, and by the time the celebration was over, Dean Clopp was asleep in a Front Lat Pulldown machine with a half-eaten turkey wrap in one hand, David Wheeler's underpants in the other, and his head filled with dreams of Italy. He had thought he was going to die in his office at Manhattan Law School, but Henry Steele had given him a way out. Now he could die like everybody else, in a nursing home, alone. He couldn't wait.

A PUBLICATION OF THE OFFICE OF COMMUNICABLE MESSAGING AT THE MANHATTAN LAW SCHOOL

A PUBLICATION FOR GRADUATES OF MANHATTAN LAW SCHOOL AND THEIR HEIRS.

Alumni *Deaths*
and other news

Guess what????

One of our students got a summer job!

Ann Marie Kowalski, a member of the *Law Review*, set a new precedent this semester at Manhattan Law School by getting hired by an actual law firm for a paid summer position.

The firm of Cranberry, Boggs & Pickel LLP of the actual island of Manhattan has plucked Ms. Kowalski from our student body and blessed her with the opportunity to perform legal work this summer, at a market rate of compensation.

We at *ALUMNI DEATHS AND OTHER NEWS* congratulate Ms. Kowalski on her unique achievement and hope she inspires other MLS students to follow her lead and actually go to class.

Ms. Kowalski was unavailable to sit for a photograph.

We apologize to our readers.

TREE WATCH
Yes, that is a tree growing from a crack in the sidewalk approaching the law school's main entrance. We'll see if it can break the record set by the moss from 2008 and survive more than one semester.

21

Does Never Work for You?

ANN MARIE LISTENED INTENTLY, ARMS folded across her breasts in a defensive posture, while Henry Steele held court at a makeshift lectern in the *Law Review* offices. Even in normal circumstances the office was cramped and poorly ventilated. Now, with the entire *Law Review* present, the room resembled a broken-down subway car during summer rush hour—sweaty bodies crammed together and one guy in the corner with his possessions in a trash bag.

Steele, however, appeared cool, calm, and collected. His porcupine hair was brushed back neatly from his forehead, and his cheeks shined with the vigor of the newly shaven and recently exercised. His teeth were white and even, and clicked precisely when he spoke. He wore a dark blue suit which was creased so sharply it could cut paper, along with his trademark lavender tie. The only imperfect thing about him were his eyes: they darted from point to point like a hummingbird, or a man looking to make a quick escape.

Steele's skittishness was understandable. He had come to tell the editors about his purchase of the law school and to recruit them as poster children in his plans for scholastic domination.

He didn't care about their education, but he needed them, and worried that his desire was unrequited. After all, most of them had paid double the normal cost of law school tuition and now were facing a lifetime of unemployment and penury. They could rightly blame the lightly regulated educational market, in which Steele thrived. He was like a politician preaching the values of fiscal conservatism to an audience of auto workers while cutting import taxes on Maseratis.

But he needn't have worried. They loved him. His attention lavished upon them the illusion that their lives had meaning and their careers promise. If such a well-coiffed and dentally hygienic businessman sought to curry their favor, then they must have something worth currying. They beamed in his reflected glow, and gazed at him like lambs before the slaughter.

Ann Marie, however, felt herself growing cold, then hot, and then finally steaming. She couldn't believe what she was hearing, and yet everything suddenly made a sick kind of sense. The furtive glances, the closed doors, the whispered voices. It was like awakening from a dream to discover the world in which she lived was just a computer simulation.

Asher Herman stood, and thanked Mr. Steele for taking the time to talk to the *Law Review*. "What you're doing here is very important," he said. "I know I speak for all of us when I say we're proud to be part of your vision."

"Thank you, Asher. I believe in meritocracy. It's what's made this country great. If you've paid for something, you deserve to get your money's worth."

"Agreed, sir. There are too many people with their hands out."

"Precisely. Given the expense of higher education today, we owe it to this generation of students—and parents, I might add—to eliminate the guesswork from the evaluative process. If we can quantify the inputs, we should be able to quantify the outputs. It's simple math. A plus A equals twenty thousand dollars." He chuckled, then continued. "What's made the system here work so well is that students know the exact dollar value of their education. I want to implement that system across the country, beginning with law schools but moving eventually into graduate education everywhere. With your help, Manhattan Law School will lead the way, shining its light down a rocky yet fruitful path."

There was much applause, followed by whistling and stomping, and even a few yodels.

Finally, Ann Marie raised one trembling hand. Steele's eyes lit like a shaman's as he called on her.

"Are you saying we've been living a lie?" she asked.

The room quieted. "Define lie," Steele responded.

"A fraud; a sham; a mockery. A false representation of reality."

"Most of you have, yes."

"But that's . . . that's awful. Monstrous."

Steele shrugged. "It's what you paid for."

Asher interrupted. "Ann Marie is one of our grade-ons," he explained.

Steele looked at her with a mixture of sadness and pity. "You seem like a sensitive young woman," he said. "Look at it this way: You've been lucky enough to win the lottery. But what about your peers who haven't been as fortunate?"

"I haven't won a lottery," she said. "I worked for my grades."

"You mean you scribbled some sentences into a blue book which a professor tossed down the stairs and then picked up and scrawled a letter onto it?"

"No. I mean I studied my ass off while these jerks were out drinking."

Hoots and jeers, followed by catcalls and farting noises.

Steele raised one hand to quiet the angry throng. "Now, now. That's not fair. Drinking games are part of the educational experience. Perhaps you should have gotten out more."

"Why? So I could waste my parents' money getting wasted? At least I have a job."

"Ann Marie accepted an offer from Cranberry, Boggs & Pickel," Asher explained.

"Congratulations." Steele's smile was all incisors, pointed and deadly like a shark's. "That's Howell Goldreckt's firm."

Ann Marie nodded weakly. "Yes."

"Howell, of course, is one of the program's biggest contributors, if you know what I mean."

"I'm not sure I do." What was Steele saying? Suddenly, Ann Marie felt queasy. When she was hired by Goldreckt, she became a minor celebrity at the law school—walking proof that all was not lost. For days she moved as if on air, gliding effortlessly through her classes like the patron saint of legal reasoning. Even an accidental Gary sighting did nothing to dampen her mood. She assumed Goldreckt hired her because she was smart and industrious, a *Law Review* editor, and top-ranked in her class. But now the doubts crept in.

"I could never have made this acquisition without his blessing," explained Steele. "His commitment to *augmenting* the resumes of students who have paid for the privilege is crucial to the success of the program as we move forward."

"He knows?"

"Yes, he knows."

Ann Marie's stomach knotted and for a moment she feared she might have to dash to the bathroom. She clenched her legs until the feeling passed, but it left her hollowed-out and wretched. Men had always misjudged her—mistaking her good looks and eagerness to please for stupidity. She spent her college years fighting off advances from professors and frat boys who took a polite smile as an invitation. Gary was the first man who valued her brains, not her body. It explained a lot about why she stuck with him even after her friends (and his social worker) told her to flee. Now, after finally succeeding on her own terms—or so she thought—it turned out her job offer was just another excuse for some cretin to get into her pants.

She stood. She was furious. Her hands shook and her lips had gone white. But when she spoke her voice was clear and strong.

"You should be ashamed of yourself. Peddling your lies. This isn't Wall Street. It's a school; a place of learning. You can't change the truth by buying it."

More boos, louder this time, along with shouts to "shut up!" and "sit down!" and "take off your shirt!"

Ann Marie turned and faced her peers. "You should all be ashamed. You think you're getting something for your money, but you're not. You're getting screwed. How much did you pay for your A's? Ten thousand? A hundred thousand? For what? How many of you have jobs? How many of you will be living with your parents next year? This man is talking like you should be grateful for his plans, but when you're gone he'll be laughing behind your backs. The joke's on you—on all of us!"

There were a few grumbles, and several students even nodded their heads. But someone else tossed a half-eaten wad of sandwich that narrowly missed her, and a group of boys in the back started chanting "blow job."

"You're being unfair to Mr. Steele," said Asher. "He's investing a lot of money in the law school."

"Henry, please," said Steele.

"Henry," said Asher, smiling shyly at the older man, who towered over him like a sequoia.

"Why don't the two of you get a room?" said Ann Marie.

This time the other half of the sandwich hit her in the side of the head. It was chicken salad on soggy white bread and it wasn't thrown very hard, but it felt like getting hit by a rock. Her cheek stung and her eyes filled with water, but she refused to cry. Instead, she shook one fist at her fellow editors and stormed out of the room.

Safely in the hallway, however, she burst into tears. Even at her lowest point with Gary—Methodist Hospital at 4 AM—she had never felt so humiliated. At least then she was needed and respected, her value measured by more than her waist size.

Now what was her value? Another dumb blonde for Howell Goldreckt to grope and fondle? He didn't respect her. He didn't care if she was intelligent, or even if she could speak English. She had come this far, only to have a man treat her as a doormat—again.

But she wouldn't stand for it. Not anymore.

She climbed out of the basement and emerged through a fire exit on a side street. She ignored the alarms and hailed a black livery cab that was idling at a stop light. The driver wore mirrored glasses and a plastic gun dangled from his rear view mirror (at least she hoped it was plastic), but she bargained the fare down to twenty dollars. The ride to Manhattan was potholed and broken, and the cab's shock absorbers not much better. Each bump made her teeth ache. On a hard curve the passenger-side door popped open, and the driver leaned dangerously across the seat to close it. He kept up a steady patois with a colleague on his cell phone, and nearly sideswiped a half-dozen cars on the FDR Drive. By the time they were crossing west on 53rd Street, Ann Marie's organs were jumbled and her brain hurt.

Finally, the driver pulled to a stop at the corner of 54th and Sixth, although the cab continued bouncing like a toddler on a ball. The driver swung around in his seat and demanded forty dollars.

"We said twenty," she said.

He grinned at her. "Okay, I say for you, pretty lady, thirty."

She stared at him for a moment, then slowly, without moving her eyes, she withdrew a twenty from her wallet.

"It's illegal for a black car to pick up a street fare anywhere in the five boroughs," she said. "Section nineteen dash five-zero-six, NYC Administrative Code." She handed the driver the twenty. "Have a nice day."

He stared at her wide-eyed as she skipped out of the cab and made her way into the glass and steel skyscraper.

Through the revolving doors, into the chill of the atrium, across the marble lobby. The guards at the security desk ignored her while they texted their girlfriends and watched highlights from last year's Puppy Bowl. Ann Marie strode past them purposefully and didn't look back.

Up, up, up, she flew in the elevator. The metal box was a silent transporter between two worlds. In one, she was an impoverished law student; in another, she would become a well-paid attorney. The decision was hers. She had worked hard for the choice, and believed she deserved it. But the just in justice had gone sour, leaving the desserts with a funny smell.

The doors opened. Harried looking women in heels wobbled past and glanced at her sympathetically, while men in shirts starched stiffly as corpses leered. Across the floor the receptionist perched like an exotic bird.

"May I help you?" she asked in a frosty tone that suggested she had no interest in doing so.

"I'm here to see Howell Goldreckt."

"Mr. Goldreckt is in a meeting," said the receptionist without missing a beat.

"How do you know?"

"Sweetheart. That's my job."

Ann Marie frowned. "Do you know when he'll be available?"

"No, I'm sorry; I can't help you."

"Can't or won't?" The question slipped out before she could stop it.

"Is there a difference?"

Ann Marie was about to respond when she heard a familiar voice booming down the hallway.

"A five iron in a sand trap! I told you the woman's an idiot."

A round of guffaws, and then four men came into view around the corner.

"Well, here's a surprise," said Goldreckt, stopping in his tracks. "Hello. Isn't your start date next month?"

Behind Goldreckt's back the men winked at each other knowingly.

"I need to talk with you," said Ann Marie, ignoring the free-floating testosterone and extra chromosomes.

"What about?"

"About that start date."

Goldreckt looked at his watch. "Give me twenty minutes."

"Now." She held Goldreckt's eyes until he blinked first. Then he turned to his partners and told them he would catch up. He led Ann Marie down the hallway to his office. Although it had commanding views North and East, the office looked and smelled like a locker room. In addition to the sofa which Goldreckt used as a bed, his squash sneakers were on a shelf next to a fistful of socks. The sneakers were cracked and hardened like rosin, and there was dried blood on one toe.

"Is there a problem?" the partner asked once he had safely closed his door and she was seated.

"Is it true?" she asked.

"True? Is what true?"

"That you're behind Pay for an A?"

"Ah," said Goldreckt, fingering his chin.

Ann Marie stood up. "I should have known."

"Wait! I've got nothing to do with it. I know about it, sure. But everyone knows about it."

She turned and took a step toward the door.

"Don't go!" For a large man, Goldreckt moved quickly. He was down on one knee in front of Ann Marie before she could stop him.

"I need you," he said.

"Yech! Gross." She could barely contain the bile. "Get up."

"I'm serious. I think about you all the time. I can't think of anything else."

"You're making me nauseous."

"Those are butterflies."

"No, it's vomit."

"I count the days waiting for you to work for me."

"I would never work for someone who hired me when he thought I bought my grades."

Goldreckt gazed up at her. His face, in the weak afternoon sunlight, seemed like a small child's. There was even a misshapen halo around his head, as if he were an angel who had collided with a wall.

"I don't think you bought your grades," he said.

"You said you did."

"No, I didn't. I said I knew how the *Law Review* worked. But I never thought you were part of it."

"You're so full of it."

"I'm telling the truth! Why would I hire someone who bought her grades?"

Ann Marie glanced down at her breasts, then flicked her eyes back to Goldreckt. "I'm not an idiot," she said. "I know what I look like to you."

"You're beautiful." Goldreckt's voice caught in his throat. "But I'm a businessman. I let my competitors hire the idiots."

Ann Marie placed one foot on Goldreckt's forehead, the point of her heel inches from his right eye. She felt powerful, as if she could kick a hole right through his skull. Perhaps she would.

"If there's one thing I've learned from law school," she said, "it's that a fact without support is just someone else's lie." Then she pushed hard against Goldreckt's forehead, and he toppled over.

She left him there—on the floor—and walked briskly to the elevator, a spring in her step, a song on her lips. The tune she was whistling sounded like freedom.

CASE DISCUSSION
Western Pennsylvania Regional School of Medicine
Clinical Skills Center

B.W., a 69-year-old woman, arrives at the emergency room via ambulance after a motor vehicle accident.

Patient presents with minor cuts and bruises under her eyes, and sulfur burns on her wrists, consistent with a motor vehicle accident in which the airbag deployed. She appears cognitively intact, and claims to have "never had anything like this happen before." A review of her chart reveals three similar trips to the ER within the past two years, all precautionary visits after car accidents, discharged without admission each time.

When asked about the previous incidents, she denies their existence, and adds, "my son is a lawyer, and he will be arriving soon to help me escape from here."

No psychiatric history noted in the record.

Patient was aware she was in a hospital and properly oriented to date and time.

Patient requested an organic meal for lunch.

Patient requested an extra pillow for her emergency room stretcher.

Patient requested more "intelligent" reading materials.

Patient requested the air-conditioning be turned down.

Patient requested a different nurse.

Patient requested a different nurse.

Patient requested a different nurse.

Patient discharged after no notable findings on examination and released to son.

Good luck to him.

22

saving Mrs. Palsgraf

THE PLACE WHERE ADAM GREW up couldn't be reached by subway, bus, or Pony Express. Nor by airplane, Amtrak, or Greyhound. The town had its own post office and small bank, but no town hall, municipal courthouse, or even a public library. When Adam graduated there were forty-eight students in his class, a third of whom hadn't shown up to school in months, and another third who were either pregnant or responsible for it. On a typical Saturday night there were bar fights and drag races, and on Sunday mornings Adam and his brother would find beer bottles, skid marks, underwear, and broken teeth on the streets near their house. Once they found a finger, neatly severed with the nail polish unchipped. Adam wanted to bag it and bring it to the police station (which, conveniently, shared space with the town liquor store), but his brother convinced him to leave it where it lay so the owner could come retrieve it (and, indeed, a few hours later, she did).

When Adam went to college, he swore he wouldn't return, and though he was forced over the years to make the occasional exception, since his father's funeral he hadn't been back.

Until the morning his cell phone buzzed as he waited for Laura in the hallway outside the faculty meeting. He had bolted as soon as the vote was taken, and assumed she would, too. While he waited, he prepared a little forgiveness speech: Yes, she had taken the cowardly way out by accepting the job at Berkeley, but at least she stood up for her principles in the end. Yes, she could buy him a drink. Yes, if she insisted, he would go home with her and they could have make-up sex. But she ended up trapped in the doorway by David Wheeler, who held a sandwich wrap in each hand like a billy club. Adam hesitated, then her eyes caught his, and he pushed his way against the crowd just as his phone began buzzing. He glanced down and saw Sam's number flashing.

"Sam," he said.

"It's Mom."

"Is she okay?"

"She's alive."

Adam moved to an alcove and cupped his hand over the earpiece to block out the noise of the faculty party. His brother explained there had been an accident, and their mother was unbowed but not unbroken. Then there was a polite but intense argument about which brother was too busy to rent a car and drive two hundred miles, which Sam won by playing the doctor card. Although Adam's students were suffering, none were on life support. More important, none would sue him if they died.

There was an Avis near his apartment, and it only took about three hours and an FBI background check to rent a car. He meant to call Laura during the ordeal, but it required all his patience and concentration to avoid a fistfight with the clerk and then with the other customers when a solitary car rolled into the lot. Finally, safely on the road, he was too agitated and distracted to speak with anyone, and drove in silence—without even the radio—at eighty miles an hour.

He found his mother at the regional hospital where she was propped up in bed, giving the nurses a hard time. Gauze wrapped her hands where they had been burned by the airbags, and bruises darkened the skin below both her eyes. Although he called her faithfully every Sunday, he had not seen her for two years—since her last "theater weekend" in New York City with two of her neighbors. The bruises shocked him, but worse was the way her hair had grayed and thinned.

"Adam!" she cried. "Could you please tell these people that I am fine? Give me some band-aids and pain killers, and let me go home, for Chrissakes."

"As soon as the doctor reviews your chart you can go home," said one of the nurses, a heavy-set woman in her mid-forties. "We've already explained that to her," she said apologetically to Adam.

"I'm sure it will be soon," said Adam.

"Hah! I was married to a doctor, in case you forgot."

"No, Mom. I didn't forget."

"With your father it was always late, and later. Medical time, we called it."

Adam didn't have the heart to remind her that his father hadn't practiced medicine for the last twenty years of his life; that, in fact, his sons barely recalled the life they lived in Manhattan and were forced to leave when Adam was only five years old. There were enough new wounds without raising old ones. Instead, he held her hand and listened to her talk until the doctor finally arrived. He was a young man who looked about sixteen, with thin wisps of hair growing from his chin. He took Adam's mother's pulse and listened to her chest with a stethoscope.

"There's nothing the matter with my heart," she said.

"Mom," Adam cautioned.

"What? I've been in a fender bender. I didn't have a heart attack."

"It wasn't exactly a fender bender."

"A few coats of paint and the car will be fine."

In fact, the car had been totaled, and his mother was driving with an expired license. She had forgotten to renew it in time, and then failed her driving test twice. But she neglected to share this information with anyone—including her insurance company—until she was hospitalized and facing criminal charges.

His mother was not yet seventy, but she had bad eyesight, and terrible coordination. Adam and his brother long feared the phone call that would tell them she broke a hip, fractured an elbow, cracked her skull. Instead, they got calls about traffic accidents. Small ones, and then big ones, although never her fault. This one was driving too quickly; that one stopped too short; the last one didn't see her signaling.

"Mom, you turned left on red," said Adam.

"But he plowed right into me."

"He couldn't stop in time."

"Exactly."

The doctor poked and prodded while she talked, eliciting various howls of protest, until he finally declared her free to leave. Adam signed a dozen forms, pledging his 401(k) and a pint of blood as collateral should her health plan choose not to pay the bill. A nurse brought a wheelchair, which his mother adamantly refused. Instead, Adam helped her limp to the elevators and then to the front entrance where she waited on a bench while he got his rental car.

It was touch and go getting her into the passenger seat, but finally after reclining it nearly flat she was able to slide inside. On the ride home she talked about the new car she would buy with the insurance money. An electric one, of course, "with a dimmer switch to save energy."

Adam didn't tell her she was probably uninsurable, even if she could get her license back, which he doubted. She would need a driver, and probably rehab. His father had died suddenly of a heart attack, with no time to prepare. Now, it felt like his mother was at the beginning of a long, slow decline, and he was overwhelmed by it. Equal parts grief, sadness, and practical concern. For a moment he wanted to stop the car and get out, run for the woods, be anywhere but the claustrophobic front seat where he was belted beside his mother and stuck behind the wheel.

But then the familiar landscape opened in front of him: craggy hills and rolling meadows, family farms with their crooked silos and dark earth, one-block townlets with their filling stations and grocery stores. Soon, he was listening to his mother tell him about her plans for opening a yogurt bar/bookstore—"because who isn't buying books these days?"—and he couldn't help smiling. His mother's energy never flagged—even in the darkest times. It wasn't that she overcame obstacles; she simply ran right through them.

They drove up the gravel road to the weather-beaten Cape Cod hidden behind ash and elder trees. A rusted bicycle leaned against the garage, and several broken folding chairs lay scattered in the side yard. The house was about ten years overdue for a good paint job and, from the look of it, new gutters. Adam had been living in apartments for the last two decades, but the green-brown streaks down the sides of the house were unmistakable and ominous.

He parked as close as he could to the front door, then got out to help his mother. It was tough going on the slippery wooden steps, and he could see that would be another logistical problem that needed a quick resolution.

Once they were safely inside, and his mother seated at the kitchen table with a cup of tea and a plate of her favorite biscuits, he called his brother to report her condition. He took the phone into his old bedroom for privacy, but when he emerged the first thing his mother said was, "I am not an invalid. I do not need a nurse, or a wheelchair, or a cemetery plot."

"Glad to see you've got no problem with your hearing."

"I'm fine. I told you there was nothing wrong with me."

"Except for the walking part. And the driving."

"What's wrong with my driving?"

"For one thing, you don't have a license. Or a car."

"That's two things."

"How are you going to get around?"

"You'll help me get my license back. You're the lawyer."

"Mom, I've got a job. I've got to get back to the law school."

"I thought you were on break."

"I canceled my classes for the week."

"That's plenty of time. We can go down tomorrow and I'll take the driving test. It's like riding a bike."

His mother was in no condition to take a driving test—or ride a bike. Even if she could walk, she obviously couldn't drive. She could barely see. When he pointed that out, she said, "We'll go to the ophthalmologist first. I've been meaning to check my prescription anyway."

"When was the last time you went?"

She thought for a moment, then shrugged. "Twenty years ago? Twenty-two?"

"Are you serious?"

"I never needed to go."

"No wonder you keep getting into accidents."

"No." She shook her head. "It's not my eyes. I'm a bad driver."

"I can't believe you're admitting it."

"I have terrible spatial perception. That's why your father always drove."

"You used to fight about it all the time. You were a miserable backseat driver."

"I couldn't judge distances. Still can't. Of course, I never told him."

"I'm sure he knew."

"Yes."

They were silent, but Adam knew they were both thinking the same thing. His father was the elephant in the room, the skeleton in the closet, the Emperor's new clothes. They never talked about the past, but it hung over their home like a shroud, a rarely told tale that darkened their memories. Years ago his father had shared a medical practice with a classmate in lower Manhattan. This was before the days of hospital mergers, when a couple of general practitioners could make a decent living treating sick people. They weren't rich, but they did well enough that they could afford not to accept insurance. At least that's what Adam's father thought. Until one day he discovered his partner was billing Medicare for procedures that patients had already paid for out of pocket. He reported the fraud immediately, and for his diligence both men lost their licenses. The partner, after a messy divorce, decamped for Florida and made millions selling snake oil to the elderly. Adam's father didn't lose his family, but he went from being a doctor in Manhattan to a pharmacist in Nowhere, Pennsylvania, hoping everyone would forget the press coverage.

It didn't seem right. His father had done nothing wrong; he was guilty only of naïvete. So why did he accept his punishment? Why didn't he fight back? Surely, he could have at least kept his license. How different would their lives had been then? Adam could have grown up in an apartment with Central Park views, instead of spending his weekends working in the back of the pharmacy, wearing a smock and a name tag, fending off classmates who'd beg him to sneak them narcotics.

His father refused to discuss it. "What's done is done," he would say, leaving Adam to fumble for answers in the press clippings, but finding only unjust character attacks and mean-spirited labels.

"There isn't a day I don't miss him," his mother said into the silence. "He was very proud of you. Both of you boys."

"I thought he hated lawyers."

"No. He didn't hate anyone." His mother drained the rest of her tea. "Your father wasn't a complicated man. He didn't agonize over his choices. He made them, and moved on."

"That still doesn't explain why he let them take away his license. He could have hired a lawyer and sued. He probably would've won."

"Adam, you know that wasn't your father."

"I don't know anything."

"He didn't like confrontation. You remember he used to leave the house when we fought. But that wasn't the only reason. He knew the toll fighting would take, and he couldn't go through it."

"Because he was afraid?"

"Because he loved us. He didn't want to drag his family through years of hearings and court cases, and let his problems take over our lives. He wanted to spare you and Sam by making a clean escape."

"But he gave up everything. Look at where we lived."

"Was there something so wrong with it? He wanted you to grow up in a place where you could make your own lives and not be saddled with his. He believed the best thing for the two of you—for the three of us—was a fresh start someplace new.

The only way he could get through his pain was by knowing he'd spared his family."

Adam considered this. It wasn't that he doubted his father's love—even though it was rarely expressed—but the idea that his father might have sacrificed himself to save his family greater pain was something new. It made a certain sense, though, and Adam could understand how saving yourself at the cost of hurting people you cared for was actually more painful than accepting the consequences, however unfair. "He didn't want to drag us through the mud," Adam said.

"And, really, what good would it have done? Maybe he'd still have his job, but at what price? Years of public battling, details about his business practices, all to satisfy his own ego? I didn't care if he was a doctor or a hobo. You don't do that to someone you love."

Adam nodded. Slowly, then all at once, he told her about Pay for an A. The floodgates opened, and, somehow it all gushed out, relief at being able to finally tell the truth to someone. Her eyes widened and her jaw dropped, but she didn't say a word until he was finished, which was probably a personal record.

"Bastards! It's always the rich and entitled who think they aren't rich and entitled enough."

"What should I do?" Adam asked, surprised he was asking his mother for advice, and yet more surprised that it felt so normal to ask.

"You have to turn them in."

"And then what? Become like Dad?"

"You may find this hard to believe, but your father was happy. We were happy. We raised our children and made a life here. It was our home."

"But I'll lose my job."

"You'll find another one. Life isn't about what you do, it's about who you are. You don't love your father any less because he was only a pharmacist. If he made one mistake, it was that he truly thought he wouldn't be blamed or lose his job, until he did. But once it happened, he made the best decision he could. You can find a new job, be safe no matter the fallout. And, you know, you can always move back home with me."

"Mom."

"I make some mean pancakes."

"Mean" was not the word he would use, but he didn't say anything. He also didn't tell his mother that Goldreckt promised to make finding a new job impossible. And even if he could, there was still Laura to consider. No cause is without its effect—wasn't that what he taught his students in Torts? A man trips carrying fireworks, and hundreds of feet down the platform a woman is knocked unconscious. The law holds him blameless, but is he? What about Mrs. Palsgraf, her head bloodied and ringing? Who will care for her? As she staggers to her feet she curses fate, the railroad, and the ignorance of her fellow passengers who think they can play with explosives without getting hurt.

Outside it was growing dark. Adam was tired and hungry. His last meal had been a plastic-bagged sandwich from the hospital cafeteria. It made the food served in the law school faculty dining room seem like filet mignon. He scavenged his mother's pantry and found some pasta and a barely-expired can of tomato puree. In the refrigerator she had a head of iceberg lettuce and some radishes. There was an ancient jar of dried basil sticking out of the spice rack, and an old tin of anchovies in the back of the cupboard. She was not a cook, but his father had been, and Adam inherited a bit of the cooking gene from him. In half an hour he managed to make dinner for both of them, and his mother's praise for the meal was entirely genuine. Afterwards, he cleaned up while his mother returned phone calls from various well-wishers. Then he helped her get upstairs (another problem to be remedied), washed, and into bed. He brought his own reading, and looked forward to a couple of quiet hours catching up on the academic journals, but he was asleep before his head hit the armrest on the comfortable couch downstairs.

Two days later he took his mother to the optometrist where they discovered her vision was 20-200, and her prescription strength had tripled. She bought stylish new glasses (clunky black frames; all the rage in Williamsburg, he assured her), and the next day she passed her vision and written tests at the DMV. Although it was still difficult for her to get in and out of the car, they practiced driving for the next three days, and on the day Adam was supposed to leave, scheduled a driving test with the help of a former patient of Sam's who pulled some strings at the DMV to bump his mother to the head of line.

The singular focus on his mother's needs was a pleasant distraction from the criminal enterprise that was Manhattan Law School. In addition to driving, he went food shopping for her (new basil, better tomato sauce), cleaned up the yard, and got several estimates to have the house painted in the spring and the gutters reattached. His brother arranged for a caregiver to come for four hours a day, and although his mother moaned and groaned about it, Adam could tell she appreciated the help. It also gave Adam a break, which he spent taking long walks in the woods where there wasn't even cell phone service. The silence and isolation was a tonic of relief, and it reminded him that there was a world outside Gowanus—a place where things could still be pure, simple, and clean. And he knew then what he needed to do.

The day of the driving test Adam's mother drove them to the DMV office. She ran a stop sign, and nearly sideswiped a parked car. Bad omens for sure. Her usual confidence and bluster were gone, replaced by something he was surprised to recognize as nervousness.

"You'll be fine, Mom," he said, with as much false confidence as he could muster.

"Of course I will," she snapped.

And she was. The DMV examiner agreed, even though she failed to parallel park correctly ("Who parallel parks anymore?" she asked). They left the office with her shiny new license, and the safety of other drivers in the hands of the State of Pennsylvania and Geico Insurance. He kissed her goodbye and promised to visit more often, which, just for the moment, he truly meant.

As he drove home across the George Washington Bridge, with the sun setting red over the Hudson River, a plan had begun to assemble in his mind. The pieces clicking into place like a children's puzzle. But first there was something he needed to do, a person he needed to see. Without her, there would be nothing.

outsourced
associates

Welcome to Outsourced Associates and your role as a "Document Champion." You may think you're just a legal monkey, but we assure you that the work you are doing is extremely important—and quite valuable to the firms we contract with, and to us. In order to receive your full $28/hour payment for your work, there are a number of rules you must follow:

1. The computers are for document review only. They have been equipped with filters that prevent any other programs from being opened or the Internet from being accessed. Any attempts to circumvent these filters will result in nonpayment and immediate dismissal.

2. You are entitled to one (1) thirty-minute break each day for lunch and two (2) five-minute bathroom breaks. You must clock in and out using the automated machine by the door and the timecard which has been placed at your workstation. You are not required to take these breaks, but you will not be paid any additional money if you skip them.

3. Any and all materials you encounter during your work with us are considered confidential. If you attempt to remove any materials from the office, you will be prosecuted to the full extent of the law.

4. We believe in a friendly and open workplace. Please place your cell phones in the box by the entrance. They will be returned to you at the end of the week.

5. The time you spend reading these rules is not considered working time and will not be compensated.

(PAGE 1 OF 16)

23

Hail Mary

LAURA WAS NOT IN HER office when Adam returned to Manhattan Law School. He had texted her about his mother's accident, but otherwise they hadn't communicated since the faculty meeting. Twice he picked up the phone to call—late at night after several, or perhaps more than several, sorrowful beers—but then lost his nerve and had to use the bathroom, anyway. Besides, he wasn't quite sure how to begin. *I'm sorry. You're sorry. What are you wearing?* Thinking about her only made sleeping in his old twin bed as painfully uncomfortable as his senior year in high school when every girl wracked his hormonally addled dreams.

He wandered the law school, searching for her. It was too late for lunch. The library was recently closed for fumigation. The streets deserted. Eventually, her faculty assistant took pity and called up Laura's teaching schedule. She was in the small conference room preparing for her DLS seminar. He found her leaning over a casebook, highlighter in hand, lips pursed in concentration. Her other hand played with a curl that corkscrewed over one ear.

"Hello," he said.

She looked up, eyes still focused on legal citations, and then she saw him.

"Adam," she said softly. "You're back."

"I'm back."

"How's your Mom?"

"She's fine. It's the other drivers I'm worried about."

She smiled politely at his joke, then tugged again at her curl.

"Anyway," he said, "I wanted to thank you for standing up at the faculty meeting."

"You don't have to thank me. It was the right thing to do."

"Too bad the sale was approved."

Laura shrugged. "Maybe not. With Clopp gone things might change."

"Not as long as Jeffries stays. Besides, it shouldn't matter to you. You're leaving." He didn't intend it, but some of the bitterness crept back into his voice.

"Is that why you're here?"

"No. I came to say thank you."

"You're welcome."

"I don't want to fight with you anymore, Laura."

"We're not fighting."

"You know what I mean."

"We both said some things we probably regret. I forgive you."

"Water under the bridge."

"Exactly."

"It's kind of convenient, though, don't you think?"

"What does that mean?"

Adam shrugged. "You go off to some cushy professorship miles away where you never have to deal with what's gone on back here."

"You think I should stay?"

"No. But I think you should do something."

"Do what?"

"Take responsibility. Acknowledge it was wrong." The conversation was going in a direction Adam hadn't intended, but he couldn't stop. "You were wrong."

"If it makes you feel better, I admit it. I was wrong. I got wrapped up in the nonsense of this place. But at least I'm getting out. What are you doing?"

"I'm not taking money to give out fake grades."

"Neither am I."

"But you did."

"Never! What do you think I am?"

"You're tenured."

"I earned my tenure," she said. "The old-fashioned way. I wrote a book, in case you didn't know—a pretty good one—and a bunch of articles. But I never did Pay for an A. Never. I refused to take the money, and I graded my own exams. Jeffries told me I wouldn't get tenure, but then he changed his mind. He made me a deal and I took it, even though I knew it was wrong. Yes, I'm guilty for keeping quiet. But I never sold my grades, and I never would. I can't believe you would even think that."

"What did you expect me to think?"

"I expected you to know me better than that."

"Well, if you really thought Pay for an A was wrong, you wouldn't be ignoring it—you'd be stopping Jeffries from using the law school as his personal ATM."

"Maybe I will!"

"You should!"

"Okay!"

And then they kissed. For ten minutes. They kissed, and didn't say another word. Their lips locked, and the world spun, and gravity loosened its grip. Adam felt as if he were floating, high above the earth, the moon beside him like a fat old friend. They kissed until Adam was dizzy, and he imagined a student's voice calling out to him through the haze.

"Professor Wright?" asked the voice.

Laura nudged him, and Adam peeked out from behind her neck. The young woman he imagined standing in the doorway was tall and blond, and looked very uncomfortable. He wanted to reassure her that as a figment of his imagination she had nothing to worry about, but the longer she stood there awkwardly, the more his brain resumed its normal activity, and he realized that she was a very real student and he was really embarrassed.

"I'm sorry to interrupt," she said. "The website says you have office hours, but you weren't in your office. Professor Stapleton's assistant said I could find you here."

"She did?"

"Yes."

"Well, Professor Stapleton and I were just discussing a few things." Adam straightened his hair and did his best to look professional, while Laura tried to suppress the giggles. "How can I help you?"

"I'm Ann Marie Kowalski. I'm not one of your students, but I'm on the *Law Review*, and Staci Fortunato mentioned—"

Upon hearing Staci's name, Adam flinched. "Whatever Staci told you is incorrect. And I have to warn you that campus security can be here in ten seconds." It was an empty threat, of course. The phones hadn't worked in the security office since Hurricane Sandy flooded the telecommunications equipment with sewage.

"This is awkward," she began, and glanced at Laura. "Is there somewhere else we can talk?"

"If it's a personal matter," said Adam, "it might be better to speak with a professional. A licensed professional," he added.

Ann Marie hesitated. She seemed pained, and Adam waited. Finally, she said, carefully, "Staci mentioned you didn't give her the grade she expected in your class."

"I hope she isn't still trying to get me to change it. It's a little late for that."

Ann Marie's laugh was soft and nervous, like a bird landing on a pillow. "No, no, that's not why I'm here. I was just interested in talking to you about the grading system." Her eyes flickered again to Laura.

Suddenly, Adam realized he knew this Ann Marie. She was the young woman Goldreckt had hired. Was it just a coincidence that she was here? Now? He eyed her warily.

"What about the system?" he asked. "I heard it worked out for you."

"I turned that job down."

"You did? Why?"

"I had my reasons."

Laura inched closer, and Adam could feel the fabric of her shirt brushing his arm.

"I don't think our students can afford to be turning down jobs," he said.

"Maybe I should go." Ann Marie made a move for the door.

"Wait," said Laura. She was still holding her highlighter. Her lipstick, Adam noticed, was smeared and several strands of her hair had come loose. She looked as if she had just returned from a night of drinking. Soon, he knew, she had to teach. That meant more students coming in to gawk at the two professors making out like high school kids. Laura, however, didn't seem to care. She waited until she clearly had Ann Marie's attention, then spoke very deliberately.

"If you know something—something about the grading system—it could be very important. Professor Wright and I care about the school, and we could help you."

Ann Marie took a deep breath, and then plunged ahead.

"Staci told me Professor Wright wouldn't change her grade—even though she paid for it."

"That's true," said Adam.

"Then you've got to stop it."

"Stop what?" He was being cautious.

She gave him a pitying look. "Pay for an A, of course. You can't let it go on."

"You know about Pay for an A?"

"Everyone knows about it! That's why the *Law Review* editors were so busy at the copy machines. I thought it was for cite-checking, but I should have known something was rotten. I feel like an idiot! They were always sending me out of the office—up to Columbia, and Pace! Have you ever been to Pace? They don't even have books. And now someone's buying the school who's going to make things ten times worse."

"Henry Steele."

"Yes." Ann Marie's eyes unexpectedly started to well up with tears. "That's why I came to talk to you. Mr. Steele spoke to us on the *Law Review*. He said Pay for an A was his model. He wants to spread it across the country, to all the schools he owns. He says it's the 'free market,' and the future of education. Can you believe it? He actually thinks schools are cheating students who pay big tuition bills and don't get good grades. He thinks he's a revolutionary!"

Laura withdrew some tissues from her handbag and passed them to Ann Marie. The young woman blew her nose, and continued.

"It makes me angry, really mad. I worked hard to get to law school and get good grades here. It's not fair that people who don't deserve it can buy the same thing."

"No, it's not," Adam said quietly.

"What happened to fairness, equality, justice? Isn't that what you teach? That's why I went to law school. Because I believed in those things." Ann Marie's face had reddened and her eyes were a vivid ultramarine. "Instead, we don't learn anything on *Law Review*. We can't get jobs because firms know our grades are a joke. And if we do get hired, it's only because some partner wants to sleep with us."

Goldreckt was a letch, but as far as Adam knew, he sinned with his eyes, not his hands. "I'm sure you're more than qualified for the job Howie offered," he said.

"I don't care. I'm not working for that firm."

"He'll be upset to hear that."

"He won't stop calling me."

Adam was familiar with Goldreckt's obsessive qualities. It's what made him a relentless dealmaker as well as one of the world's leading collectors of Jerry Garcia ties. Once he had his eye on something—or someone—good taste did not stand in his way. "He can be hard to ignore," Adam agreed.

"It's wrong. The whole system is wrong. You can't stand here and let it go on."

"She's right, Adam," said Laura. "We have to do something."

"I know." In fact, he had known for some time, but he hadn't wanted to hurt Laura, or end up like his father. That life—hang your head, bear your sorrows, slouch off to the far reaches of another state—was not for him. Yes, his father was a good man, but Adam was not a martyr. He wouldn't go quietly into the night. The student standing in front of him was reason enough to do something, if more reasons were needed.

But the plan he had concocted was marginal, at best. A Hail Mary pass with three seconds remaining. He had never been a quarterback, or much of an athlete in general, and he preferred his sports as metaphors rather than the dirty, painful reality. Yet Laura and Ann Marie were looking at him as if they expected him to lead the drive downfield. He met their eyes, and realized that maybe he did indeed have a winning play. It would take good timing, and great coordination, but with the three of them they might be able to pull it off. Or so he hoped.

"Listen," he said, and then he explained.

He finished just as the students trickled in to Laura's seminar. They glanced at him briefly, but most were so downtrodden they could barely lift their heads. They probably assumed he was another Associate Dean who had come to berate or flunk them. Laura gathered her notes and cleared a space at the head of the seminar table, transitioning seamlessly into her professorial role. Ann Marie, on the other hand, stood like a deer in the headlights, her face visibly paled.

He was about to reassure her—her part in the plan was without risk—when he noticed the clean-shaven, recently showered, young man in a suit at whom Ann Marie stared.

"Hello Professor Wright," he said jauntily. "Good to see you again."

"Gary?" asked Laura.

"I know I've missed the past few classes," he said to her. "I was in rehab."

"Rehab?"

"My girlfriend made me go. You wouldn't believe the kind of people you meet there—I have so many future clients lined up."

He extended his hand to Ann Marie. "Hi, Ann Marie. How are you?"

Adam cast a glance at the young woman to see if she was okay, or if he needed to throw his body between the two of them and absorb the blows.

"Girlfriend?" she asked.

He nodded. "I'm sorry to spring that on you. It just seemed like it was time to move on, you know?"

"It's okay," said Ann Marie, a bit flustered. "You look really good," she added.

"Thanks. You look great, too. I hope it's okay for me to say that."

"Thank you, Gary."

The entire class was watching now, spellbound, including Adam and Laura. Even those who didn't know the specific details of their relationship had heard the tale—now an urban legend—of the stalker and the first-year. It had made the rounds of the legal blogs—and the local police blotter—and was even a case study at NYU's psychopharmacology program.

"I understand now how my obsession over you was really a struggle with my own insecurity during my first year of law school and my problematic relationship with my parents."

"That's okay, Gary."

"Really? Because in my group we talked a lot about the collateral damage of substance abuse. Hurting people you love, damaging heavy machinery, things like that."

"I'm fine, Gary. And your parents' insurance paid to repair the bulldozer."

"Good. It's important to make amends. My girlfriend says we shouldn't fixate on the past, but I think we shouldn't ignore it, either."

"It was an interesting year," agreed Ann Marie. "We learned a lot, and grew up a lot. I know I did."

"There's still so much more to learn, though. Don't you think? We won't be in school forever. And then what? What will we do? What kind of people will we become?"

"That's a good question."

"I'm excited to see what happens next. Aren't you?"

"I am."

"Um, Gary," said Laura, breaking the spell. "Class has begun?"

"Oh, I'm sorry Professor Stapleton!" He laughed almost normally. "I'll take my seat. It was nice talking to you again, Ann Marie."

"Nice talking to you."

Adam watched him take little goat-steps to an open chair on the opposite side of the table. Then he withdrew a shiny laptop from his backpack, a casebook, a legal pad, two pens, and a highlighter. He arranged them in perfect square angles, then sat up straight and gave Laura his full attention. His face was beaming.

In that moment, Adam saw the future, and knew it was theirs to lose.

Law Schools Raking in More Than Just Tuition

By D. CAMPBELL
WILEY

Last year, there were 354 crimes reported along the Gowanus Canal, according to the New York City Police Department. Eighteen murders, including six beheadings, almost three dozen iPhone thefts, two deadly crocodile attacks, and one case of smell death, a disease that was thought to have died out in the 1600s, but that made a surprise appearance on a warm afternoon this past August when a woman was overcome by the toxic fumes and her body simply stopped functioning. She remained seated on a bench, overlooking the water, for eleven days before someone finally noticed she wasn't moving and called 911. Sixteen hours later, an ambulance arrived and she was removed from the scene with a spatula.

A grisly year, certainly, topping the 321 crimes a year ago by more than ten percent. But the numbers don't include the biggest crime of all. Manhattan Law School, a barely accredited institution that calls this area of Brooklyn its "temporary home, until we can afford a better facility," according to the school's dean, Aloysius Clopp, is a true scandal of higher education.

It is often said that law school grades are random. Students at schools around the country joke that professors throw the exams down a staircase and assign grades based on where the papers land. But a months-long investigation by *The New York Times* has uncovered evidence that for many students at Manhattan Law School, grades have been far from random. They are involved in what inside sources call "Pay for an A," a widespread, carefully plotted scheme where students pay the law school and their professors thousands of dollars in exchange for guaranteed A's, A minuses, and B plusses (depending on how much they can afford) in their required courses.

These falsely inflated grades helped a record twelve percent of Manhattan Law School graduates find full-time employment after graduation, and have made the school profitable enough that, multiple sources revealed, the school is on the brink of being sold to Steele Educational Enterprises, for $250 million. According to Professor Adam Wright, a critic of the system, who spoke freely with this reporter, the price reflects a cash flow of more than four million dollars annually in additional revenue from unwitting parents who believe they are paying the additional cost of *Law Review* membership, an honor traditionally bestowed upon the highest-ranking students.

In discussing "Pay for an A," Wright implicated a number of his colleagues, including Associate Dean Jasper Jeffries (profiled in this newspaper's Sunday Routine column last May), as well as longtime professors Rick Rodriguez and David Wheeler. "I would say they're good people trapped in bad circumstances," noted Wright, "except they're not."

Would the students have earned these grades if not for the payment scheme? "Not a chance," said Wright. "We have some perfectly well-intentioned students but, unfortunately, most of the ones with the highest grades are simply not capable of doing *Law Review*-level work."

So while hipsters and artisanal pickle-makers traverse these streets on a typical weekday afternoon, they should know that behind those unlabeled doors are victims of a scam, the likes of which the law school community has never before seen.

When asked for a comment, retiring head of the law school Dean Clopp said, "I don't have a stapler. Ask my secretary." Yet, according to multiple sources, the origins

Continued on Page B7

CORRECTIONS: In a previous version of this article, the number of beheadings this year in the Gowanus area of Brooklyn was incorrectly listed as 600, not 6. "Brooklyn" was also misspelled twice.

24

Down and Out in Gowanus

THE LAW SCHOOL LOOKED AS if a bomb had exploded in the main entrance. Papers were scattered everywhere; chairs were toppled; and the guards had abandoned their posts. When Adam pushed through the front doors, a glass pane broke with a sharp crack that sounded like a gunshot and left a spider web across its surface. The security turnstiles were stuck, and his ID didn't work, so he scrambled over them awkwardly, tearing a hole in his trousers in the process.

He walked to the stairs without seeing a soul. The only sound was a low growl, like someone praying, dying, or worse. But when he opened the stairwell doors, there was no one inside. Instead, it reeked of stale sweat and marijuana. Someone had taped the article from *The New York Times* across the fire alarm and scrawled "Manhattan Law Skool Sux!" in a black marker above it. At least there were still students who read the printed paper, although the bad handwriting and spelling suggested it could be a professor.

The faculty, of course, had plenty of reasons to be angry. Two hundred and fifty million reasons, to be exact. The article single-handedly killed the sale of the school to Steele Educational

Enterprises, Inc. In light of the bad publicity, the estimated value of the institution fell by eighty percent. Unlike other schools with valuable real estate, or at least a name with valuable goodwill, the law school had few assets besides the cracked and stained furniture it could sell on Overstock.com and the expired snacks in its vending machines. The day the article was published, Steele exercised his termination rights under the contract's "morals clause." He had promised the tenured faculty $100,000 for each year of service to eliminate tenure, end the school's 401(k) contributions, and accept at-will employment status. The old guard would become millionaires, while new hires would become wage slaves, and everyone could be fired for publishing the type of claptrap that gave the eight-point law journal font a bad name. But now the older faculty's fantasies of riches—sold on their younger colleagues' backs—vanished in a flash.

Everyone's dreams had died. The students, who had few jobs to begin with, found their offers revoked. The faculty, both innocent and guilty, were immediately tarred by Pay for an A and rendered unemployable. The school instantly became the subject of a joint investigation by the Department of Education and the District Attorney's office, and an accreditation review by the Association of American Law Schools. Even the faculty dining hall was shuttered when the school's outside food vendor (a company dealing with its own legal crisis, as dozens of office workers in buildings it served had come down with a rare strain of feline hepatitis) demanded payment in cash up front.

"My God, what have you done?" Laura asked Adam when the article appeared.

"We," he said. "Remember?"

"I do, but now I'm wondering what we've gotten into."

"It's not too late for you to jump ship."

"Of course I won't. I just hope you know what you're doing."

"I knew he couldn't keep my name out of it. A guy like Donald can change his accent, but he can never change his stripes."

In violation of his promise of confidentiality, D. Campbell Wiley had revealed the source for his article. Since then, Adam's phone had not stopped ringing with other reporters, angry alumni, and enraged colleagues. Former colleagues, actually, because one of the callers had been Jasper Jeffries, who informed him he had been fired. "Just as soon as you make up some grades for the idiots in your class," he added.

Now, as he made his way to his office, Adam was no longer as confident in his plan. It was a Tuesday morning, but the halls were deserted. He passed a seminar room where there was normally a document drafting workshop and saw a student sitting alone sullenly smoking a cigarette, which of course was prohibited indoors. The student spotted him, then slowly and deliberately flipped him the middle finger. Adam was, he realized, the scapegoat for all that had gone wrong.

Had he done the right thing? Certainly the student didn't think so. Whatever teaching prospects Adam had were gone, and the law school's name was like a scarlet letter burned into his chest. But the students didn't have jobs to begin with, and they were laboring under an illusion that hurt all of them, even the ones who paid for their A's. Unless there was real change, they were all on a sinking ship where even the rats would drown.

Adam was halfway down the hall when the door to the bathroom opened and Professor Rodriguez emerged. He looked wild-eyed and unshaven, and his normally lacquered black hair was tangled and dulled. Adam nodded politely and tried to slide by, but Rodriguez put out a hand and stopped him.

"You've really fucked us, haven't you, Wright?" he said.

"Not me," said Adam.

"*Not me,*" Rodriguez mocked him in a whiny, sing-songy voice. "You've fucked us, Wright. Yes, you have. Right up the ass. The ass. Where people get fucked. But you'll get yours. I promise you that."

"Thanks for the warning."

"It's not a warning. You won't see it coming. We'll slam you so hard your shit will come out of your ears."

"Is that so?"

"Yes, it's so."

Adam had never liked Rodriguez. Like Wheeler and Jeffries, teaching was an excuse to pursue his own esoteric interests while his students floundered and sank. The truth was most of his colleagues were in the teaching business for all the wrong reasons, concerned more with their obscure political agendas and solipsistic scholarship than imparting anything worth learning. Adam felt an enormous freedom knowing he wouldn't miss them. Which explains what he said next.

"Let me ask you something, Rick. Were you born a pompous prick or did you just become one?"

He saw the punch coming from a mile away. Rodriguez was not quick, and he wasn't athletic. He punched like a kangaroo, all hopped up on his toes. Adam sidestepped, and Rodriguez's fist went right into the wall—the thin coating of plaster no match for a human hand. Unfortunately, the plaster was just a veneer for the discolored, but still solid, brick beneath. The crack of bones was unmistakable, and both men stood looking at Rodriguez's hand as if it were a foreign object for two silent seconds before Rodriguez let out a howl.

"You moved!" he cried.

Adam shrugged. "You missed."

"You broke my hand!" He put his knuckles in his mouth, sucking on them like a baby.

"Sorry." Adam left him there, doubled over in pain.

In the safety of his office, Adam shut the door and collapsed into the bean bag chair Facilities Maintenance had given him to replace his creaky desk chair. Although the "beans" gave off a plastic chemical smell, it masked the moldy bacterial smell of the carpet. In fact, the guy from Facilities informed him that the chemicals in the chair would kill the mold in the carpet, and reassured Adam he would be fine as long as he didn't spend more than two hours with the door closed.

And yet he would miss the place. There was a certain satisfaction to being down and out in Gowanus. Like the Bad News Bears or the '63 Mets, the school's haplessness was its draw. The

211

promise of better things glowed faintly in the distance if you squinted your eyes hard enough. A fan just had to believe.

He took another minute to compose himself, then reached into the back drawer of his desk and found the digital recorder, which he pocketed in his pants. Then he turned and left his office.

He had no difficulty hailing a livery cab on the street where they circled like flies hungry for a fare. Business was bad, and the driver spent the first half of the ride complaining about Uber and the second half complaining about lawyers. "Jackals and thieves," he spat. "The devil take them." Then he quoted Adam a fare that was double the price they had agreed on.

Adam didn't have time to argue, and the driver appeared slightly unhinged. He gave the man his money.

As he approached the building, he could see the tall blonde woman standing alone and aloof at the far corner of the security desk. In heels, she was taller than many of the men who leered at her while pretending not to. Regal and statuesque, she was like a fairy tale ice princess from a Northern land.

Yet Ann Marie was nothing like that, as Adam had learned. She was, instead, the type of student he had gone into teaching to teach: committed, curious, law-abiding, and impassioned. It wasn't her fault she attracted men like Goldreckt, men who preyed on her natural empathy and her inability to kick a man to the curb.

But that was about to change.

She saw Adam and waved. "Professor Wright!"

He smiled and walked over to her, ignoring the stares like daggers from his fellow members of the male species. Men always acted true to character. At least that's what he was counting on.

"Ready?" he asked.

Ann Marie made a face. "I guess so."

"It will be fine," Adam promised her. "He'll behave."

"That's not what I'm worried about."

"He told you the truth. If there's one thing I know about Howie, it's that charity is not in his nature."

Ann Marie sighed. "What if I still don't want to work for him?"

"If the plan works, you won't have to."

"And if it doesn't?"

"We can both get jobs at Starbucks."

When she smiled, her whole face shone, and Adam felt woozy from the reflected glow. He steadied himself with one hand against the wall until the blue spots quit dancing in his peripheral vision. Then he straightened his spine.

"Let's go make a deal."

They took the elevator to the thirty-fifth floor. They rode together in silence, contemplating the LCD screens that flashed news updates and, once, the headline, "Law School Grading Scandal." Adam winced, but was glad to see that Ann Marie had missed it. They stopped at thirty-two to pick up a harried-looking young man who ignored them because he was too busy chewing his nails. When they got off, he was unlacing his shoes.

The receptionist on thirty-five nodded vaguely when she saw them, and Adam realized she had been his suite-mate's secretary many years ago. But she gave no hint of recognition, and simply called Goldreckt's office to announce their arrival. They waited a few minutes in the richly appointed reception area, with its nautical themed prints, musty leather-bound books, and astringent smell of floor cleaner. An associate passed in the hallway, then stopped quickly when he saw Adam.

"Dude!" he said. "Returning to the scene of the crime?"

Adam introduced the associate to Ann Marie, whom the associate already knew from interview season. "How could I forget?" he asked. "They're already scalping tickets for the pool party."

Ann Marie smiled politely, and Adam steered the conversation in a different direction.

Finally, another secretary came to fetch them. The poor woman looked like a trauma victim, with bald patches on her scalp and red patches on her face. She spoke extremely quickly and quietly, as if words hurt her tongue. When she walked, her feet appeared to be running away from each other. But she calmed down when Ann Marie lightly touched her forearm, and managed to correctly steer them in the direction of Goldreckt's office.

When they entered, the first thing Adam thought was that he had never seen Goldreckt without his usual bluster and spittle. But there he was, sitting at his desk, hands steepled, thumbs twiddling, hair partially combed. If Adam didn't know better, he'd say the man looked nervous. He had even cleaned his office—or at least stacked things into assorted piles that teetered dangerously on the verge of collapse. He took one look at Ann Marie, and his mouth appeared to tremble and he blinked rapidly. In fact, Adam could swear he saw tears, although the lawyer quickly blew his nose with a used paper towel on his desk.

"Fucking *New York Times*," he grumbled.

"Not the best PR," Adam agreed.

"And you! What the fuck were you thinking?"

"Please, Mr. Goldreckt," said Ann Marie. "Cursing is counterproductive. And not at all attractive. Professor Wright is here to help; he has a plan."

Goldreckt's face fell, and he looked for a moment like a child caught with his hand in the cookie jar.

"You're not still angry with me?"

"Not if you keep quiet and listen to Professor Wright."

Goldreckt clamped his lips shut tight and raised his eyes beseechingly at Ann Marie. She let him sit there in silence for a full minute before she nodded at Adam to continue.

"You always told me the best time to make a deal is when the market collapses," Adam began. "Prices are low; sellers are desperate; there are no white knights."

"They've fled for the hills," agreed Goldreckt.

"That's why now is the time to buy Manhattan Law School."

"What? Are you crazy?"

"I'm just following your advice. The school's on the verge of closing and no one will touch it, but the fundamentals are sound. The building and faculty aren't going anywhere, and the students are stuck, too. Sure, some of them will drop out, but most have already invested too much to leave. And going to school is better than scrambling for a job anyway. But their parents need a reason to keep paying tuition. That's where you come in. You swoop in with a plan to save the place, clean up its reputation, and preserve their investment. You'll be a hero."

"You'd be *my* hero," Ann Marie echoed.

Goldreckt looked from Ann Marie to Adam to Ann Marie again. It was a little disgusting, really, the way they were toying with his affections, but he deserved it. Plus, Adam had crunched the numbers, and he knew the deal could work if certain bloated faculty salaries were allowed to sink into the canal.

"Where do I get that kind of money?"

"You can get it."

"Not all at once."

"A structured transaction. Pay out the bondholders over time, stepping down the interest rate for certain milestones like bar passage rate and job to homelessness ratio."

"How much you think they'll take?"

"Pennies on the dollar. It's a fire sale. They don't have a choice."

Goldreckt gnawed on his lip for a moment while his brain did the math. "You think I should do it?" he asked Ann Marie.

She gave him her sweetest smile. "Yes, *Howie*. I think you should."

If a man could turn to jelly, Goldreckt would have been a quivering blob. He sighed hopelessly.

"But what about the bad press? Even if we can keep the school open, applications will dry up. No one's going to apply to the school after the hatchet job in the *Times*."

Adam withdrew the tape recorder from his pocket and set it on Goldreckt's desk. "Leave that to me," he said.

Then he pressed "play" and told them about the rest of his plan.

Boalt Hall

Laura,

Given the circumstances, I hope you understand that we have
no choice but to rescind your offer of employment. The official letter
is enclosed, but I wanted to make sure you knew that there were no
hard feelings, and I hope we can still be the best of friends. Do give
me a ring if you ever find your way out to the West Coast again.
Perhaps we could meet for a cup of organic cocoa and you can catch
me up on whatever it is you end up doing with yourself after all of
this scandal blows over.

I'm also sending you a few jars of that chocolate spread you
seemed to love while you were out here. Consider it a gesture of
friendship and an apology for ever getting you all excited about
Berkeley in the first place. I should have realized that the Gowanus
and Berkeley are two very different worlds, and it probably wasn't
the right match to begin with, regardless of everything that's
happened.

Take good care of yourself. And don't lose faith—even felons
deserve people who love them.

Rosie

25

A Light Shines in Brooklyn

O N A CLEAR DAY YOU could see New Jersey.

It made Laura happy—knowing there were worse places in the world. Gowanus might have been a dump, but at least it didn't pretend to be the "Garden State." And, as hard as it was to admit, there were things she liked about the place. In fact, the other day she had noted an art exhibition at a new gallery in a converted waste transfer station. Black-clad hipsters stood smoking outside, while a velvet light strobed through the open door. "Hey there, law lady," one of them had called. "Buy me a drink?"

She was too old to be offended by the catcall, too young to need to buy a guy a drink. Besides, she had Adam to do the buying. Very unfeminist of her, she knew, but a girl needed to feel like a woman every now and then.

She smiled at the memory as she gazed out the window of her apartment. The sun was a fat fruit sinking on the horizon, and pink clouds skidded across the sky. Across the rooftops she could see flowers growing, trees in bloom, and what seemed to be a mugging in progress—but even that couldn't spoil the view. She loved this time of summer. Thick August heat. A lush darkness settling. August was the reason she became a professor. Long summer days with nothing to do but read and lounge until nightfall; late mornings lingering over strong coffee; a good afternoon nap. And no one trying to schedule committee meetings.

Monk barked, drawing her attention away from the view.

"Okay, little man. I'm done mooning."

She fastened his leash and left her apartment. In the lobby she ran into a neighbor, an older woman who was struggling with the door while pushing her shopping cart. Laura held the door while the woman slipped inside, and then the two of them chatted while Monk yipped at the woman's ankles. After a few minutes, satisfied that her neighbor could make it upstairs in the elevator, Laura said goodbye and headed outdoors.

A warm breeze eddied in currents along the sidewalk, blowing bits of paper and leaves in tight circles. Laura headed west, toward the river, while Monk more or less cooperated. At the corner she saw another familiar face, and stopped for another moment. Across the street a shopkeeper waved to her, and a man on a bicycle rang his bell as he zipped through the changing light. They said New York was a town of strangers, but she knew better. New York was thousands of different towns made up of people of every shape and flavor who came together, split apart, overlapped, reconfigured, reinvented, grew, thrived, changed, were broken by scandal but recovered, eventually, fully—and stronger for having had the experience. It was the magic of the city, the dynamic that powered it. Nothing that could be imagined was impossible; no problem unsolvable; no condition that couldn't be cured. It was what she loved about New York, and what inspired her and kept her. If she could make it here, she could make it anywhere. And the truth was, she didn't have much of a choice anyway.

She wasn't surprised to get Rosie's letter. After the exposé of Pay for an A she assumed her teaching career was over. Although not guilty of participating, she was guilty of turning a jaundiced eye, and truly believed she deserved her fate. Her penance would be banishment. She was prepared for it.

The light changed, and she crossed Columbia Heights, the smell of salt and sea air carrying in the drafts off the water. Manhattan was an island, but so were all the boroughs except the Bronx, part of an archipelago whose deep channels and calm harbors brought adventurers to their shores. It was easy to forget New York's nautical history while in the shadow of skyscrapers and brownstones, but a walk to the waterfront—or a hurricane—quickly brought it back.

She turned down Doughty Street and was briefly sheltered from the wind, then the promenade opened before her. Once again she was struck by its beauty—both man-made and natural. Directly in front of her were deciduous trees and rows of blooming flowers. Beyond them, the slate gray calm of the Hudson River. On its far shore the skyscrapers and spires of Wall Street rose like conquerors, citadels to wealth, vanity, and power. Finally, to her north was the Brooklyn Bridge, its twined cables glinting silver in the setting sun. Over 130 years old, it was the first land link between Manhattan and Brooklyn, and led to the creation of New York City. Without it, there would have been no New York Marathon, no New York bagel, and no Manhattan Law School. And she, Laura, would have been jobless, which, technically, she wasn't, at least not yet.

Grateful for small favors, she tightened her grip on Monk and crossed into the park. Elderly couples strolled hand in hand while kids ran unattended as if dodging an obstacle course. Young lovers swooned on benches while old friends gathered over food and concealed beers. A man with a steel string guitar played a folk song badly while a woman read lines for a dramatic monologue like a professional. All in all, another brilliant evening in Brooklyn.

Laura made her way to the river and stood at the railing. She took deep steady breaths of the sweet fresh air. At the far end of the promenade a man with curly brown hair and a lanky walk waved to her. She would have recognized him anywhere. Monk started yapping, and Laura released his leash. The dog ran swiftly toward Adam, and Laura followed.

HIRE THE SERVICES OF A PULITZER PRIZE WINNING* REPORTER

➢ Expose corruption at the highest levels of government
➢ Post a really long Facebook update
➢ Take down the world's most powerful business leaders
➢ Polish your child's preschool application
➢ Gain access to global nuclear codes
➢ Perfect your grandfather's eulogy

Whatever the occasion—I'm your man. I've gone undercover with the secret militia in Antarctica (still a secret!), been embedded with the Canadian Royal Post, and was once taken prisoner by an angry Swede. I've won every award there is to win in Slovenian journalism—twice.

And now, I'm available to you, for all of your writing and editing needs. Give me a shout for rates and details, along with dozens of impressive testimonials I wrote myself—proof of the very type of work I am able to do for you!

I am also your man for delicious appetizers and cocktails at the Tassie Lassie Bar & Grill, in downtown Hobart next to the art supply store, where I'm biding my time until the next big scandal calls me, or the international desk at the Herald Tribune lifts the restraining order.

* Full disclosure: I won the Pulitzer Prize in a poker game off Maureen Dowd—right before we had sex. And more sex. I am also available for sex. Just give me a call.

Call Wills
1300 62 5547

Call Wills
1300 62 5547

Call Wills
1300 62 5547

Call Wills
1300 62 5547

Call Wills
1300 62 5547

26

Snap, Crackle, and pop

ADAM SURVEYED THE ROWS OF students sitting in front of him. Laptops open, hats on backwards, body parts exposed. There was a boy with a tattoo of Homer Simpson on his forearm next to a girl with the lyrics to a Taylor Swift song hennaed across her midriff. In the rear of the room, the backbenchers had their feet on the seats and giant buckets of soda perched precariously at the edges of their desks. All in all, a typical morning in the life of the beleaguered twenty-first century law professor.

And yet so much had changed since he and Ann Marie left Howell Goldreckt's office with the rough outlines of an offer in their hands. Three days later, with few other options, the Board of Trustees overrode the faculty and sold the law school to Goldreckt's ragtag group of investors, a hastily organized collection of persuadable clients, indebted colleagues, and intrigued alumni, all willing to give Howell the chance to turn a school from a laughingstock into something better. A small band of faculty members, led by Jasper Jeffries, threatened to sue, but they were quickly dissuaded when Clopp's long-suffering (and frequently forgotten) secretary, Lucinda Morris, produced several volumes of ledger entries detailing all the unreported (and untaxed) payments that would surely be Exhibits 1–100 at their depositions. As it was, the ensuing IRS and DOE investigations into how Pay for an A funds were accrued and accounted for would consume their time, money, and lawyers for years to come.

With only a handful of innocent faculty remaining, the law school struggled to close out the academic year while fighting off an audit, an accreditation review, and a class action filed by students who weren't involved in Pay for an A. In the end, the court dismissed their claims because, it held, students had no expectation of any particular grade and therefore no standing to challenge the allocation of grades based on financial payments. "It may not be fair," the court wrote, "but neither is our educational system. The wealthiest have always been able to afford superior schools, hire tutors for their children, and buy access to better information. If something is rotten, it's rotten throughout the kingdom."

Despite their victories on and off the court, it was touch and go whether the school would open in the fall, and whether any matriculated students would actually attend. The copy center shut down when it ran out of toner, then paper clips, then staples. Faculty were forced to piggyback on the unsecured Wi-Fi of someone named "BritneyBitch" when Internet service was canceled. To save money, the school outsourced its health-care services to a webcam clinic in India and sold off its prized collection of Thomas E. Dewey memorabilia. It rented out the student cafeteria for a scene from *Law & Order* that called for "INT. DILAPIDATED DINING HALL IN STATE MENTAL INSTITUTION." Still, it was weeks since anyone had received a paycheck, and some joker taped a sign on the lobby doors that read: "Last one to go pleaz shut off the lights."

The survivors sat in limbo, between a rock and the Gowanus Canal, when *The New York Times* published a follow-up to its scathing exposé of the school. Written by D. Campbell Wiley, the article appeared above the fold on the front page of the Business Day section with the headline, "Law School Back From The Brink—Rumors of its Death Greatly Exaggerated."

In May, Lucinda Morris, assistant to the dean of Manhattan Law School, tried to make a reservation for a conference the dean planned to attend in Denver. The school's credit card was rejected. It had just suffered through the worst scandal in its history—indeed, one of the worst scandals in the history of higher education—after it was disclosed that professors had been selling grades for money in a scheme called "Pay for an A." Most of the faculty resigned or were fired in disgrace, and the school was bombarded with lawsuits and demands for tuition refunds. "We were surviving on fumes," said Professor Adam Wright, who was named the school's 32nd dean by an investment group that purchased the school in the wake of the scandal. But in a textbook example of crisis management, the new administration instituted a series of concrete changes in teaching policies, including giving more responsibility to students for their own learning, under a program designed by Professor Laura Stapleton. The result has been a leaner, more vibrant curriculum that has begun to draw notice and raves. Even some potential employers have reached out, hoping that a set of better-educated law school graduates might be exactly the young associates they would need.

Although the article struck some as cloyingly deferential, it was the opinion of the *Times* legal department that a single (non-precedential) puff piece was a small price to pay to resolve an expensive (and embarrassing) claim for breach of contract. Of course Adam never threatened to sue the *Times*—he was too big a fan of the First Amendment to be so blunt—but the lawyers paid attention when he played his tape recording of D. Campbell Wiley's promise of confidentiality. "An oral contract is binding with valid consideration," he reminded them. "See *Cohen v. Cowles Media*." The lawyers didn't need the citation; they knew the case law. But it was a nice flourish to accompany a stack of solid evidence, and it clinched the deal.

Within hours following the article's publication, students started emailing the school to ask whether their acceptance letters were still valid. Long-overdue course selection forms suddenly appeared in the registrar's office. Parents who had stopped payment on their deposits called to say it had all been a terrible bank mistake. The stink of scandal began to lift, and a bit of light shined through the bird-shit stained windows. Even the canal smelled fresher.

In the end, although it had gone down to the wire, things unfolded just as Adam planned. He had done enough deals with Goldreckt to know the lawyer could seize an opportunity when he saw one. Of course it helped that it was Ann Marie who made the offering. Corraling the *Times* was more difficult, but Adam knew his old chum Wiley would act true to character, and his bosses would prefer a quiet resolution to a public shaming. Once Adam convinced the in-house lawyers that a follow-up article was both newsworthy and would release all claims whether known or unknown throughout the universe in perpetuity, the tuition dollars followed. Wiley disappeared soon afterward, and he was last seen tending bar in the former British colony of Tasmania.

But the best part of Adam's plan was persuading Laura to stay. After Berkeley withdrew its offer she had contemplated leaving New York anyway, going on a long-deferred Himalayan trek or African safari, anywhere without Wi-Fi and running water. "You said you wanted to change the system," he reminded her. "So, let's change it."

They were at dinner at his brother's apartment, an Upper East Side co-op fit for a successful young doctor and his girlfriend-of-the-moment. It was during one of the couple's lovey-dovey moments when Adam cornered Laura on the couch. "The school needs you; the students need you; I need you," he pleaded.

"I bet you say that to all the girls."

"Only the ones who can teach Civil Procedure."

Laura pulled him close for a lengthy kiss that was only interrupted by Sam's loud and theatric coughing fit when he and his girlfriend returned to the room.

Adam remembered that moment fondly as he faced the class. Lost in his daydream, he was interrupted by a knock on the door and the entrance of the *Law Review*'s new Editor in Chief, Ann Marie Kowalski. These first-year students in Adam's classroom had been her peers until they were stripped of their credits and threatened with expulsion. Now they were starting again. Granted amnesty under the condition that they return to school and retake their classes, they were also given tuition credit for their previously completed semesters. Yet not everyone had returned. Some, better suited for lives as strippers, squeegee men, or three-card monte dealers, returned to the streets, joining the hustle and flow of the big city and providing future clientele for their former classmates.

Because it was the first day of a new school year, Adam had invited Ann Marie to welcome the new students, and to say some encouraging words about the journey that awaited them if they worked hard, stayed straight, and persevered. She had brought her managing editor with her, a young man Adam never expected to see alive, let alone in a clean shirt with his teeth brushed. But the meds and Gary's girlfriend had straightened him out, and Laura's tutoring helped him write his way onto *Law Review*. As for Ann Marie, with Goldreckt's assistance she was applying for federal court clerkships, and had promised to give his firm another look the following year. In private she told Adam she didn't think she was meant for Big Law, but he told her to keep her options open, grateful that the school still had students who actually had options.

The class listened to Ann Marie's short speech, and one student even raised a hand to ask a question about future issues of the *Law Review*. Ann Marie said they were still soliciting manuscripts and organizing a symposium in the spring with Professor Stapleton.

"If you need any help with the planning or anything, let me know," added Asher Herman. "I have some experience with that kind of stuff."

Ann Marie smiled sweetly and said she would keep it in mind, while Gary fixed his former rival with an indignant glare. Then the two *Law Review* editors left, and Adam turned to face his new students.

This is it, he thought. A new beginning. A fresh start. The first day of the rest of their lives. It was a frightening concept, but it was also an exciting and empowering one. He would show them how the law worked, unfold it, and demonstrate its ticking parts, and then they could put it together in new and interesting ways, adapting it for different times and shaping it to serve—dare he say—truth and justice.

"*Palsgraf v. Long Island Railroad*," he began. "Who wants to tell us about the facts of that case?"

Ten hands shot in the air, overeager and ramrod straight. Adam looked over the room, suddenly crackling with energy, alive and engaged. He chose a young woman sitting in front who was taking notes by hand in an old-fashioned spiral binder.

"Ms. Fortunato. Please, come up here and tell us the story."

Then Adam yielded the lectern while Staci stood before the class and began to teach.

FRIDAY 9 A.M.
CLOPP HALL

COMPLIMENTARY BREAKFAST WILL BE SERVED

MANHATTAN LAW SCHOOL LAW REVIEW PRESENTS:

Law, Like Love: Indefiniteness and Legal Theory*

A discussion with
Dean Adam Wright and Professor Laura Stapleton-Wright

Law, say the men in their dark suits and ties
Law is what we declaim and devise
But it's not what they do,
Not what they say
Law is alive; we renew it each day.

-- Ann Marie Kowalski, MLS Law Review

Luke and Leia and Chewy and Han
Flew faster than light to meet Obi-Wan
Committed a tort
Got sued in a port
In personam jurisdiction *sine qua non.*

-- David Wheeler, Professor Emeritus

Who stole the soap?
Who ate my bread?
Who took my blankie?
And smothered my head?

-- Jasper Jeffries, Sing-Sing Correctional Facility

Do all poems rhyme?
Is this a poem?
If it's not
Can I get an extension?

-- Asher Herman, MLS student

There once was a Prof from Nantucket
Who could have been rich but said stuff it
He gave me a C
But now look at me
Too bad he's in love or I'd hump him.

-- Staci Fortunato, MLS Law Review

I loved someone once
But never loved myself
It was easier loving her
Because she was not me
And didn't have to bend so far

-- Gary Deranger, MLS Law Review

The law is a troubling institution
And has nothing to do with love
I have no interest in attending this panel
Also, this is not a poem
I do not write poems

-- Richard Rodriguez, Professor Emeritus

Roses are red
Violets are blue
I am the Dean
And who are you?

-- Erwin Clopp, former MLS Dean

* With apologies to W.H. Auden. *See* "Law Like Love" (1939).

Acknowledgments

We wish to thank: Jesseca Salky, for her unflagging support and enthusiasm, her insightful notes, and her kindred spirit; Leigh Eisenman at HSG Agency; Jon Malysiak and his team at Anker-wycke, including Jill Nuppenau, Kaitlyn Bitner, Elizabeth Kulak, and the designer of our wonderful cover, Elmarie Jara; David Lat, for his advice and encouragement; Lenny Beckerman at Lotus Entertainment; Christine, Simon, Lulu, Nina, and Micah, for their good humor and patience; and each other, for making this book something more than either one of us would have written alone.